A Detour Home

A Novel

A Detour Home
A Novel

Norma Murphy

ISBN: 979-8-9891648-1-3

Also by Norma Murphy:

A Better Life
The Price of Secrets

Dedicated to my boys, Jason and Matthew.
I am so grateful every day to be their mother.

Acknowledgements

The first person I want to thank, every time, is my husband Garry. My partner, my friend, and always my first reader. Special thanks also to my writers' group, Gemma Lury, Brenda Hummel, and Katherine Holtzman, who have been with me from the beginning, providing invaluable insights and encouragement. I also want to thank Ann Murphy for feedback on early drafts, Kevin Murphy for his legal expertise, Jess Lamond for helping me gain a better understanding of the foster care system, and Kerry Blodgett for sharing her knowledge of counselling procedures and ethics. And I am forever grateful to my talented developmental editor, Sharon Umbaugh, for her expertise and guidance in helping me make this novel the best it could be.

Finally, very special thanks to all my readers who enjoyed my first novel, *A Better Life*, and have expressed their genuine desire to know what happened to Jenny and Margaret. Here you go.

Prologue
13 Years Earlier

It only took Jenny a few seconds to open the car door. It was a heavy door, but it didn't make a sound. The girl was buckled into a car seat and Jenny squeezed the plastic piece that held the straps in like she had done it a hundred times before. Then she pushed the button on the front, slid out the buckle. The straps over the little girl's shoulders were already loose and slipped off easily. Jenny picked her up and eased her out as carefully and gently as if she were her own sweet child. She weighed nothing at all, and when the little girl rested her head on Jenny's shoulder and didn't wake up, maybe that was the moment.

Chapter 1

I don't want to go home. Not yet, maybe not ever. I wish I had somewhere else to go, and I wish I had never found out my whole life has been a lie.

The woman behind the ticket counter stares at me as if she didn't hear me, so I make my voice stronger and ask again for a ticket to Pittsfield, slide a twenty and a five under the glass between us. Maybe she's about to question me, ask how old I am and if I'm alone. I stare back and wait, ready to tell her I'm sixteen, but she slides my ticket and change across to me without a word. I scoop everything up and thank her, take a deep breath as soon as I turn and walk to an empty bench along the back wall.

I look up when a guy walks in alone and stops just inside the door, scans the room like he's not sure where he is or why he's there. He takes everything in, then walks over to the ticket window. He's maybe late twenties, thirty at the most, tall and thin with short brown hair.

Once he has his ticket, he turns and scans the room again. I feel his eyes on me for a second, then he walks towards me. My heart starts racing. Did he see me watching him? Did Jenny report me missing? Is he looking for me? For the first time since I left home I feel like I might be in trouble.

He sits next to me as if there's nowhere else to sit, which there is. He's not too close, but I slide down to the end of the bench anyway, keep my backpack on the seat between us.

"Ah won't bite," he says.

He sounds like he's from the south. His smile looks real and his voice is gentle and he doesn't look dangerous, but that doesn't mean anything. Jenny has warned me so many times about talking to strangers, I'm pretty much suspicious of everyone.

He's wearing blue jeans and a light blue dress shirt, a navy-blue suit coat. Even his eyes are blue, the color of a summer sky. What does he want?

I pretend I didn't hear him and wish I had brought my headphones. I keep my head down and look at the bus schedule. Again. It feels like part of my hand now. My stringy hair hangs down and covers the side of my face, and I hope he doesn't recognize me from that show about missing kids. I wish he would just read a newspaper or look at his phone, but his eyes are on me.

"Where are you headed, miss, if you don't mind my asking?" Could he be the police?

"Home." I take in his face for a few seconds. He's not exactly handsome, but not ugly either. His nose is a little crooked, his blue eyes soft and kind looking.

"Lucky girl. And where might home be?" As if it's any of his business.

I wonder again if he's the police, but I don't think so. Why is he talking to me? A plain teenager nobody ever notices? There's no way he's trying to pick me up or anything. It's the middle of the day and there are plenty of people around and nothing is going to happen. "Do I know you?" I know we never met.

He tilts his head and studies my face. "You do look slightly familiar, but I don't believe I have had the pleasure." His words are slow and drawn out, and even though he sounds a little phony, I kind of like his accent and his smile, his white teeth. "I'm Jack." He slides down a little closer and puts his hand out.

I look at it for a second before I decide to shake it. No point in being rude. "Nice to meet you." I turn back to my bus schedule as if it's the most interesting thing in the world. I wish I had a book.

"You are very smart not giving your name. There are far too many predators out there, especially when they see a pretty girl like you."

A pretty girl? Like me? Right. "Thanks." I'm not sure what I'm thanking him for, that he called me pretty or that he said I was smart. Either way, I feel my face getting hot. I'm relieved when his phone rings and he answers it.

The only person who ever called me pretty was Gene, a long time ago when I was little. My eyes are the color of milk chocolate mixed with green. Hazel. An awful name for an awful color. My face is thin and pale, and my straggly hair doesn't help.

Jack tells whoever it is that he will have it ready by the end of the day. He sounds normal and professional, but he's a stranger, and I'm not stupid. When he says he is very glad he could help, I'm curious about what kind of help, where he works and what he does, but I'm not about to start a conversation with a stranger who might be a serial killer for all I know.

I pull out my prepaid cell and swipe the screen as if I'm scrolling through emails and texts so he won't think I'm listening or alone in the world. I pretend to text someone so I seem normal, and when my bus is called, I wait a few seconds, keep my eyes glued to my phone.

Jack stands, picks up his briefcase and says, "Nice to meet you, miss." He heads out to the bus before I do, so I know he's not following me. I wait until a few more people head out, get in line behind a woman with short black hair holding a little girl's hand.

After I give the driver my ticket, I see Jack about six rows back, in the aisle seat. He's reaching down, probably into his briefcase. I slip into a seat two rows ahead of him, slide over to the window and set my backpack on the seat next to me. In a couple of minutes, everyone is sitting, the door squeals and snaps shut, and we are on our way. I take out my schedule and stare at it, even though I know it by heart. I went such a short distance, stayed in the same state, and feel like I'm a million miles from anywhere.

I watch the world go by, the houses set back from the road, the trees still bare, a few patches of snow from the last storm refusing to leave, everything holding onto the last dregs of winter like a prize.

The next stop is quick, with only one person getting on, a kid who sits three rows up from me and is alone too. His hair almost reaches his shoulders, dark brown and thick and wavy. I would do anything for hair like that. He turns to look out the window as the bus pulls away, then the man across the aisle says something and the boy turns and laughs—quick and real and a little self-conscious. His laugh and his hair weirdly make me think of Jenny, who is probably going nuts right now, wondering where I am.

A few more people get on at the next stop, and no one gets off. The seats are filling up now. I don't want to sit next to anyone and have to make small talk, try to answer questions about myself and my life. I'm a stranger to myself, so I might as well be a stranger to everyone.

I keep my eyes focused out the window, even though there's not much to see—an empty bench under a little shelter, a panel with a map of the bus route protected from the weather by yellowed plastic. When the bus pulls out again, I still have my seat to myself.

There's a man sitting next to the boy now. He has white hair so fine and wispy it seems to float around his head like a halo. They are already having a conversation, and I'm glad he didn't sit next to me. Sure enough, the man is asking the boy all kinds of questions. I can't hear every word, just enough to know he's asking where he's from, where he's going, how old he is, as if it's any of his business. It's amazing how much old people can get away with.

Instead of answering like a good little boy, he asks, "How old are you?" I smile for the first time in a while.

The old man laughs and says he will be 87 in August. Like everyone else on the planet, they talk easily. They have known each other about two seconds and are more comfortable than I will ever be with most people.

I rest my head on the back of the seat and close my eyes, listen to the voices around me. Small talk about work, the weather. A woman says, “It’s almost April, and it feels like spring is never going to come. But that’s New England, right?” She sounds so sad.

Jenny used to talk about moving somewhere warm, Florida or California. She wanted so badly to get out of the trailer park, out of the life we had, and she did, finally. But she’s still not happy. She’s one of those people who will never be happy, no matter what.

The brakes squeal and I feel the bus come to a stop again. I turn around and see Jack is still there. His eyes meet mine and he smiles and waves as if we are friends. I wave back to be polite, but I don’t smile. My heart starts racing, and I’m not sure what I’ll do when I reach my stop if he follows me off.

The guy with the white hair gets off, and some women are climbing onto the bus now, laughing and shouting as if everyone is deaf. They all have puffy white or gray hair, shopping bags and huge purses. As they start down the aisle looking for seats, the boy turns around and our eyes meet. He looks a little panicked. I stare back at him, set my backpack on the floor and tilt my head towards the now empty seat. He nods, and in a second he is sitting next to me. It feels like we are saving each other.

“Thanks.” He has dark eyes and thick lashes and a shy smile, and he smells like spearmint gum. He’s also not as young as I first thought, a year or two older than me, I think. No threat.

“No problem.” We watch and listen as the women get settled, six of them, and I feel safer by the minute from Jack. “They look like they’re having a good time,”

“It’s their weekly shopping trip to the outlets,” he whispers. “Every Wednesday. Shopping, lunch, Manhattans.”

One of the women stops and puts her hand on his shoulder with a smile. “Hello, dear.”

He looks up and pats her hand. “Hey. Good shopping?”

“Always, dear. Always.” She continues down the aisle.

"Are you on this bus every Wednesday?"

He nods. "I have p.t."

I wait to see if he's going to explain, but he doesn't say what his p.t. is for and I don't ask. It doesn't look like there's anything wrong with him, but I nod. You can't see everything.

"I'm Adam." He doesn't put his hand out, which is fine with me.

I only hesitate a couple of seconds. "Meg." It's what I want to be called now. Not Margaret. Not Meggie. Meg.

"I haven't seen you before," he says. "Do you live around here?"

"No. I went to see an old friend. Now I'm going home. Not that I want to." *Why am I telling him this?*

"Where's home?"

I look down at the bus schedule spread out on my lap and don't answer. I feel so lost.

"It's okay. You don't have to tell me." Adam smiles as if he understands perfectly.

Maybe a stranger is exactly who I need to talk to. It's not like I'm ever going to see him again. "It's just that I went to find some answers about myself and I didn't. It's frustrating. And complicated."

"I get it," he says. "You don't want to go home yet until you do what you set out to do. I get that."

"But I have no choice. I don't have anywhere else to go. I'm going to have to wait until I'm older to get any information. About myself. It isn't fair."

"Sucks."

"How old are you?" I didn't plan to ask him this, but I'm really curious.

"Why does everyone ask me that? How old are you?"

"16."

"I'm 17."

"You seem way more mature than the boys I know in school."

That makes him laugh. "Mature? Tell that to my grandma."

"You live with your grandmother?"

"She raised me. When my mother was 15 she got pregnant and was going to get rid of me. My grandma, her mother, told her if she had me and still didn't want me, she would find a nice family to adopt me. She thought once my mother saw me, she would suddenly fall in love with me and want to be a mother. Not."

"I'm sorry."

"Don't be sorry. If my mother didn't want me, I'm better off without her. I'm lucky I didn't end up in foster care." He doesn't sound angry or resentful. He actually sounds proud of his beginnings. At least he knows who he is and where he came from.

Adam looks past me, out the window, and I turn and look out there too. We're passing a group of low buildings set back, surrounded by a chain-link fence with three rows of barbed wire on top. At first I think it's a prison, then I see a sign that says Wheeler Manufacturing and I wonder what they manufacture. I glance down at the schedule again. One more stop before mine.

I lean back and close my eyes for a few seconds, think of Adam's mother not wanting him. Was that what happened to me? Did my mother give birth then not want me? Maybe she had no family like Adam's mother had, no one to take me in and raise me. Or do I have a grandmother out there somewhere who doesn't even know I exist?

When I open my eyes, Adam is looking at me. "So, is someone going to meet your bus?"

"Not that I know of." An hour ago, I couldn't imagine telling anyone anything about my life, but now I find myself wanting to share it, at least some of it. I could never tell Adam about Jenny taking me from the back seat of a car and keeping me. It sounds so bad. "I sort of took off, so, no. She doesn't know where I went or that I'm on my way back. I did leave a note, though, so she wouldn't worry." As if that would be enough.

"Your mother?"

I sigh. "The person I thought was my mother. That's why I left, to try and find out who my birth mother is. It turns out I was in foster care before she adopted me. She wants me to believe I was born the day she got me, when I was three. Like I didn't exist before that. But I did. I feel like my whole life has been a lie, and I don't know who I am."

Adam has been staring into my eyes the whole time I'm talking. It feels good to have someone really listen to me. "You know who you are."

"I know who I am now, I guess. I want to know where I came from, who my parents are, and how I ended up in foster care. I feel like if I know the truth, then I'll know who I really am."

"Are you sure you want to know the truth?"

"Aren't you glad you know?"

He surprises me with a smile. "Hell, yeah. I'm a survivor. You are too."

"You think so?"

"For sure. Hey, you think your adopted mother knows and just isn't telling you? Like she doesn't want you to know?"

I shake my head. "I don't think she knows. She doesn't want to know and she doesn't want me to know either. That's the problem." How could I possibly explain Jenny to anyone? How she's not like a normal mother, how I have always taken care of her more than she has taken care of me, how she has trouble facing things she's done or tries to deal with things after the fact, when it's too late? None of that is his business. "She says I am who I am and nothing is going to change that. She raised me and that makes her my mother and there's no reason to go looking into things that would probably hurt me."

"Sounds like she cares."

"She tries." In her own way, Jenny has always tried.

"You're lucky," Adam says. "Here I thought you were pretty much alone, like me."

"I've felt pretty much alone all my life. I never felt like I belonged anywhere. That's why I want to find out who I am and where I came from."

"Maybe ah can help." Jack is right behind us now. He must have heard our whole conversation, and I was so focused on spilling my guts to Adam I didn't even notice.

Chapter 2

"I'm Jack." He leans forward and holds his hand out to Adam.

Adam looks at Jack, then glares at me as if I'm guilty of something. "You know this guy?"

Jack says, "Yes" and I say, "No" at the same time. For some reason, Jack thinks this is funny and laughs. What did he mean he might be able to help?

"What can we do for you?" Adam asks. *We?* He sounds protective, almost jealous.

"I couldn't help but overhear about your dilemma. Sorry, but it is a public place, right?" Jack keeps his eyes on me.

"What did you mean, you might be able to help? Help with what?" I ask.

"I heard what you said to your friend here, about finding who you are. Maybe I could help with that, help you find some answers."

"How?" Not that I'm going to give him any information. "If you're looking for money, I don't have any."

Jack reaches back and pulls his wallet out of his back pocket, unfolds it. For a second, I think he's going to give me some cash, but he takes out a card, hands it to me. I hold it out so Adam can read it too. *Jack Doolin, Investigator*, and a phone number, the same area code as me.

"Are you the police?" Adam asks.

Jack laughs. "Do I look like the police?"

It's not exactly a no. Should I be nervous? Would Jenny have called the police, reported me as a runaway? "I told you I don't have any money, if that's what you want."

Jack leans in a little closer, lowers his voice. "I don't want your money. Look, I'm new around here, in case you couldn't tell. I recently moved up from Georgia. Savannah, to be exact. Have you ever been? It's a beautiful city, full of charm and—"

"So, you're not the police," Adam interrupts.

"Not even close."

I want him to explain more, about who he is and what he wants. "I still don't see how you can help me."

"I heard you say you wanted to look into your adoption, find your birth parents. Is that right?"

"It's not that simple." I'm whispering now.

"You're not gonna trust this guy," Adam glares at Jack. I can't tell if he's angry at Jack for intruding, or me for talking to him.

Jack ignores Adam and focuses on me. "Look." He holds his hands up in front of him. "I don't blame you for being cautious. If I do end up doing work for you, though, I will need to at least know your name." He gives me a smile and I fight to hold mine in. "Just think about it. I'm pretty sure I can help you. At least I would like to try."

I study Jack's card again. Anyone can have cards made. It doesn't mean anything. And no one does anything for free, especially not for someone they just met. "I'm all set."

Jack nods, and I watch him walk back to his seat. I feel bad now. What if he's for real? "Thanks anyway."

"Of course." Jack nods. "If you change your mind, give me a call."

The shopping ladies get off at the next stop, and all of a sudden the bus is dead quiet. I turn around and see Jack looking out the window. I'm not sure how I feel about him. I need to be careful, and I absolutely can't get my hopes up.

Adam frowns. "What a creep."

"I wouldn't say he's a creep." I slip Jack's card into my jacket pocket.

"You're not thinking about calling him."

"I don't know."

"You really think he's gonna do anything for free?" Adam shakes his head like I'm stupid, or at least naïve.

"I told him I don't have any money."

"That was smart."

"It was the truth."

Adam narrows his eyes like he doesn't believe me. "What about a credit card?"

"I don't have a credit card either."

He thinks about this for a few seconds. "Well, no one does anything for free."

"He seems like he really wants to help." I wish I could believe there are good people in the world. I don't want to be like Jenny who always thinks the worst, thinks everyone is out to get her.

I glance at my phone. We'll be at my stop in about five minutes. I have almost a three-hour wait there before the last bus takes me home. I'll have that much more time to practice what I'll say to Jenny. I wish I could tell her it was all worthwhile, that I found what I was looking for and everything is good, but I'm no better off than before I left. Maybe worse for taking off like that and upsetting Jenny for nothing. When the driver announces my stop, I pick up my backpack and hold it on my lap. "I'm getting off here."

"Me too," Adam says. He looks happy about that. We step off the bus and stand outside while Adam checks his phone, texts something, then turns to me and asks if I want to get something to eat. He sounds like a lonely kid.

"Don't you have p.t.?"

"It was cancelled. Come on. I'll buy you a sandwich." He starts walking before I have time to answer or think. "There's a place up here with the best Cubans."

I have heard of a Cuban sandwich, but have never had one. For some reason, I keep up with him, even though I'm not sure about this. I should just wait inside the bus station, but I have hours to kill. Plus, I'm hungry and I don't feel like being alone, eating out of a machine again. "Do you live around here?" I don't know anything about him except his first name and that he lives with his grandmother.

"Not far." He turns to me. "You hungry?"

"A little." I'm starving.

We walk a couple of blocks in silence. The clouds are darker now, lower, and the wind has picked up. Adam has his hands in his sweatshirt pockets and hunches a little, as if he's used to being hit by the cold. I look around at the buildings, mostly brick and mostly abandoned. Am I an idiot for going somewhere with this guy? When we come to the next corner, Adam stops. A hand-painted sign over the door says, *Tito's*. The one window is covered by a dirty curtain.

"Here we go." Adam opens the door for me and I walk in first as if I planned to be here all along, as if I'm comfortable with this. I wish I were back at the bus station.

It's a small place that barely fits the two square tables on the left and a high counter in the back with a menu on the wall behind it. There's a door on the right, probably the bathroom. The place smells like grease and some kind of meat, spices I can't identify. There is no one else here, and I'm getting a bad feeling, then a really big woman wearing a filthy apron appears behind the counter. Her face is red and sweaty. She must be the cook, or maybe the owner? Adam walks up and orders while I wait just inside the door. I think about turning around and walking out, but I take another step inside when the woman looks over and stares at me for a couple of seconds. She says something to Adam I can't hear before she turns and disappears into the back.

Adam takes a seat at the table closest to the counter, leans back and smiles at me like everything is perfect. "Have a seat," he says. "It won't take long."

I tell myself to relax, not to judge. I've been in worse places with Jenny. I sit down across from Adam, hang my backpack on the back of my chair.

"You're gonna love this," he says.

"I never had a Cuban," I tell him. I'll eat half of it here so I don't hurt Adam's feelings and bring the other half back to the bus station to wait. I might call Jack, just to see what he could possibly be able to do. It won't hurt to listen.

The door opens and I'm glad someone else has come in, but when I turn around I see an older guy, maybe in his 40's, with a shaved head and a small gold hoop in one ear. He's wearing a tight black tee-shirt and looks like he spends every day at the gym. He stares at me a few seconds, then nods at Adam and walks to the counter. In a minute, the woman walks out with our sandwiches on flimsy paper plates.

Adam steps up to the counter and says something to the guy. They both turn and look at me before they walk to our table. "Meg, this is Mike. Mike, Meg." Adam sets the sandwiches down, sits and takes a bite out of his. Mike scrapes a chair over from the other table, sits close to me with his legs spread wide, and I feel trapped.

Everything in me screams to get out of there. Now. Instead, I sit frozen and say, "Nice to meet you." Can he hear my heart pounding?

Mike looks over at Adam and smiles. He's missing a few top teeth. "You been holding out on me?"

"We just met," Adam says. "On the bus." He sounds defensive, maybe scared.

I am so stupid for coming here. I can hardly breathe as I push my chair back and stand, pick up my backpack. The woman is nowhere in sight and it's just me and these two sketchy guys. What is wrong with me? "I'm sorry. I have to go."

Mike stands too. "What's your hurry, Meg? We just met." He grabs my arm and I notice his dirty fingernails. "You haven't had your sandwich." He steps closer, his fingers still wrapped around my arm.

I pull my arm away and he must hear my heart pounding out of my chest. I glance down at my sandwich, the grill marks on the bread, the handful of chips next to it. "I'm not hungry. Sorry. I just realized I'm going to miss my bus." I wish my voice was stronger. I look over at Adam, focused on his phone, his sandwich nearly gone. He's all done with me. Did he make everything up? About his mother not wanting him, his grandmother raising him? I actually felt a connection. What is wrong with me?

Mike steps over to the door and blocks my way, his meaty arms folded across his chest. He has a smirk on his face as if this is a game and he's the one who made up the rules. He's not going to let me go. His sweat is strong and sour, or maybe it's mine. He is going to make me go somewhere and I can't let myself think about what he might make me do. How could I be so stupid? I look over at the still deserted counter. Should I scream? Is that woman part of all this, too, whatever it is?

I get ready to swing my backpack at him, then I hear, "Mike!" The woman is back, and her voice is loud and angry.

Mike gives her a mean and dirty look. "Get back in the kitchen."

She glances at me, glares at Mike for just a second and shakes her head, then she's gone again.

We're both startled when the door swings open. Mike stumbles back a little but doesn't fall. It's just enough to take his attention off me.

"Sorry I'm late," Jack announces, taking everything in, then focusing on me. I have never been so glad to see anyone in my life. "I got here as soon as I could. Good thing you have that tracking device on your phone. Let's go. Your brothers are on their way."

Mike's face is red, his eyes bulging and angry. "Hey!" is all he gets out before Jack pulls me out of there and we walk quickly down the street, back towards the bus station. Jenny always told me the world is a dangerous place and now I get it. I really do. Finally.

"Are you okay?" Jack is cool and calm, as if he saves people all the time.

All I can do is nod and try to breathe. I turn away so he doesn't see the tears streaming down my face. I feel so stupid and so lucky and still so scared.

We walk fast and I'm afraid to turn around, expecting Mike and Adam to rush up behind us any second. When I do get the courage to glance behind us, the street is empty except for a young girl in a red hoodie walking a tiny dog.

I am so relieved to be out of there, relieved Jack came to my rescue, but I remind myself he's still a stranger. I need to be careful. What if he's dangerous too? We turn the corner and slow down a little and I find my voice. "How did you know where I was? What was that about a tracking device and my brothers?"

"I followed you. I had a bad feeling about that kid. I'm pretty good at improvising."

"I guess I'm not a very good judge of character. I feel like an idiot for trusting him."

"Don't be too hard on yourself. The important thing is you're safe, and you probably learned a valuable lesson, right? They didn't hurt you, did they?"

"No. But if you didn't come, I don't know what they were going to do. That big guy? His name was Mike and he wasn't going to let me leave. He was blocking the door. And Adam wasn't about to do anything. He was the one who brought me there. Oh my God. I was so scared." I swallow hard and the tears come again and I can't stop them. They are more than from what happened with Adam and Mike. It feels like they come from somewhere deep, waiting for a long time to be set free.

"Do you want to call the police?"

"No. No police. I just want to forget it. Please."

"Whatever you say."

By the time we reach the bus station, the tears are finished and I'm finally able to breathe normally again. "Thank you. I owe you a lot. I don't even want to think about what would have happened if you—"

"It's over. You don't have to let those punks take up any space in your head, okay? They're not worth it. Do you want me to stay with you until your bus comes? I'm happy to."

I do and I don't. I'm not used to anyone, especially a stranger, being so kind to me. I look in his eyes and all I see is a nice, sincere guy. But what do I know? "Why?"

"Just in case they decide to come back. Not that I think they will. I just thought it would make you feel better."

"I mean why are you being so nice to me? You don't even know me."

Jack looks into my eyes before he looks down and focuses on his shoes. "I had a sister. Maybe you remind me of her."

"Did something happen to her?"

Jack looks at me again with a sad smile. "She was such a good kid. You are too. Just steer clear of strangers."

We stand outside the doors and Jack puts his hand out. "You have my card, right? You be careful. If you need anything, or if you change your mind about my helping you, I'm only a phone call away."

I take his hand and shake it. "I'm Meg."

Now he smiles and it's real. "Nice to meet you, Meg."

Chapter 3

I pull open the door and step inside the bus terminal, take a deep breath and let myself get swallowed by the crowd, random pieces of conversation, busses being called. The voice over the loudspeaker is deep and calm and somehow comforting.

I choose a seat along the back wall where I can watch the front and side doors. There's no way Adam and Mike would come here, not with all these people around. I'm fine. Hungry. I buy a root beer and a bag of corn chips from the vending machine and take deep breaths, try not to focus on what an idiot I was, going with Adam like that. It's over. I'm safe now, thanks to Jack.

A woman who looks about Jenny's age with a little boy on her lap sits two seats away. She has curly blonde hair and a worried look on her face and keeps glancing up at the clock. I wonder if she's in trouble, if she's running from someone. The boy stares at me, then turns and buries his face in his mother's neck.

There are still more than two hours before I get on the bus to take me home. Back to Jenny and my fake life. After I eat my chips, I wipe my hands on my jeans and pull out Jack's card. Bright white. No address. Just his name, phone number and *Investigator*. I like that word. I look up at the clock again, the minutes going faster now. It's just a phone call. I tap in his number before I think myself out of it.

"Jack Doolin." His voice sounds professional and friendly at the same time.

"It's Meg," I say. "From the bus?"

"Meg. Are you okay? Those guys didn't come back, did they?"

"No. I'm fine. I'm waiting for my bus and I was just wondering about what you said, how you think you can help me?"

"I will need you to fill me in on a few things, but if I'm not mistaken, you are looking for your biological parents? I can certainly try to help you with that."

"And you know I don't have any money to pay you, right?" I am so sick of saying that.

"I know. And I truly understand. It's okay. Really."

I want to trust Jack, but I still don't know if I can. No one does anything for free. That's one thing Adam was right about. "Why? Tell me why you want to help me. There must be something in it for you."

"You are awfully young to be so skeptical of people, if you don't mind my saying. I know those guys scared you, and maybe you've had other bad experiences, but I hope you know there are good people in the world too."

"Like you?"

"I try to be. Sometimes it gets me in trouble, but, yes, I consider myself a good person. In any event, I'm glad you called. Do you want to meet and talk about how I can help you? Hold on just a second, would you?"

I hear another voice, a man's voice, then Jack is back. "I can be there in about 20 minutes."

"Can you find out why someone was in foster care? I mean whether the parents gave her up for some reason or if she was taken away from them? And can you find out who they are?"

Jack and I have the bench along the back wall all to ourselves. The woman with the little boy is gone and I'm glad there's no one close enough to hear. Not that anyone is paying attention to us, and why would anyone care? He holds his briefcase on his lap and turns to me, looks me in the eye.

"First of all, I want you to know I don't do anything illegal."

"I just want to find out who I am, who my parents are, and why I was in foster care before I went to live with Jenny and Gene, the people who raised me. That's not illegal, right?"

"Not technically, no, but unfortunately the powers that be don't bestow those rights until you're 18. You know for sure you were fostered before you were adopted?"

"I just found out recently. I always thought Jenny and Gene were my real parents. They raised me since I was about three, so they're all I remember. I didn't even know I was adopted." Saying *adopted* comes easy now, and sounds so much better than *kidnapped.*

Jack looks at me closely. "How old are you, exactly?"

"Almost 16. I'll be 16 in June. At least that's what it says on my birth certificate."

"And your adoptive parents, Jenny and Gene you said? Are they willing to try and get that information for you? It would seem that would be the easiest route, depending on the terms of the adoption."

If I were adopted legally, it probably would be, but I wasn't and there's no way I can tell Jack how I ended up with Jenny and Gene. What I told him already is as close to the truth as I can get. Maybe I already got too close. "You know what? I don't think this is going to work. It's too complicated. I'm sorry I wasted your time. I don't want to get anyone in trouble." I stand and pick up my backpack, as if I have somewhere to go.

Jack stares up at me. "It has been my experience that most goals worth pursuing seem too complicated at first. And as I said, I don't do anything illegal and I surely have no desire for trouble. Truth be told, I was in a bit of trouble myself in Georgia. That's why I moved up here. A fresh start."

I sit back down but keep my backpack on my lap and stay on the edge of my seat. "What kind of trouble?"

Jack takes a deep breath, looks me in the eye. "I worked for an architectural firm after college, in their IT department. It was an entry level position, not that there's anything wrong with that, but it took very little intelligence and even less imagination. I wanted to do more, and I guess I became what you would call a hacker. Have you heard that term?"

“They break into computer networks to get people’s information and steal their identities, right?” *Who is this guy?*

“That’s exactly right. Well, the first part anyway. There are a lot of people out there who are up to no good, but I swear I didn’t do anything like that. I was only trying to expose vulnerabilities in their software. I brought it to my boss, thinking I would be some kind of hero, maybe even get a promotion. I meant no harm, but they fired me and threatened to file charges. So here I am.”

“You said you were an investigator.”

“I am. At least that’s what I’m working towards. But right now I work at a small startup company, just to pay the bills and save a little money. There are three of us, working out of a garage doing computer repairs, software installations, that kind of thing. My goal is to open my own investigative firm. You are my first client, if you still want me.”

I glance over at the clock. A little less than an hour now. This could be my best and only chance to find the truth. “Okay.”

“Okay?” Jack’s face lights up as if I’m the one doing him a favor. “Okay then.” He opens his briefcase, lifts out a laptop. “The logical place to start is where we have at least some information. That would be your adoption.”

“What if it wasn’t exactly a legal adoption? I mean, what if the people who adopted me didn’t go through like a regular adoption agency?”

He stares at me for a couple of seconds. “A private adoption. It’s actually more common than you think.” He opens his computer, presses a button, and a picture of the night sky fills the screen. “It’s what is referred to as the gray market. There is usually some kind of go-between, a lawyer or a doctor. Is there anyone you remember?”

I don’t remember any doctors when I was a kid, but I do remember Gene’s friend Sam, who said he was a lawyer. He always scared me, made me feel like a bug he wanted to swat away. He has to be the one who did all that paperwork Jenny showed me—my birth certificate, vaccination records, even a social security card. She said if anyone ever questioned us, she had everything she needed to prove I was her daughter, as if fake paperwork was all it took.

"There was this guy, Sam, who used to come over, and I'm pretty sure he was a lawyer. It seemed like he always had papers for Jenny and Gene to sign. I don't even know his last name."

Jack's face lights up again as he stares at the computer screen and starts tapping keys. "Not a problem. It's something. And Sam, Samuel I assume, isn't that common a name, I don't think. He practiced in Massachusetts?"

"I think so. We lived in Greenville at the time, so maybe western Mass?" I feel like I'm actually doing something now, maybe getting somewhere. I watch as Jack scrolls through lists of names. At the top of the screen, it says, *Massachusetts Board of Bar Overseers.*

"Here's a Samuel Evans, but he's in Gloucester. There's a Samuel Smith. He has an office in Houghtonville. Let's see. It's about 40 miles northwest of here." He taps more keys and doesn't take his eyes off the screen. "Would you mind getting me a cup of coffee, please?" He reaches in his back pocket for his wallet.

"I'll get it. The least I can do is buy you a cup of coffee."

I break my last twenty, and when I get back with Jack's coffee and a bottle of water for me, he is frowning at the computer screen. "If this is your guy, he's not the most reputable. He had his license suspended for three years, from 2005 to 2008. It appears he co-mingled his personal funds with client funds. But it does say he is fully licensed now."

Even though I was just a kid, I always had the impression he wasn't a good guy. He was too big, too loud, and when he was there it seemed like there wasn't enough room or enough air to breathe in the trailer. "It sounds like it could be him."

"Let's take a look at his web site."

I laugh. "Sam has a web site?"

"Everyone has one these days. You can set one up for next to nothing." Jack clicks some more keys, then there's Sam looking out from the screen, his finger pointed at me. His eyes look angry but his mouth is almost like a smirk. *Have YOU been hurt in an accident? Injured on the job? Call me NOW and I WILL get you the compensation you deserve.* His hair is white and he seems smaller, but he's real.

"That's him. That's Sam."

"Okay, so, if he did any kind of paperwork for your adoptive parents, there's a pretty good chance he would know something."

"Maybe. Gene could have asked him to see what he could find out."

"Do you think Sam will remember you? And, more importantly, do you think he would be willing to tell you anything?"

"I think he'll remember me, but I'm not sure how much he would tell me." I look up at the clock and see there's only a half hour until my bus. I can't leave. "I'm going to see if I can exchange my ticket."

When I come back, Jack takes out his phone to call Sam. He turns down the volume, puts it on speaker, and we lean in close. Sam answers, "Law Office," and his voice is like a ghost.

"I saw your website and wanted to see you about an accident I had this afternoon," Jack says. "This guy rear-ended me, then started yelling at me about his Bentley. He's the one who hit me. And my neck is pretty sore. I wanted to consult a lawyer before I saw a doctor, see if you can recommend anyone."

"Well now, I just happened to have a cancellation for this afternoon. What time can you be here?"

Jack tells Sam he can be there within the hour. He's as excited as I am as he packs up his laptop, drinks down his coffee. "My car is in the parking lot."

"Wait. You have a car? Then why were you taking the bus?"

"We call it our company car. We take turns using it when we need it. It's a good write-off too." He stands and throws his empty cup in the trash, takes a step and stops and turns when he sees I haven't moved.

Am I about to make the same mistake I just made with Adam? This time getting into a stranger's car?

Jack sits back down, turns to face me. "I know you're nervous after what happened earlier. And rightly so. I surely understand if you don't completely trust me. Actually, I admire you for it. You did trust me with personal information, though, and that's a huge step. Do you want me to go see Sam myself? I'm happy to."

I stand. "No. I need to do this." We walk outside the terminal, past the busses and around to the parking lot in back. Jack walks up to a silver Nissan and opens the passenger door. I slip in before I change my mind.

Sam's office is in a strip mall, along with a dry-cleaner, two empty places with signs in the window saying they are for lease, a nail salon, then a sign that just says, *LAW OFFICES*.

As soon as Jack parks, he opens his door, steps one foot out.

I put my hand on his arm. "Maybe I should go in myself. He might be suspicious if you're there. He might feel sorry for me if I'm alone."

Jack turns to me, nods. "Maybe so. I'll be right here."

When I pull open the door, Sam is sitting behind a table in the back of the room, papers and folders and books piled everywhere, two folding chairs in front of the table. He stands when I walk in. "Can I help you, miss?"

His deep voice brings me right back to the trailer, unwrapping hamburgers, the smell of French fries, then Sam sending me outside with a red popsicle. Instead of the wrinkled white suit I remember, Sam wears black pants and a light green shirt with the sleeves rolled up. And he isn't the giant I remember either.

"Hi, Sam."

He narrows his eyes, tilts his head and half-smiles. "Do I know you?" Of course he wouldn't remember me after all these years. He sounds a little nervous, like he's expecting trouble, and it makes me feel stronger.

"Remember your friend Gene? And Jenny? We lived in a trailer park in Greenville? I'm Meg. Margaret."

Sam takes a minute to study my face, then puts on a fake smile as if he's glad to see me. "Margaret. Of course. How've you been? How are your parents?"

"I go by Meg now. And that's why I'm here, to find out about my parents. I mean, my real parents."

His smile is gone, then he stares past me towards the window. "I'm expecting a client any moment, but in the meantime, why don't you tell me what I can do for you." He picks up a stack of folders from one of the chairs, sets it on the floor. "Excuse the mess. My secretary up and quit and I'm in the process of setting up a new office here."

I sit in the chair he cleared off and start talking before he's back in his seat. "I want to know about my background, about my birth parents. I know Jenny and Gene aren't my biological parents, which I'm sure you already know."

Sam's face drains of color and I wait. I'm not so nervous anymore. I feel like he owes me something, and I think he feels it too. "Now why would you assume that?"

"Because you made all that fake paperwork for them."

"Now look, Meg. Everything I did for Gene and Jenny was completely above-board. I went strictly by the information they provided. I didn't knowingly falsify anything, if that's what you're implying."

Of course he did. But I don't think he knows how Jenny got me. Maybe he thought I really was their daughter and they really did lose their papers. He probably wouldn't have bothered to check. He leans back in his chair, folds his arms across his chest and stares at me. "I don't want any trouble here. And I do have a client due any moment, so if you don't mind." He raises his eyebrows and stands.

I stay sitting. "I'm not here to cause trouble. I just want to find out if you know anything about me from before I was with Jenny and Gene. When I was in foster care."

Sam stares at me and frowns. He really doesn't know. Then his expression smooths out, and he sits back down. "Well, I couldn't tell you offhand, of course. I had no idea you were in foster care. But I can certainly look into it for you. I handle many cases like this."

"You really don't know anything? You don't have like a file on me?"

"I know as much as you do, but as I said, I would be happy to look into it. In fact, it's one of my specialties."

"You'll really help me?" I can't believe it.

"It's what I do. Now my usual up-front retainer is $3,000, but seeing you are what I consider a friend of the family so to speak, I would offer you a discount and only charge two." He's serious.

"You want $2,000 to find out who my parents are and why I was in foster care? Wouldn't it just take a phone call or something to DCF? They won't give me any information because I'm a minor, but you're a lawyer. They'll give it to you, right?"

"It's not that simple, Meg. You see, there are issues of confidentiality, as well as the rights of the birth parents. There is much more red tape than you could possibly imagine, especially when it comes to these government agencies. There's a mountain of paperwork, bureaucracy to contend with. It's much more than a phone call, believe me."

I should have known he wouldn't help me for free. "You won't even try to help me unless I give you $2000?"

Sam smiles, leans back in his chair. "You didn't think it would be free, did you little lady?"

"I don't have that kind of money."

"Well, if you change your mind." He pulls a card from his pocket, holds it out. "You seem like a resourceful young lady. Perhaps you could find a way to get the money."

Chapter 4

I slip into the passenger seat of Jack's car and slam the door shut. "What a jerk."

"I take it he wasn't forthcoming? Do you want me to talk to him?"

"No. I don't think he knows anything. He seemed a little nervous when I mentioned the paperwork he did saying Jenny and Gene were my parents, but I think he just took their word for it. He was surprised when I said I was adopted and that I was in foster care before that. But he would be happy to look into it if I gave him $2000. The family discount."

Jack frowns, taps his hands on the steering wheel a few times like he has a song in his head. "So, is there anyone else you can think of who might know anything?"

"No. Not really. But we can't just give up. I mean, we can do some more searching on the computer, right? There are a million websites out there with information on missing kids."

"Of course. But don't you want to go home? Maybe try to get more information from Jenny?"

"I can't go home yet. I just can't. And Jenny doesn't want me to find anything. She wouldn't help, even if she knew something, which I don't think she does. You probably think I'm crazy."

"I don't think you're crazy. I think you are stubborn. I think you are brave, and I think you are someone who doesn't give up. I admire all those things, but at your age, you don't have a lot of options."

"I know. But I can't wait until I'm 18 to get information about myself. That's not fair. Plus, they would ask me a million questions I wouldn't be able to answer. Will you help me?"

Jack's eyes lock on mine. "If we are going to get anywhere, I need you to tell me everything you know." He knows there's more. Of course he does. "I need you to be completely forthcoming and honest with me, which means you have to trust me completely."

I look away. "I know."

We both turn and look straight ahead, where tiny drops of rain speckle the windshield. He sighs, turns the key in the ignition. "Okay, then. If you're not going home, then where?"

"I don't know." I must sound desperate. Or stupid. When Jack doesn't say anything right away, I know I'm expecting way too much. First I want him to work for free, now I'm practically asking him for a place to stay. "I'm sorry. You must have better things to do than babysit me."

"That's not how I see it. You are on a mission, and I truly want to help."

Sitting here with Jack, thinking about all we have gone through in the short time we've known each other, I feel like some divine force put him in my life, even though I don't really believe in all that. I don't even know what to say.

"Okay," Jack says. "How about this? I understand you want to see this through, at least as far as we can, and you don't have money for a place to stay. I have been there myself. I have a spare room, and you can stay with me on two conditions: One, that you call Jenny and let her know you're okay. The last thing I need is the police breaking down my door looking for you. And, two, if we don't find anything by Friday, you will go home and we will think of a way to do this that doesn't involve you being gone from home. That's only going to bring trouble."

I dread calling Jenny, but I know I need to. It's better than going home and facing her. I can't tell her about Jack, though. She'd go nuts and would probably call the police. "All I can tell her is I'm okay and not to worry, but it won't be enough. It might even make things worse."

"Maybe so, but that's the deal. She must be worried sick about you. She deserves to have some peace of mind."

As soon as Jack pulls out onto the street, I call Jenny. She answers on the first ring but doesn't say anything right away, like she's expecting bad news.

"Mama?"

"Meggie? Oh my God. Finally. Are you okay? Where are you?" She sounds frantic, and now I'm glad I called. I think.

"I just wanted you to know I'm fine. That's why I called, so you wouldn't worry. How are you?"

"How am I? How do you think I am? My 15-year-old daughter is missing, and I've been going out of my mind with worry. Other than that, I'm great."

"I'm almost 16, and I'm not missing. I left you a note."

"Tell me where you are. You're not with Gene, are you?"

She doesn't sound like she's been drinking, but Gene? Really? "Why would you think that? How could I be?"

"I wouldn't put it past him."

That makes no sense, but I don't want to talk about Gene. I want to get off the phone. I look over at Jack, focused on driving, the rain heavier now. "I'll be home in a few days, okay?"

"No, it's not okay. You need to come home right now."

"I'll try to call again before I come home. I just wanted you to know I'm okay so you wouldn't worry."

"You think you can just take off like that, then waltz back in here whenever you feel like it? You can think again."

"Now you don't want me to come home?"

"Whatever you're looking for, you're not going to find it out there." She sounds so angry and hurt it scares me.

"I just need a little more time."

Jenny doesn't say anything for a few seconds, then, "If you don't come home right now, don't bother to come home at all."

Her words hurt, even though I know she doesn't mean them. They probably hurt her more than me.

"See? This is why I haven't called. I knew you'd be like this. I promise I'll be home in a few days. Friday at the latest. I need you to trust me." I end the call before she says anything else. I know that will make her even angrier, but she could fight all day.

Now Jack turns to me. "Well that could have gone better."

"It's what I expected. But I'm still glad I called."

It takes about an hour and a half to get to Jack's apartment. He lives in Denton, only a couple of towns over from where Jenny and I live. His apartment is in one of three brick buildings on a side street and isn't much different from ours and probably a million others. The kitchen is open to the living room, separated by a little counter with two stools. There's a short hallway on the right, a bedroom on the left, and an office at the end of the hall. The office is a little bigger than the bedroom, with a beige couch on one wall, a bed pillow and blanket on top, as if he were expecting someone to sleep over. A desk sits in front of the window with a computer, a stack of notebooks and binders lined up. Then I notice a picture in a gold frame. I lean in closer to see it's a little girl, seven or eight. She has high pigtails, soft blue eyes like Jack's, and a sweet smile. I turn to Jack, ready to ask if that's his sister, but he's already heading out the door.

"I'll show you the spare room."

"I can sleep on the couch."

"I wouldn't hear of it. I usually work late and crash on the couch." We take the few steps to the bedroom, where a blue and white quilt covers a twin bed. There's an alarm clock on the table next to the bed, a lamp. On the dresser sits a jar of change and a hairbrush. Not a bit of dust or clutter anywhere.

I set my backpack on the floor next to the bed. Jack and I stand inches from each other in the small room, and my heart starts racing. I don't think he's going to want anything from me, but this would be his perfect chance.

"Thank you. For everything." I know there's so much more I should say, but I don't know what, and I don't know how.

"How about I make us something to eat, then we'll make a plan?" Jack turns and rushes out to the kitchen as if he's more uncomfortable than I am.

We eat bologna and cheese sandwiches and pickles at the counter while Jack tells me about Savannah: the narrow streets, the old homes, the history. "And lots of tourists who come for the horse-drawn carriages and the southern charm."

"Were you born there?" I ask.

"I was born in Atlanta, but we moved to Savannah when I was two, so I consider it home."

"Do you miss it?"

He sighs. "In many ways I do. It is taking a little getting used to living here, but I'm settling in." He takes the last bite of his sandwich. "What can I offer you to drink?"

"Anything is fine. I don't want to be any trouble." I glance into the refrigerator when he opens it, see a carton of lemonade, a gallon of milk, a couple of plastic containers. No beer.

"No trouble." He pours us each a glass of lemonade and sits back down.

"I don't even know where I was born, isn't that weird?"

Jack picks up our empty plates, sets them in the sink. "We will do our level best to find out." He turns and stares at me, his blue eyes focused on my face, so serious. "I hope you're ready to trust me now. That's the only way I can help you, if I know all the facts."

"I know. It's just that I don't want to get anyone in trouble, especially Jenny."

"I'm not the police."

I take a deep breath and know I will tell him everything. I have to now. "I wasn't legally adopted."

Jack nods, puts a finger on his upper lip and waits.

"This sounds really bad, but Jenny took me from a foster family when I was three." I stop and search his face for a reaction—doubt, anger, surprise—but I don't see any judgement. He patiently waits for more.

"I was in foster care, like I said, and the people who were supposed to be taking care of me left me all alone in the back of a car. Jenny saw me and pulled me out of there and basically saved my life. She and her boyfriend Gene raised me. I always thought they were my parents. So, that's why there wouldn't be any adoption records or anything."

Jack blinks and his face turns serious. "I take it they didn't call the police?"

I shake my head.

"But it must have been all over the news. The foster parents certainly would have reported the kidnapping of a child. And the foster care agency must have searched for you. How did they get away with it?"

"The foster family didn't report me missing right away. They wanted to keep collecting the checks. Then when DCF finally checked on me and I wasn't there, they supposedly did an investigation." I shrug. It's too unreal to think about. "I think they just forgot about me after a while. Then a few months ago, they started doing news stories about kids missing from foster care. They showed all the missing kids, hundreds of them, and for some reason they chose a picture of me when I was three and did one of those age-enhanced things. It looked just like me."

"And did they identify her?"

I nod. "Adeline Jenkins. That's who I might be. But I don't know for sure."

"Okay then." He turns around, reaches up into the cabinet and takes down coffee, filters. I watch him fill the coffee pot with water, spoon coffee into the filter. "Well, that certainly makes things a lot easier. Maybe we can find out one way or the other." He walks down the hall to the office and I follow, then he stops short and turns to me. "I bet it's a relief for you, to share this secret, to trust someone."

On top of feelings of excitement and dread, I do feel relief, something I never expected. "It is. I'm sorry I didn't tell you right away. I just—"

"I can certainly understand. It's quite serious, what Jenny did. I'm sure you realize that if anyone found out, she would be charged with kidnapping."

"But she actually saved me."

"Maybe so."

I sit next to Jack while he turns on the computer, types Adeline Jenkins into the search bar. I watch his determined expression as he scrolls through the headlines, all the old articles I have read dozens of times. *Girl Missing from Foster Home, Foster Parents Investigated in Missing Child Case, DCF Faces Growing Scrutiny Over Missing Children.*

When the age-enhanced picture of Adeline Jenkins fills the screen, Jack turns and stares at me. "It does look like you."

"I know."

"Okay, give me a few minutes to read these, okay?"

Jack frowns at the computer screen when I come back with a mug of coffee. He is trying to figure everything out, when the girl in the story might be sitting right next to him. He turns to me, an angry look in his eyes. I don't blame him for being upset. I should have told him everything in the beginning.

"So," he starts, "the people fostering you finally admitted to leaving you in the car while they ran into the store, supposedly for just a few seconds, and when they came out, you were gone, and they never reported it? They endangered your life, and all they got charged with was fraud for continuing to accept checks from DCF?"

"I guess."

"Okay. Let me make sure I have this right. Jenny took you from that car, believing you were in danger, and she and Gene raised you as their own daughter. Now you want to know who your biological parents are and how you ended up in foster care." He totally gets it.

"It's really messed up."

"I would say so."

Jack takes a sip of coffee then gets back to the computer, types in *Massachusetts foster care system.*

The top headline is new to me: *Birth Mothers Speak Out About Failed Foster Care System.* Jack opens the link to the article, published yesterday in the Boston Globe. It says it's the third in a five-part series. This one is about mothers who either gave up their children or whose children were taken away and put in foster care. Now the children are missing, and the mothers blame the foster care system for failing to take care of their children. We read it in silence.

When I gave up my son to foster care, he was 11. I had no family and was on the verge of homelessness. I thought they were going to place him with a good family. I thought he would have a better life than I could give him. Instead, they stuck him in this group home where he was bullied and who-knows-what else. He ran away after a year and no one has any idea where he is.

And,

What kind of a system takes away your two kids, saying they're being neglected, then splits them up so they never see each other again? And if that's not bad enough, now both of my boys have gone missing and no one has any idea where they are. Talk about neglect.

And,

They said I couldn't keep my baby, my own daughter, because I was only 15 and in the system myself. They said they would find a good family to foster her and eventually adopt her. This great foster family lost her. She was only three.

The article makes everything more real, more personal. It's all about the mothers, including maybe mine. I scroll back up to the quotes and read the last one again, the short one. *My daughter. She was only three.*

"That could be me," I say, to myself as much as to Jack. "It kind of fits. I was with a foster family, and I was three when

I disappeared." I try not to get too excited, but I have a strong, strange feeling in my chest. Something like hope?

"Of course there wouldn't be any further information here, but let's see what we can find out." Jack scrolls to the bottom of the article, where the reporter has his email address. He clicks on that and a new window opens. "The reporter's name is Eric Roberts. What do you think? Do you want to see if he'll meet with us?"

"I don't know. I mean, what would we say? What would we have to tell him?"

"We don't have to tell him anything you don't want to. He may insist on some details, of course, some facts before he tells us anything, but it's totally up to you as to what you want to share."

I think about it for a few seconds. What else do I have? "Okay." I feel like I'm being pulled, or pushed, not by Jack, but by some force or something, some wave I'm riding. I can't think about it too much or I'll change my mind.

Jack starts typing. *Would like to discuss your recent article about birth mothers and foster care. I may have some information about one of the missing children.* "That will surely get his attention." Before he sends it, he turns to me. "You're sure?"

I read it over one more time and nod. My heart is pounding, but I also feel calm, so grateful to have Jack helping me. He's the only person on the planet who knows all my secrets.

He presses a button and the screen changes. *Message sent.*

I check the corner of the screen. 11:53. "It's late. He probably won't even see this until tomorrow."

"He's a reporter." Jack takes a sip of coffee. "Reporters are always looking for the next story."

At exactly midnight, we get a response from Eric Roberts. *Are you local? Willing to meet in person?*

Jack types, *We could meet you in the morning in Greenfield, if that is convenient for you. Millie's Diner on Parker Street at 9:00?*

Eric responds right away. *See you then.*

I try not to get my hopes up, but I can't help it. It feels good to be able to hope. A voice in my head says it can't possibly be this easy. I tell the voice to shut up, that it's about time something is easy.

It isn't until I'm in bed, under the covers, that I realize how tired I am. Today feels like it lasted a week at least. Thoughts of Adam and Mike push their way in and I push them right back out. I'm safe. Thanks to Jack. I fall asleep thinking about Jenny. I wonder if calling her made things better or worse. It must have made her feel at least a little better, hearing my voice, knowing I'm okay. And I am okay. Here I am staying with a guy I just met today, sleeping in a strange bed, planning to meet with a reporter tomorrow, and somehow I'm okay. I fall asleep telling myself that.

Chapter 5

Jack parks the car just past Bob's Hardware Store, wheelbarrows and rakes lined up out front. "The diner is just a couple of blocks from here. I thought it might be better if Eric doesn't see the car. You can't be too careful."

I'm not sure what he's talking about, but I'm too distracted by what I'm doing, what I might be getting into, to ask. The more I feel like I'm making a huge mistake, the faster I walk. We turn down a quiet side street with only one car parked on it, one of those tiny cars that look like a toy, shiny red. I think about walking with Adam, going into Tito's like an idiot, that woman behind the counter. Mike with his mean eyes and dirty fingers.

"Are you okay?" Jack's voice is soft and reassuring.

I try to smile but can't.

"I'm sure you're nervous, but remember, you don't have to tell him anything you don't want to, and anytime it feels like too much, we can leave, okay?"

"I wanted answers so badly, but now it feels like it's happening too fast."

We stop and stand in front of the door to Millie's and face each other. "Do you want to leave?" Jack asks. "It would be rude, of course, but it's completely up to you."

I shake my head. "We're here."

Jack nods, pulls open the door, and we step in to the smells of coffee and bacon. I have a memory of another diner just like this when I was a kid, with Jenny and Gene. We were on an adventure. A stack of pancakes, a tall glass of cold milk, Jenny's pink lipstick on the rim of her coffee mug. Gene was asking someone if they had a map. I wish I had a map.

Everything in Millie's is gray and white and clean—the linoleum floor, the counters and stools rimmed in shiny chrome. We stop just inside the door and look around. A man sitting in a booth in the back stands and looks our way, shoots his hand up like kids do in school. He's kind of old, 60's maybe, and his hair is mostly white, but thick, and he has bushy white eyebrows.

We introduce ourselves with first names and shake hands. Jack and I slide into one side of the booth, Eric in the other. In a few seconds, the waitress appears with a pot of coffee, turns over the thick white mugs. I ask for a ginger ale and she says she'll be back in a jif. The door jingles and I turn, picture Jenny walking in and seeing me with two strange men. She would have a fit and drag me out of there, no questions asked.

Jack starts. "First of all, thank you kindly for meeting with us. We wanted to talk about the article you did on the mothers with kids in the foster system. It was pretty amazing, hearing from the mothers."

"You said you may have information about one of the missing children?" Eric nods at Jack, then focuses his eyes on me.

"I think I could be one of the missing kids," I say. My voice is barely above a whisper.

Eric's calm expression doesn't change. No shock or surprise, just a tiny nod as if he hears things like this all the time. His eyes are watchful, waiting for more. He takes out a notebook and pen, which makes me a little nervous, but I think it also means he's taking me seriously.

I take a sip of ginger ale and clear my throat. "I found out recently I was in foster care when I was little. I want to find out who my biological parents are, but I need to be 18 to get any information from DCF. I was living in a foster home when I was a baby, then I went missing when I was three. In your story, you interviewed a mother who said her daughter went missing from the foster system when she was three. I think maybe I could be her."

Eric scribbles something down, frowns. “You must have more than that, more than a feeling. When you say you *went missing*, what exactly do you mean?”

I take another sip of ginger ale, getting watery now, and thankfully, Jack takes over.

“Obviously she can’t know anything for sure, being so young and all, but we thought you might be able to—”

“How old are you, Meg?” Eric interrupts.

“I’m almost 16.” I dread the question I know is coming.

“Where have you been for 13 years?” Before I can answer, Eric turns to Jack with a frown. “Has she been with you?”

Jack shakes his head. “Meg and I just recently met. I’m an investigator. When she told me she was looking for her birth mother, I offered to help. That’s all.”

“I’m not accusing you of anything,” Eric says. “I’m just trying to get all the facts here. You contacted me, said you may have information, but so far you haven’t given me anything. I need you both to be straight with me. Understood?”

I make my voice strong. “I just recently found out I was adopted when I was about three. That’s where I’ve been, with the people who adopted me. I was in foster care before that. I’m trying to find out who my birth parents are and how I ended up in foster care.” Am I telling him too much?

Eric makes a note, stares at it a few seconds, then looks at me. “Would you mind clarifying a few things for me? You said you might be one of the missing foster children. I need to know who you think you are and why you think this. And you said you were adopted after being in foster care. I need to know how that came about, whether it was a legal adoption, and through what agency.”

It’s about as far from legal as it could be. I take a deep breath. “I was only three, so I don’t know about an agency. Can you just tell me how I can contact the woman in the article?”

Eric signals the waitress, who brings another ginger ale for me and more coffee for Eric and Jack. He waits until she walks away before he stares at Jack. "I agreed to meet you because you said you had information about one of the missing foster children, but it's becoming clear that you only want information that I believe you know I can't give you. These women spoke to me on the condition of anonymity. They all have pasts they're not proud of, and some may think they deserved to have their children taken away. The last thing they need is more scrutiny and judgment."

"We are not here to judge anyone," Jack says. His voice is soft, calm. "It sounds like these women would welcome finding out their child is safe, right? If we can do that, it would be a good thing, wouldn't you say? Let me ask you, Eric, what was the purpose of your article if not to help find these missing children?"

Eric shakes his head, takes a sip of coffee. "First of all, it's my job to write the news, follow stories. It's what I do. Secondly, this series is intended to shine a light on flaws in the foster care system. Oftentimes, the only way to make needed change is by getting stories like this in the public eye. If it helps these particular women, or any parents, all the better, but I can't in all honesty say my purpose was to reunite these women with their children."

"Even if you are able to put them in touch with their children who have been missing? Who disappeared without a trace from the foster care system?" Jack asks.

"There are far too many variables, details of their lives I'm not privy to. I'm not painting the system as the demon here, Jack, but DCF is seriously understaffed and underfunded. Reforms are definitely needed, and I believe the public needs to know the truth."

"If there was a way to help Meg find out if this is her biological mother, wouldn't that be another good story for you?"

"Possibly. But, as I said, these women don't want their identities out there. You can understand that this is sensitive information. But Meg, if you believe you were in a foster home, went missing, then somehow ended up with the people who you say adopted you and raised you, I would need to know the how and the why. I need all the facts before I could even consider taking this to my editor. Some proof that you are who you say you are."

"But that's the thing," I say, my voice breaking. "I don't know."

Eric looks down at his notebook, then at me. "To be honest, Meg, there are too many missing pieces of this puzzle, and frankly, I think you know more than you're saying. If you disappeared from a foster family when you were three, how exactly did your adoptive parents get you?" He taps his pen on the table. "There's too much you're not telling me. I think I'm wasting my time here." He puts his pen down, closes his notebook.

I stir the ice in my glass with my straw and try to think of what to say next. If I tell him about Jenny and he tells the police, she'll be arrested for kidnapping, and I couldn't do that to her. I believe her when she said she was saving me, or at least I believe she believed that. We didn't have an ideal life, but I'm sure it would have been way worse if I stayed with the people who left me alone in the back of a car.

"If I told you anything, you would have to keep it confidential, right?" My voice is soft, and Eric leans in closer. "I mean, whatever I said, you would protect me and the people who raised me, right? Just like you're protecting the women in the story?"

Eric stares down at his notebook again, picks up his pen and taps it on the table. "I can't guarantee anything at this point, Meg, based on what I know so far, which is next to nothing. But to your question, yes, you would be protected as a source, just as the women in the story are. As far as the people who you say adopted you and raised you, I would need to know more, especially how, exactly, they ended up with you."

"All Meg wants is to find out whether or not she is the woman's child, the one in your story. I would think the mothers you interviewed would be happy to know their child is alive and well, right? Maybe even be reunited?" Jack is trying so hard to help me.

Eric sighs. "Back to that. Listen, it's a long, hard road for these women. Some of them are now in stable relationships and want to forget the child they gave up or that was taken from them. Then there are some who are angry, isolated, dependent on drugs or alcohol, which could be why their children were taken in the first place. These are generalities, mind you. I am not in any way talking about the women in my story. But if you do somehow find your biological mother, be prepared. And, as I said, if you want my help, you need to be honest with me. I don't do one-sided stories. I need all the facts if I'm going to get into this with you."

"I don't want to get anyone in trouble."

Eric smiles for the first time since we walked in. "Then let's find a way not to, okay?"

I try to smile back, but I'm not sure what I'm doing or what I'm getting into. How close can I get to the truth without hurting Jenny? "I need a couple of days. I have to talk to someone."

Eric's smile is gone and he gives me a hard stare. He's probably not happy he came all this way for nothing. "I can give you until tomorrow. These stories have a shelf life."

"We just need to check a couple of things," Jack says.

"I know it's not always easy to do the right thing." Eric stands, puts his notebook and pen in his pocket, picks up his briefcase and looks at me. "Tomorrow, then? 10:00?" He pulls out his wallet and lays a twenty on the table.

"We'll be here," Jack says, and we all shake hands and walk out.

I want to believe everything will be okay. I want to believe that I can somehow tell the truth and find the truth without getting Jenny in trouble. As we walk to Jack's car, I start to form a plan, a way to give Eric his story and find out if I really am Adeline Jenkins.

I could say it was Gene, that he was the one who took me from the car, that he thought he could get some kind of ransom. I could say that Jenny had nothing to do with it. Gene could have come up with all kinds of stories about where he got me—on the side of the road, from a friend who couldn't take care of me. He always had a story.

They probably couldn't find Gene, he's so good at hiding out, and if they did, they probably wouldn't believe him when he said he had nothing to do with it, that it was all Jenny. Plus, all the paperwork Jenny has that says I'm hers was forged by Gene's friend Sam.

I need to talk to Jenny before I meet with Eric again. I owe her that. More than that. She needs to understand how important this is to me and how close I might be to getting answers. She'll be mad, even more than she already is, that I met with a reporter and plan on meeting with him again, but hopefully she will listen.

Chapter 6

"I dread seeing Jenny." I stare at the ground in front of us as Jack and I walk back to his car. This time we're walking slowly. "But I can't tell Eric anything until I talk to her. I am done with secrets. I'm going to tell her everything, about you and about Eric and his story and how he is probably the only way to find out who I really am." I can already imagine Jenny's reaction, how upset she'll be, even more than she is now, and when she's upset she doesn't listen, doesn't hear or feel anything but her anger.

We stop at the corner and wait until we can cross. There's a lot more traffic now, people with places to go. People who know exactly who they are and have somewhere they're supposed to be. Jack turns to me, his face serious. "You are very brave. I admire you for that. I think you are the bravest person I have ever met."

I stare into Jack's face, his kind blue eyes. *Where did you come from?* "I'm not brave. I feel scared most of the time, and when I'm not scared, I probably should be."

"You'll feel better after you talk to Jenny, and I'm sure Jenny will too. People surprise us sometimes. Maybe she wants to be done with secrets as much as you do."

I look up at the blue sky, a few clouds that make me think of cotton candy. The sun is warm on my face. "You don't know her. She's afraid. I don't blame her. She could spend years in jail for kidnapping if anyone finds out."

The light changes and we cross the street. There's a tiny park up ahead on the right. A small rectangle of grass with a tree and a bench in the middle. It's between two buildings and set back from the street like a secret spot. The empty bench is painted dark green and we walk to it without a word and sit, as if we had planned to come here. A robin lands in front of us, pecks in the grass a few times before it flies away.

"This has to be difficult for you," Jack says. "You must have a lot of conflicting thoughts in your head right now."

"Ever since I found out about how Jenny got me and kept me, raised me like I was her own daughter, I've had a million thoughts in my head. I mean, I was shocked. I think I still am. And I was so mad that she never told me. I'm old enough to know. I still can't believe she just walked up to that car and *took* me. If I didn't see that show about the missing foster kids, she probably never would have told me."

"It was pretty brazen. Did she say why she didn't just call the police when she found you alone?"

"She said at the time all she thought about was getting me out of that car to somewhere safe. Then after she got me home, she knew if she called the police that she would be the one who got in trouble. She would be the one they arrested. Then when she found out I was in foster care, she knew if she gave me back they would put me right back in, maybe even with the people who left me there in the first place. All she thought about was saving me." I stare straight ahead as I talk, at the cars going by, the antique store across the street. Three girls wearing green plaid school uniforms and backpacks walk by, glance over at us for just a second. "It makes me feel like my whole life has been a lie, which is what Jenny doesn't get."

"Oh I'm sure she gets it. She just doesn't want to lose you. And, of course, she doesn't want to go to jail. I'm sure you're right about her being afraid. Anyone would be."

"I wouldn't do anything that would get her in trouble. And I told her a million times she isn't going to lose me. No matter what I find, I'm not going to abandon her. I just want to know who my parents are and why I was in foster care. I feel like I'm missing part of myself."

"I understand."

"I wish Jenny did. I wish she could understand it has nothing to do with her."

Jack squints like he's trying to figure something out. "Now there I would have to disagree. When Jenny took you from that car, essentially pulling you out of foster care, she changed the entire course of your life. She raised you as her own for 13 years. You can't say she doesn't have a stake in what happens to you. A pretty big stake, I would say."

"I just mean that nothing will change between us."

Jack makes that face again. "Not to argue here, but you can't really know that. Have you thought about what you'll do if you do find your biological mother?"

I have had so many different scenes in my head, always with just my biological mother, no father. She's usually single and young and almost always glad to see me. "I want to talk to her, and hopefully get some answers. I want to know who she is and who she was when she had me. I want to know the reason she gave me up, or if I was taken away from her."

"You might find some answers you don't want to hear."

"Like what? That she didn't want me? That I was a mistake? If that's how it was, at least I'll know. Plus, it's been a long time. She might feel differently now about having a daughter than she did then, right?"

Jack opens his mouth, then presses his lips tight like he doesn't want his next words to escape.

"What?"

"Let's take it a step at a time, okay? I don't want to invent things that might not happen. But remember what Eric said, about being prepared? It was good advice. I hate to say it, but after all your efforts, she might want nothing to do with you. Are you prepared for that?"

"It's better than not knowing."

Jack nods. "Maybe so. When do you want to go see Jenny?"

"Today. Before we meet with Eric in the morning. I still have no idea how I can tell him anything about Jenny without getting her in trouble."

"I'm sure all kinds of thoughts are running through his head too. And as far as him keeping things confidential, I'm sure he would do his best, but protecting sources can get a little fuzzy when it comes to reporting crimes, especially Federal crimes like kidnapping."

"I hate that word. And that's not how Jenny saw it. She saw a baby all alone in the back of a car with no one around and she got me out of there. I could have been one of those kids who died. Jenny showed me all these news stories she cut out of the paper about parents forgetting to drop off their kid at day care and leaving them in the car while they went to work, or shopping or gambling or whatever." The more I try to explain, the more I want to defend Jenny.

I wait for some comment from Jack, agreeing Jenny did the right thing, that she shouldn't be arrested for it, but when I turn to him, he's leaning forward, staring down at his shoes. I'm not sure what else to say.

"I hate that word too," he finally says. "Let's not use it, okay? If I hear you right, you believe that sometimes abducting a child is justified?"

When he puts it like that, it makes me a little less sure, but I say, "I—maybe. I mean, if it's to save someone's life, then yes."

Jack turns away like I said something wrong, and he sounds funny when he answers, like his words are stuck in his throat. "Maybe so." He keeps his head turned away, and I'm not sure what to say. Obviously, Jack has secrets too. Everyone does. It might have something to do with his sister. He said he *had* a sister. Did she die? Was she kidnapped? I put my hand on his arm, the first time I've touched him since the day we met and shook hands. Was it really only yesterday?

Jack takes a deep breath before he turns to me. "Are you ready?"

I don't move. "You know you can tell me anything, right? Everything has been about me. What about you? Do you want to talk about anything? I'm a really good listener. And I'm excellent at keeping secrets, as you know."

That makes him smile. "Not just now, thanks. Let's focus on you."

"I never had anyone I could depend on like you, someone I can totally trust." I feel a twinge of guilt at saying this. Jenny would be angry and hurt and say, *What about me?*

"Well, that's a shame. I'm glad I can be here for you." The sun peeks out from behind a cloud just as he says this, and we both look up at the sky like little kids at recess. We stand at the same time and start walking again.

"I actually have an idea of what I can tell Eric so Jenny won't get in trouble." I'm not proud of it, but I tell him anyway. "What if I say it was Gene that took me? I can tell him Jenny didn't know anything about it until we saw that story on television."

Jack stops and stares at me for what seems like a long time. "Do you really want to complicate things by lying? Lies have a way of coming out eventually, and end up being much more destructive than the truth would ever be. And I don't believe you want to lie. You said you were done with secrets."

"I am. I want to be. I just don't want Jenny to get arrested."

"You don't have to tell them what Jenny did, but you also don't have to lie. Listen, Meg, some people are born liars. I don't believe you are one of them."

I want this to be true. "I'm not the innocent little kid you think I am."

Jack laughs. "I don't think you're innocent, or a little kid for that matter. But I'm a pretty good judge of character and I don't buy you being able to set someone up like that. What exactly was Gene's role in all this?"

"Jenny said he *let* her keep me at first because he thought there would be a reward. Then, when they found out I was a foster kid and there was no reward or anyone that would pay a ransom, he wanted to leave me in a church. By then, though, Jenny and I had bonded, I guess, and leaving me wasn't an option, at least not for her."

"Okay. So let's imagine how this would play out and the questions Eric might have if you told him it was all Gene. What did Gene tell Jenny when he just showed up with a three-year-old girl in his arms? What did Jenny say and do? Why didn't she call the police? Do you see how much simpler the truth is? Jenny saw you in danger and got you out of there. She may very well have saved your life."

My life. I want it to feel like my life. I have gone over and over what I remember of my life, every memory, things I will never forget—the trailer, sitting at that little table in front of the window coloring or doing puzzles. The door that swung open wide and banged against the side of the trailer whenever Gene finally came home, the screen door squeaking. A welcome warning that everything was about to change.

"Maybe it will be a good thing for Jenny as well as you to talk about all this, especially now that you may have a possible lead on your birth mother."

"I know Jenny, and I can't see her ever wanting what she did to come out. But if Eric can keep it secret, our identities I mean. If we're protected, she might be okay with it. After she thinks about it." We are back at Jack's car. It feels like days instead of a couple of hours since we parked here.

"There's only one way to find out." Jack unlocks the car doors and we slip inside. Before he turns on the ignition, we turn and face each other. "I know there's a lot on the line here, Meg. Truth be told, I don't think Eric is out to get anyone in trouble.

He wants the story, but I also detected a lot of empathy for these women. And, of course, the children."

I think about what Jack said about lies being more destructive than the truth. "I'm sure Jenny never wants anyone to know the truth. And if the truth did come out, I don't want to be the one to get her in trouble."

"All we can do right now is see what she says, then go from there. You might be surprised. Are you familiar with that expression, *I'll take that secret to the grave with me*?"

"Sort of."

"It rarely happens."

I think about that for a few seconds, not sure I believe it. "Will you come with me to talk to Jenny?" I blurt this out before I think, then feel so selfish for asking. But I can't imagine going ahead with any of this without him.

Jack's eyes widen in surprise. "You want me to get arrested for harboring a runaway?"

"I'm not a runaway. I left Jenny a note and I called her. You didn't do anything wrong. All you did was help me."

"Would Jenny believe that? Or would she call the police, thinking some pervert befriended you?"

"I can't see her calling the police, but you're right about what she would think. She wouldn't trust you, not for a second. I'm sorry I asked. You already did too much. You have your own life to get back to."

"I know we haven't known each other long, but I hope you consider me a friend. I don't believe there's a limit on what a friend can do. And I don't want you to think I don't want to go with you. I just don't want to make things worse between you and Jenny. And, of course, I don't want to be arrested. You are still considered a minor after all."

"I know. It's okay." I don't want to beg him, and I don't want him to feel bad, but my eyes fill up and I'm close to crying. "I still have my bus ticket." I pull the bus schedule out of my pocket, pretty worn and wrinkled now. I have studied it so many times, I should know it by heart. A tear escapes and I brush it away. I'm not a crier.

"Hey." Jack puts his hand on my arm. "It's going to be okay."

"I know." I blink to keep the rest of the stupid tears in, try to focus on the schedule, but it's blurry now. "Do you think you can drop me off at the bus station? Or wait. Maybe I can walk. Maybe there's a bus stop closer to here and—"

"Meg. Stop. How about if I drop you off at my place for about an hour while I check in at work. You can have some time alone to think, then I'll take you to see Jenny."

"You don't have to. You already did too much."

"I feel like I got you into this whole situation with Eric and all. The least I can do is see it through."

"I still don't know why. I mean why you care so much. And I know that's what Jenny will ask. *Who are you and why are you so involved?* According to Jenny, everyone on the planet has an ulterior motive, and no one does anything unless there's something in it for them."

"You need help, Meg. I saw that the first day we met. And I truly believe people come into our lives for a reason. And truth be told, the more I get to know you, the more I realize how much you're helping me too."

"How?"

"It's a little complicated to explain now. I'm still figuring it out myself, but one day I hope you will understand."

Chapter 7

I don't know what the hell is wrong with me. Meggie finally calls and I was so relieved to hear her voice all I did was yell at her. It happened so fast I didn't have time to think. Then she hung up and now she's gone again. I can't believe I actually told her that if she didn't come home right now, not to bother coming home at all. Sometimes I feel like I'm not in control of my own mouth. I don't blame her for hanging up on me.

When I tried calling right back, I got a message from a recorded voice that the person I was trying to reach is not available. No kidding.

For the hundredth time since she's been gone, I walk into Meggie's room and sit on the side of her bed. I fold my hands in my lap like I'm getting ready to pray. You'd never know anyone lived in this room, it's so neat and clean, nothing on the dresser but a brush and a box of tissues. No posters on the walls, no photos stuck to the mirror. How does a teenage girl not have a bunch of stuff everywhere? We've been here two years now, but it seems like Meggie hasn't quite moved in.

I open the top drawer, touch the pale blue sweatshirt on top, a pair of jeans next to it, underwear and socks in the next drawer, all folded neatly. Her fleece and windbreaker hang in her closet, along with a yellow dress that probably doesn't fit anymore.

Meggie has never been one to make a mess, make a fuss. Until now. I smooth the comforter, look around again. She said she's okay. She said not to worry, as if it's that easy. She has no idea. I study myself in the mirror, pull out a gray hair that doesn't belong. If it wasn't for a few small lines around my mouth no one would guess I'm 32. I look at Meggie's brush before I use it, the fine strands that look like baby hair. She'll be home soon.

In the kitchen, I glance at the clock on the stove. I have less than 15 minutes to get to my so-called counselling appointment, the part of my probation I hate most, even more than the AA meetings. My lawyer told me more than once how lucky I was not to get six months at least for shoplifting, that a year of probation, counselling and AA are a very lenient sentence and not to blow it. All I did was steal a lipstick. Not exactly grand theft. I'm glad Justin's a court-appointed lawyer and I'm not paying for those words of wisdom.

Dr. Brock's office looks like a movie set. Dark paneling and ferns and shelves full of books he probably hasn't read. He stands and says, "Jenny." He sounds like he was expecting someone else.

We sit facing each other in the chairs in front of the window, a fern on the wooden stand between us, thick and green. He asks how I am, how my week was. All good. Same old.

I watch him stare down at the top paper in the stack he has on his lap. How did my file get so big?

He finally looks up with a tight smile. "So. I'd like us to explore your relationship with Gene a little more, since he was such a significant part of your life and a huge influence on your behavior." He looks down at his notes again. I didn't realize I was that interesting. "Last week, you said he was using you. Can you tell me more about that?"

"I already told you everything about Gene." I slip off my sweater, even though it's a little chilly in here. I'm wearing my bright pink blouse, unbuttoned just enough. I uncross my legs and lean back and smile to show him how good I am, and also to lighten the serious mood he's creating. "I told you I was really young and pretty and pretty innocent when we met, and he took advantage of that. He got me into drinking and drugs, mostly pot, and he encouraged me to steal. Mostly just booze. So that's it."

"And how did you feel about all that? Were you ever afraid? Experiences like this can cause long-lasting trauma, loss of self-esteem, anxiety, a whole host of issues."

"I was never afraid of Gene. We had a great time, and we truly loved each other, Part of me wishes I had never met Gene, but there is also a part of me where Gene will always have a place. It's not a big enough part that I would ever take him back, but it's big enough so I don't feel like it was all for nothing, okay? I really don't want to talk about Gene anymore."

"What would you like to talk about then?" As if it's up to me. "You told me you don't have any siblings, but what about your parents? You haven't mentioned them at all. Are you close?"

I want to talk about my parents even less than I want to talk about Gene. "I haven't spoken to my parents in years. They disowned me because they hated Gene and I chose him. And please don't ask me how I feel about that. I really don't care." I turn and look out the window at the cars speeding down the street, people walking. A world that doesn't include me right now.

Dr. Brock stares at me, waiting for more, but I have no more I want to give him. It's not the whole story, not by a long shot, but what I told him is true.

"Jenny?" He waits until I look at him. "I can see thoughts of your parents are upsetting to you. It may be good to talk about it. There's no judgment. I'm here to listen. You're the one who needs to do the work."

"Why does it have to be work? I'd much rather have a little fun, wouldn't you?" Dr. Brock is the absolute opposite of bad-boy Gene, and isn't that what I'm supposed to be going for? I reach over and put my hand on his thigh, and he flinches as if I've burned him, pushes his chair back.

"Jenny. That is not appropriate. I think you know that." His eyes say something different. I can see he wants me, but not enough to jeopardize his precious job.

God how I hate that word, *appropriate.* I heard it more than enough in my lifetime, from my teachers, my mother, even my father in the beginning.

"Why not?" I ask. "I feel good when I'm with you. Isn't that why I'm here?" I give him my most seductive smile and lean in a little closer. "No one needs to know." I keep up my smile, even though I'm not feeling it and he's not buying it.

Dr. Brock stands, so I do, too, but when I reach for him, he takes hold of my arms, not rough, but not gentle either. Just enough so I can't get any closer. After all the time he tried to get inside my head. "This is totally out of bounds, Jenny. You know that." It isn't the reaction I was hoping for or expected or deserve.

I pull my arms away and look into his angry brown eyes I thought were so warm just a few minutes ago. "You know what? This isn't working for me anyway." I sound like I'm talking about an outfit or a job.

"Jenny," is all he says, but the way he says my name is full of disappointment.

"What?" Is that regret I see in his eyes now? He lost his chance and he knows it.

The good doctor can't seem to find any *appropriate* words, so I step away, retrieve my sweater and purse and walk out without looking at him again. I don't even slam the door. How's that for control?

I make myself slow down as I walk towards the elevators, glance at my reflection in the mirrored doors before I head down the stairs to give him a chance to come after me. Halfway down, I stop and look up, listen to the silence of the stairwell. Self-righteous prick.

Now I'll have to explain to my probation officer how I need a new counselor or therapist. Whatever. The court mandates, the patient has to find one. At least Medicaid pays for most of it. All I want is to be done with this and get on with my life, get this last shitty part of my past off my back. Ten more months of probation and counselling and meetings, then I get my life back.

The house phone starts ringing as soon as I open my apartment door. It's probably a sales call, but I grab it before I even close the door behind me, hoping it's Meggie again, apologizing and telling me she's on her way home now. But it's more likely the police telling me she's in trouble or something happened to her. It's never good when the house phone rings, but I pick it up anyway. "Hello?"

"Your father passed. I thought you should know."

At first, I think it's a prank call, some kind of scam, but it's my mother's voice, and she sounds really drunk. I don't say anything yet. I don't know what to say.

"Daddy's special little girl. Well, you don't have a daddy anymore." She sounds glad to be giving me this news, as if I deserve it. Maybe I do.

"Mom?" I close the door before I pull out a kitchen chair and sit, lean my elbows on the table and hold the phone tight.

"You lost the right to call me that a long time ago." The last time we talked, when I called to tell her she had a granddaughter and we needed help, she told me she had no daughter and hung up. Now she's crying, I think, but I'm having a hard time feeling sorry for her. It's impossible to feel much of anything for her. Or my dead father for that matter.

"What happened?"

"He had a heart attack."

There are so many things we should both say, so much time lost, but I don't know where to start. As much as I would dread going home after all this time and seeing my mother, I ask, "Is there a service?"

"It's private."

I almost laugh, but it's not funny. "Private? I can't go to my own father's funeral?" I'm relieved, and not all that surprised. Her last act of revenge.

"It's what he wanted. I just thought you should know he's gone, just in case you ever think about him. Or me." I can't tell if she's laughing or crying. Maybe both, but it sounds like she's trying to laugh, as if none of this bothers her, as if none of it was her fault.

"I try not to think of that part of my life. You chose to believe your husband over your own daughter when you found him in my room. That's on you." All the years that have passed since our last fight, the night she threw me out when I was barely 16, don't mean a thing. We are right back in the exact same place. "You knew the truth of what he was doing, but it was easier to blame me, right?"

"Of course I blamed you. You seduced him. With your skimpy little shorts and no bra. What did you expect?"

"I expected—"

My mother hangs up without another word. I start to call her back, but what's the point? And what did I expect back then anyway? That she would understand that I was a teenage girl discovering the power her body had over men? My father understood and took advantage of it. Why the hell did she have to call and bring back all that hurt and shame I worked so hard to bury?

When the tears take over, they surprise me. Then I'm crying hard and loud and I'm not sure what the hell I'm even crying about except pretty much everything about my shitty little life. It feels good to let it out and I don't try to stop. Why should I? Then it's finished as quickly as it started, and I am empty.

Once I get home from my one cleaning job for the day, I take a long, hot shower, slip on my sweats and settle on the couch. I want a drink now, need a drink, just to take the edge off. I deserve that much. A six-pack wouldn't be bad. I don't see my probation officer until next Monday, and the alcohol would be out of my system by then. My daughter is off somewhere on her own, looking for her *real* mother, and I'm not supposed to worry. I got shut down by my idiotic, self-centered jerk of a counselor, and now I have to find another one. My father just died, and my mother hates me. And there's not a damn thing I can do about anything. If anyone deserves a beer, I do.

Screw it. I grab my purse and head out to the package store. One six-pack. Maybe I won't even drink the whole thing tonight. Just enough to help me relax and forget the mess my life is right now.

I walk fast, keep my head down. I push out thoughts of Dr. Brock and replace them with thoughts of Gene. The happiest times of my life was when we drove around in his van, drinking warm cans of PBR or Bud, sharing a joint, the radio loud. Nothing else mattered then except having a good time. Everything was so simple. Finding Meggie changed all that, changed me, changed Gene. Maybe it just showed us who we were all along. The look in his eye when he saw me carrying her. *What the hell are you doing?* Whatever I was doing, it felt good. It felt right and that's all I knew.

I'm proud of myself for not getting more than a six-pack, not going out for more when that was gone. The phone doesn't ring again. I half-watch American Idol and battle thoughts of my mother and my father and at some point close my eyes. It's been such a long and awful day.

I fall asleep on the couch and dream of my father, and even though I can't remember the details, when I wake up a little after four, I'm left with a feeling of being exposed and helpless and angry. I get up and use the bathroom without turning on the light, crawl into bed and pull the covers up to my chin, but I can't get back to sleep. Too much of me doesn't want to.

After lying there for an hour, I get up and get dressed and wish I had left just one beer to even things out for the day. There's nothing like a beer first thing in the morning, then a couple cups of strong coffee and something sweet. I take out the gallon jug of water from the fridge, open it and tilt it up to my mouth too fast. Most of it gets into my mouth, some dribbles down my chin and onto my shirt. I gulp it down, burp, rinse my mouth and spit it into the kitchen sink, feeling disgusted with myself.

When Meggie comes home, I'll tell her I'm sorry. I'll tell her how much I missed her and that I'm trying, really trying, to do better to understand how she feels. I'll tell her about my father dying, and that should bring some sympathy.

After more water and a piece of toast, I go back to bed. I set the alarm for eight to give me plenty of time to get to work. I don't mind my cleaning jobs. Three houses and the common areas of our apartment building. The pay is decent, and I don't have anyone looking over my shoulder, anyone I need to talk to. It's amazing how much people will pay to have someone clean up their messes.

Then my stupid meeting at noon where I will say, *I'm Jenny, and I'm an alcoholic.* I may or may not tell them about how my father died and I drank a few beers last night and how terrible I feel about it, which I don't. They will nod and look at me with sympathy and fake understanding and tell me how they can relate to how difficult it can be to get through something like that without alcohol.

If Riley's there, my sponsor and one of the few people in this world who cares about me, she will encourage me and try to make me believe I can be better, at least for today. One day at a time. God how I hate that idea. I am so sick of my life being a constant daily battle to be good, to be good enough. One day. That's all I'm supposed to work for and look forward to. I deserve more than that.

Chapter 8

My probation officer, Mr. Brennan, calls me at 8:30. I'm on my third cup of coffee and my second piece of toast, and I don't feel too bad. I've been worse.

"I got a call yesterday from Dr. Brock, telling me he can no longer treat you."

I take a sip of coffee and wait. No sense trying to explain until I hear what he says.

"He told me what happened." Mr. Brennan sounds tired, or maybe just tired of me.

"I'm sure he told you his version. I'm sure he left out the part where he was hitting on me, right?"

"Jenny, the judge doesn't have any patience for this kind of behavior. You know the counselling is mandated as part of your probation, and you can't have a lapse in service. Last chance to make this work. You got a sweet deal, so don't blow it, okay?"

"Got it." The more he tells me this, the less sweet it feels.

"I mean it."

"I hear you."

"Find a new counselor today, and make it work." He hangs up without another word. How rude.

I look at the next name on the list of "providers" I get to choose from. *Dr. Richard Elliot.* Sounds like someone from a soap opera. I skip to the P's, just random, and try to be positive. This time, I'll try a woman. Maybe a woman won't be so condescending, and I also won't feel the need to make sure I look good. It crosses my mind for a couple of seconds that there could also be a chance I could get something out of this, but I'm not counting on it.

Besides Meggie, I have never been close to a female in my life—not my mother, not any girls in high school. I never knew how. The only person even close to a friend was Darlene at the trailer park, not that we had anything in common. That's where I would head after a fight with Gene, and Darlene and I drank gin and tonics. I guess she was a friend, now that I think about it. She was a good person, always glad when I walked over to her trailer, even if it was only to vent or ask her to watch Meggie sometimes.

I don't have high expectations as I make an appointment with a Dr. A. Phillips, surprised she can see me as soon as this afternoon. A good thing for me, so I don't have the "lapse in service," but what does it say about her? The secretary asks me to be there 15 minutes early to fill out the paperwork. Always paperwork.

Unlike the other doctors who sit behind their desks to show me how important they are as I'm ushered in, Dr. Phillips comes out of her office to greet me. Her face lights up with an expression like she has been looking forward to meeting me all her life. She's the first person in a long, long time to look at me like I matter. She wears navy blue pants and a gray cotton sweater. She's somewhere in her fifties, shorter than me, and solid. Her straight hair comes to her chin, brown with streaks of gray, and it's a little shaggy, like she might cut it herself.

She puts her hand out, and I take it for a quick shake. I hate shaking hands. It seems like such a guy thing. But Dr. Phillips takes my hand gently and adds her other one for a moment as if she already knows how hard this is for me. "You must be Jenny. Welcome."

We walk into her office, which is about as different from Dr. Brock's office as possible—a little messy, but bright and comfortable and full of light. "Here you go. Have a seat. Please." She lifts a couple of books from one of the chairs and sets them on a table in the corner.

She takes the chair next to me and we swivel to face each other. She doesn't have a notebook on her lap and a pen in her hand like the others either.

"Thanks for seeing me so fast." I want to get off on the right foot.

Dr. Phillips waves the air like there's a mosquito, folds her hands in front of her belly. "No problem. Or no bother, as they say in Ireland. Have you ever been? Absolutely gorgeous. If you ever have a chance. I had a cancellation right before you called, so here we are. Serendipity and all that. Everything just as it should be. Am I right?"

I don't know what the hell she's talking about, and I begin to think she's more nuts than I am. I smile and nod and tell myself to be good. This will be easy. Someone I don't have to impress. Start fresh. I'm surprised she's not going to write anything down or that she's not making a show of looking through my growing file, trying to make me feel embarrassed and ashamed before we even start.

I think she read my mind. "So, Jenny. First off, I want you to know I haven't looked at your file yet. I like to get my own first impression without knowing what your past is. Does that make sense? Good. I used to teach. Third grade. I never looked at a student's file until at least a month into the school year. I didn't want to label them, you see. The straight-A students and the struggling ones and the so-called troublemakers. Too many teachers I knew had preconceived notions about their kids. They thought they knew exactly who their students were before they set foot in the door. As if kids don't change over the summer. I didn't do it then, and I don't do it now."

Dr. Phillips looks at me like she's expecting some kind of response, so I say, "Okay. Thanks." I like her. A lot. She does all the talking.

"So, that's a little about me. Now tell me something about you. Tell me why you're here, for starters. And don't say it's because they made you, because it's mandated by the court, that it's part of your probation. I want more than that, okay?"

"If you didn't read my file, how do you know it's court mandated?"

"I like that you ask questions, Jenny. I didn't read your file, but I read the paperwork you filled out. By the way, I like your name. Jenny. I always wanted to be a Jenny. You know what my first name is? Agatha. Isn't that an awful name? That's why I just put "A" in my listing. And there's no way to shorten it, make it into a cute nickname. What would it be? Aggie? Agg? No thank you. My mother loved those murder mysteries."

I laugh, and she does too. This might work. "Okay. I guess I'm here because I screwed up. I made some mistakes, some bad decisions."

"That's good, Jenny. You're owning up, taking responsibility. You have no idea how long it takes some people to get to that point. So, what are you doing to turn things around?"

"I'm here. I'm going to AA meetings, even though I hate them. I'm checking in with my probation officer every week."

"Anything else?"

"Isn't that enough?"

"I'm afraid not. Not if you want to really make a lasting change. Do you? I should have asked you that first. These things are all mandated by the court. Don't get me wrong. They're all good things, put in place to help you, but in my experience, it takes more than that. But, you know what? I don't have all the answers. Maybe you do. Maybe you're one of the lucky ones who can turn things around just like that. I haven't met anyone who can do that yet, but there's a first time for everything. Am I right?"

She asks this like she really wants to know, but she doesn't wait for an answer.

"I think the best way is to find answers together. I also think you have everything you need right inside you to change your life." She pats her chest. "You just don't realize it yet."

"You don't know me."

"You are exactly right about that, Jenny. How about we fix that? Tell me one thing you want me to know about you. Or even better, tell me one thing about yourself you want to change, if you can. One thing. Big or small. Actually, I recommend starting small, then we can build on that. How does that sound?"

There are so many things, and none of them are small. Unlike the other so-called counsellors, something about Dr. Phillips makes me want to tell her everything. I take a deep breath and start. "I have a daughter. I adopted her when she was three. She's almost 16 now and when she found out she was adopted, she left home looking for her birth mother, and I don't know where she is. When she finally called me, all I did was yell at her. I told her if she didn't come home right now, not to bother coming home at all. I didn't mean it. All I want is for her to come home. No. It's more than that. I want her to *want* to come home. And as far as what I want to change, I want to stop pushing people away."

Dr. Phillips doesn't say anything right away, maybe to see if I have more, which I don't. Not yet, anyway. That was plenty. She looks shocked, as if she's looking at a car wreck. "Wow, Jenny. That's a lot. I appreciate your sharing all that with me right from the get go. Okay. Let's give this a go. I don't have kids. Never been married. But I can imagine it's hard when they start growing up and you feel like you don't have control. Am I right?"

"I feel like I have never had control over anything."

"Let's start there, then."

I don't know where "there" is exactly, but I have a feeling of hope. At least that's what I think it is. What do I know about hope? Once I start talking about Meggie, I can't seem to stop. I tell Dr. Phillips what a good kid she has always been, how strong and independent and stubborn she can be.

"Not exactly negative traits, are they? Where do you think she learned to be like that?" Dr. Phillips asks this with a straight face, a serious look.

I put on a serious face too. "I have no idea." Then we both smile and it feels good. It feels like things might have a chance of being okay.

"Here's my idea. Our time is almost up, but I want you to practice your next conversation with your daughter. Ask Meggie what she wants you to do, then try to listen. I know it might be hard because we all want what we want, but I can just about guarantee it will bring better results than arguing."

Dr. Phillips walks around to the other side of her desk, opens a drawer and pulls out a black and white marble notebook like kids use in school and a blue gel pen. She holds them out to me. "Try writing a little each day. Or a lot. When you have your morning coffee, if you're a coffee drinker, and maybe even again before you go to bed." She waves her hand like she did when I first came in, swatting away an imaginary fly. "Actually, any time you feel like it."

I take the notebook and pen, even though I don't really want them. "I'm not much of a writer."

"Don't think of it as writing. Maybe think of it as venting, getting things off your chest. Just let it rip. It can be a great release, I promise. Would you give it a try?"

"Do I have to show you what I write?"

"Absolutely not. For your eyes only. I used to only suggest keeping a journal, but then people wouldn't get around to buying one, so here you go. A gift from me. It's totally up to you, but I hope you'll try it. What do you have to lose?"

"Okay. I'll try it."

"I'm glad to hear that. You'll be surprised what comes out if you just let it. Any last thoughts before you go?"

"I think I feel better already." It's one of the truest things I have said or felt in a long time. "Thank you."

"My pleasure. Truly."

Chapter 9

"Are you sure I won't make things worse by being here?" Jack sounds as nervous as I feel. We sit in his car, the ignition off, the engine ticking as it cools, neither of us making a move to get out. It only took about 40 minutes to get here, and I'm not ready to face Jenny.

"I'm not sure about anything, except I know she's going to be mad whether you're here or not. I just hope after she calms down she listens. I feel like she doesn't hear me anymore, that it's all about what she wants, which is for me to just forget I was in foster care, forget about wanting to know who I am and where I came from."

"It's probably very difficult for her. And, if you don't mind my saying, I think you will have a better chance of her listening if you listen to her too."

"I *do*. I do listen to her. That's all I've been doing. She keeps saying the same thing over and over." I don't like how whiny and defensive I sound, but it's true.

"Maybe she feels like you're not listening either?" He stares at me, gives me a minute to think about it. "Okay, then. Ready?"

I always listen to Jenny. "I guess."

At the end of the walkway, Jack says, "I'll stay back for a few minutes, give you and Jenny some time."

I open the apartment door, half-wishing she was at work or at a meeting, but she's standing at the kitchen sink, her arms in soapy water. She turns when she hears me, surprise on her face, and relief. She looks so tired. "I'm sorry you were worried. Are you still mad at me?"

Jenny doesn't bother to dry her hands, but rushes over and hugs me. I don't remember her ever holding onto me so tight. I must have really scared her. "I'm so glad you're home and that you're okay." She pulls back and studies my face. "You *are* okay, right?"

"I am. Thanks to a friend." I turn and open the door wider, and when Jenny sees Jack, she lets go of me and takes a couple of steps back. I close the door and move into the kitchen while Jack comes up next to me.

"Who are you?" Jenny sounds both angry and afraid.

"This is my friend, Jack. Jack, this is Jenny, my mother."

"It's nice to meet you, Jenny. Meg has—"

"Meg?" Jenny interrupts. She raises her chin, narrows her eyes, looks Jack up and down before she turns to me. "You have some explaining to do, *Meg*."

She has no idea. "I know. That's why I'm here." Maybe it was a bad idea to have Jack come with me. "Can we sit down? Please?" I look around the kitchen. It's clean, and it smells like coffee and toast. Just like any normal apartment.

"I've been going out of my mind worrying about you, now you show up with some strange man and I'm supposed to sit down and chat like this is anywhere close to normal?"

"I'll explain everything if you'll just listen. I have a lot to tell you, and it's really important. I don't want to fight with you. I just want you to listen. Please."

"I hope you don't mind my accompanying Meg," Jack says.

"My daughter, who happens to be a minor, has been missing for three days now. You show up with her and you're how old? I should have you arrested right now."

"For what?" I jump in. "All he's done is be my friend."

"I'm sure. I should call the police right now."

"It's not like that, mama. Let me explain."

Jenny shakes her head. "This should be good." She surprises me when she sits down and leans back, crosses her arms and stares at me.

I sit across from her and wait for Jack to sit. "I don't want to have secrets anymore. I'm sick of living with secrets and lies, aren't you?"

"Sometimes you don't have a choice." Jenny's voice is soft now. "You're too young to understand that, but you will someday. I was crazy with worry, you know that? You can't just take off like that."

"I left you a note and I called."

"That's not good enough. You're 15."

"I'm almost 16. And you know why I left. You wouldn't help me find out anything about myself. You wanted me to forget I ever existed before I came to live with you. I need to know who I am, and I might be close to finding out."

Jenny looks at Jack. "And what's your part in all this?"

"I'm here to help, if I can."

"Jack is an investigator. He's helping me find my birth mother. I told him what happened." My voice is stronger than I feel.

Jenny's face tightens. "You told him what, exactly?"

"I told him about how you saved me."

She glares at Jack, then at me. "You told him—how could you do that?"

"It was the only way we could actually find anything. When I first left, I went to see Darlene. She was the only one I could think of who knew us when I was little, but she didn't know anything. She didn't even know I was adopted."

"I could have told you that."

"And when I was on my way home, ready to give up, I met Jack at the bus station."

"And just like that you're friends. After everything I've told you, all the times I've warned you about talking to strangers? Trusting people?"

"I didn't trust him at first."

"She wouldn't even tell me her name," Jack interrupts. "She was very careful, very smart."

Jenny gives him a fake smile. "And yet here you are."

"Jack actually saved me from this kid I met on the bus, Adam. He seemed harmless, but he was not a good guy. Anyway, if Jack hadn't been there, I don't know what would have happened."

"You got in trouble and this guy miraculously shows up and saves you."

"That's what happened."

She turns to Jack. "I don't know what your game is, but I want you to leave." Jenny stands and starts walking to the door.

"Mama. Please. If Jack leaves, I will too." I know this will make her furious, but it stops her and she turns around, holds onto herself.

I take a deep breath, determined to tell her everything. "Jack found an article about mothers who had kids in foster care who disappeared, like me. We met with the guy who wrote it, Eric. He's a reporter who's been writing about foster kids and mothers, and he might be able to help me find out who my birth mother is. Maybe. But he won't tell us anything unless he knows my whole story." All that came out so fast, I didn't have time to think about what I was saying. I watch Jenny's face change like I had just told her I murdered someone.

"You met with a reporter. You're planning to turn me in after everything I've done for you, just so you can find out who gave birth to you, then gave you up to the system? You want to send me to jail? Because that's what would happen." Jenny pulls a chair up next to me, sits back down and stares into my eyes. "I want you to listen to me. And you need to hear me, okay? I've been seeing a counselor who makes me see things a little more clearly. I'm trying to listen more. But you also need to listen to me, okay?"

I glance at Jack for a second, then focus on Jenny. "I'm listening."

"I know you want to find the person who gave birth to you, but I need you to understand how I feel. I deserve that much. You say it's important to find her. I don't think you understand how important being your mother is to me. It's everything. It's all I have. I raised you and took care of you the best I could. You're my daughter. I need you to not take that away from me."

"I told you a million times you'll always be my mother. No matter what I find out, you will always be my mother. I could never take that away from you. Even if I do find the person who had me, she isn't going to instantly become my mother. You are. I don't know how else to tell you."

"You know what?" She slaps her hand on the table. "It doesn't matter. I'll be in jail and you'll have all the time in the world to get to know her."

"I won't do anything that would get you in trouble, I promise."

"You already did. You told him." Jenny gives Jack a vicious look. "And you're planning to tell a reporter. Maybe Jack won't tell anyone, and I wouldn't count on it, but a reporter? You might as well take me to the police station right now."

"I didn't tell him anything except I found out I was in foster care when I was little and that I might be one of the kids who disappeared. I didn't say anything about you, I promise."

"But you're planning to."

"Only if I can find a way to tell him that won't get you in trouble."

Jenny shakes her head, then turns to Jack. "Why are you here, exactly?"

"I'm here because Meg asked me to come. As a friend."

"Okay. So you met in a bus station, you've known each other a couple of days, and now you're in our personal business. And I'm supposed to believe you're here out of the goodness of your heart." Jenny leans back, combs her hair with her fingers. "What do you want?"

"I want to help, that's all. And I don't blame you for being suspicious. I'd think it was strange if you weren't."

"And there's nothing in it for you." Jenny is being so rude right now, but I don't blame her too much. She hasn't had good experiences with people. I wouldn't blame Jack either if he got up and walked out, but he glances at me, then down at his hands.

"When I first saw Meg all alone in the bus station, it made me think of my sister. She would be a few years older than Meg now. She's been missing since she was seven. I'm to blame for that. So if I see a young girl alone and maybe vulnerable, I feel a kind of responsibility to make sure she's okay."

I knew it. "What happened?" My voice is soft.

"It was a little more than 12 years ago now. I took my little sister to the park. She loved to go on the swings and slide, the monkey bars and such. I sat on a bench and played games on my phone. I was still watching her. I made sure to look up every few minutes. And she was always having fun." Jack stops and I feel so bad.

I want to put my arm around him, but I can't. Jenny and I stare at him.

"This pretty young lady came over and sat down, started talking to me. She was a few years older, and I was a naive kid, flattered by her attention. We talked for a few minutes. I remember she asked about the game I was playing. I gave her all my attention, then she kissed me on the cheek and told me I was sweet. I watched her walk away, watched her until she climbed into this dark gray van that was parked across the street. Then she was gone. When I looked around for my sister, she was gone too." Jack's voice is quiet and so sad.

"I'm sorry," I whisper.

"She was my parents' pride and joy. I'll never forget their faces when I came home with the police instead of my little sister. Everyone blamed me, and rightly so. After a month or so with no word, my parents sold the house and bought a trailer and started travelling. They said they wanted to see the country, but

I know they were searching for her. I lived with my uncle until I turned 18. Alicia. Her name was, is, Alicia."

I forget all about Jenny for a minute. "That's why you talked to me? And that's why you're helping me now?"

"I wanted to make sure you were okay. Then as I got to know you, I just wanted to help, if I could. I know it won't bring my sister back, but maybe someone will come along and help her if she needs it."

"Is that why you want to be an investigator? To find people?" I ask.

Jack shrugs and tries to smile. "Maybe so."

Jenny scrapes her chair back and stands. She has a frown on her face, aimed at me. "I want to know what you plan to do."

"I'm planning to meet with Eric tomorrow. I won't tell him anything unless he promises whatever I tell him is confidential. He said he protects his sources. I would tell him how you saved me, how I was in danger and you saved me, raised me like your own daughter."

Jenny shakes her head, stares at me then looks away. "*Like* my own daughter. You are my daughter. I am your mother." She storms to her bedroom, comes back carrying her jacket and purse and is out the door before I can say anything and stop her. I probably couldn't if I tried.

Chapter 10

Jack and I stare at the door Jenny slammed on her way out, the calendar on the wall still shaking, still on March. "I may have made things worse for you."

I shrug. "I probably should have told her about you before we came. She doesn't like surprises. But then she'd be all worked up before we even got here. There was no good way." I walk over to the calendar, flip the page to April and sit back down. "I'm really sorry about your sister."

Jack nods. "I appreciate that." He looks over at the door, the sound of it slamming still in the air. "Should we go after her? Make sure she's okay?"

I wish Jenny would change her mind and come back, but she won't. She'll come home when she's ready. "She needs time to cool off. It's been a lot."

"She's scared."

"She's always been scared. She thinks she's going to lose me."

"A valid fear, I would say."

"No, it isn't. I've told her a million times she is not going to lose me. No matter what I find, I am not going to desert her. She won't believe that. She has a problem trusting, even me."

"You know that's not all she's afraid of. She could very well be arrested and charged with kidnapping. I'm sure that's a big part of her fear. She would certainly lose you then. It wouldn't be a choice."

"Eric said we can find a way to not get anyone in trouble." I want so much to believe that.

"He doesn't have all the facts, though, does he? I mean, he didn't exactly guarantee anything. He couldn't. Until he knows everything."

I sigh and Jack patiently waits for me to say something. All I can say is the truth. "You're right."

"We can still meet with Eric tomorrow," Jack says. "Maybe he has a way to make sure everyone comes out of this unscathed."

"I hope so."

"How about I go home and you stay here and wait for Jenny? I'm sure she'll come home soon. I saw how glad she was to see you. And after she's had time to think about everything, you never know, she might come around and want to help."

"Right. You don't know her."

"I know she'll be glad to have you here when she comes back. And to have me gone." He pushes his chair back and stands, and I do too. "How about I pick you up tomorrow around nine?"

"You still have the car?"

"For now."

"I'm really nervous about tomorrow."

"Perfectly understandable."

We stand there for a few seconds, both of us quiet. We've been together only a couple of days, but now I know what people mean when they say they bonded with someone. Jack reaches for the doorknob. "Promise you'll call if you need me, or if you just want to talk. I'm not much of a sleeper, so don't worry about waking me if it's late." He closes the door gently behind him and I'm alone again.

I walk around the apartment and understand what it must have been like for Jenny when I left, how scared she must have been, not knowing where I was, when and if I was coming home. I turn on the television, and a commercial fills the apartment. A man telling me I'm paying too much for car insurance. I wish.

I walk into Jenny's room, careful not to touch anything. I want to pick up the pile of clothes on the wicker chair in the corner, fold them and put them away if they're clean, put them in the hamper if they're not, but I leave them. Her dresser is covered with lotions and makeup and perfume, a box of tissues, a jar of cotton balls, a couple of magazines. The only thing on the table next to her bed is a thick book with a blue cover. I run my fingers over the raised letters. *Alcoholics Anonymous*. A wave of guilt washes over me. I know it's not my fault, but tonight it feels like it is.

I wish Jenny would come home so I wouldn't have to go looking for her. I can't wait much longer. She is most likely in a bar, because that's what she does. She drinks to celebrate, she drinks to commiserate. She'll say she deserves to have a drink. I don't get it. She deserves to hurt herself?

The third place I walk into is two blocks from our apartment. The sign over the door says, *The Kettle,* and it looks like it's been here about a hundred years. I walk in to the smell of stale beer, so familiar. I glance at the bar to the right, where three men hunch over their bottles, then I scan the room and see Jenny sitting alone at a table in the back, surrounded by dark paneling and shadows, her hands wrapped around a half-full pint glass. Before she looks up, and before the woman behind the bar says anything, I rush over to Jenny's table and sit. Besides the beer, there are two empty shot glasses in front of her.

Jenny looks up, her eyes open wide as if she's surprised to see me, as if I wouldn't come looking for her. "Well, well. What are you doing here?" She looks around. "Where's your friend?"

"We didn't finish talking." I stay calm, careful not to upset her more than she already is.

"Talking? Is that what we were doing? Okay. Let's talk. Let's talk about you. That day I found you? That was the day you were born." She takes a swallow of beer, then another one. "You ever think you probably wouldn't even be alive if it weren't for me?" She's slurring, and her eyes are glassy. I haven't seen her like this in a really long time. I hate it. I did this.

"I know you saved me, probably saved my life."

"Damn right I did. I wasn't thinking too much at the time about what I was doing. I admit that. I saw you there all alone, and I just acted. Pulled you right out of that car like I was on a mission. Pure emotion. Pure. I like that word. Don't you like that word? The nuns used to talk about being pure. They made it sound like the best thing in the world to be, but impossible." She shakes her head and takes another swallow of beer, her glass almost empty now, dried foam coating the inside. "At least for me."

It kills me to see her like this. So pathetic. It makes me angry, but really sad too. It's my fault. I knew how she felt about me finding my birth mother, but I pushed and pushed and this is the only way she knows how to cope. Get wasted and block it all out, stop thinking about it. Doesn't she see, it only makes everything worse?

Jenny looks up from her glass, her watery eyes not quite focused. "Unfortunately, I will never be pure. It's way too late for that. And you know what? I don't think I ever was pure. I think from the day I was born, I was bad. Born to be bad. That should be my theme song. Born to be bad." She frowns. "Wait. Was it Born to be Wild?" She tries to focus on my face, and one tear escapes down her cheek. "Doesn't matter. Doesn't make a damn bit of difference."

"Come on, mama. Let's go home." I push my chair back and stand, try to take Jenny's arm to help her up, then the waitress rushes over, slaps the check down on the table without a word. She looks around 50 and her jeans are at least a size too small and her hair is yellow and frizzy. She's wearing so much mascara her dark eyes look like dead spiders. She stands with her arms crossed, waiting. Jenny sits there, her head nodding. I wonder if she ate anything today. We have to get out of here while she can still walk.

I pick up the check. Three pints and two shots, plus tax. $32.50. I don't have that much money, and I don't know if Jenny does either. How could she drink so much in such a short time?

I look up at the waitress, then sit back down. "Can you give us a minute?"

"Sure." She walks back behind the bar where I know she isn't taking her eyes off us. I lean closer to Jenny. "Mama? We need to pay the bill. I need to get some money from your purse, okay?" As soon as I touch her purse, she yanks it away and hugs it to her chest.

"Come on," I say, like she's a kid and this is a game. "Here." I set the check on the table in front of her. "You need to pay this so we can leave. It's $32.50. Come on, mama, please. We need to go home."

"You pay it. You have all the answers. You pay it." Jenny stands, a little off balance, and starts walking towards the door, still hugging her purse like there's a million dollars in there.

The waitress is out from behind the bar before Jenny gets near the door. She scoops up the check, steps in Jenny's way. "Excuse me. You didn't pay your tab." She says it loud enough so the men at the bar turn around to watch the show.

Jenny turns and looks at me. "My daughter'll take care of it."

"You got this?" The waitress holds the check up and waves it at me like a prize I'm supposed to claim. "Cause I'm not gonna eat it."

I open my mouth and nothing comes out, then a man appears, leans down and says something quietly to Jenny. He's at least a foot taller than her and looks like a bouncer you see in movies: shaved head, a tight black tee-shirt and jeans. When he puts his hand on Jenny's arm, she pulls it away so hard it surprises him. Then Jenny tries to walk around him and I rush over. "Mama. We need to pay the bill so we can go home. If we don't they'll call the police." Maybe that will be enough to scare her into paying.

"Let them. I don't care. It was shitty service anyway." She makes a mean face at the waitress, who turns and walks back behind the bar, picks up her phone.

“They’ll be right here.” The waitress has a smug look like she just won something.

The police must have been right around the corner because they pull up in about two minutes, red and blue lights flashing, lighting up the wall behind us. Part of me wants to walk out the door and leave Jenny to clean up her own mess. But if they arrest her, I don’t know what would happen. She’s on probation, so they could put her in jail, and I’m a minor with no other family to call. I have no one to call but Jack.

He answers on the first ring, like he was expecting my call. “Meg?”

“I’m really sorry, but I need your help.”

“Not a problem. What’s wrong? Did you find Jenny?”

“I found her, in a place called The Kettle. It’s about two blocks from our apartment. You’ll see the police out front. I need to borrow some money to pay her tab. I’ll make sure she pays you back.”

“Sit tight. I’ll be right there.”

Jenny and I sit in plastic chairs against the wall outside the kitchen, while the big guy goes outside to talk to the police. The ugly waitress is back behind the bar talking to the men. She says something I can’t make out and they all laugh. I look outside through the dirty window, and see Jack is there, saving me again, saving Jenny.

I’m surprised Jenny isn’t yelling and screaming that they can’t keep her there, that she didn’t do anything wrong, but she leans back, her head against the wall and her eyes closed, oblivious to the trouble she caused.

In a few minutes, the police turn off their lights and drive away, and the big guy comes in and tells us we can go. “Your friend took care of it.”

Jenny’s eyes open halfway and she sits up and frowns. “What friend? I don’t have any friends.”

“Don’t come back.” His voice is low and gravelly. “You won’t get served here again.”

My phone dings, a text from Jack. *All good. Outside if you need a ride.*

Thx, I respond. *All set. Thank you so much.* Seeing Jack might set her off again, and I think the fresh air will do her good. On the way home I hold Jenny's arm, surprised she lets me.

We are both silent until we get inside the apartment. Jenny says, "I'm sorry. Sorry. I'm sorry. Okay?"

I can't talk to her when she's like this. "I'm going to bed."

"You hate me now, right? You come home, you finally come home, and I do this. You must hate me. I don't blame you."

As if I ever could. "I thought you were doing better. I thought you were getting help and weren't drinking anymore."

"I wasn't. And I am getting help. Good ol' AA. They tell us we have no control. None. Zero. I'm totally helpless. They actually make you admit that. I think that's step one, or maybe step two." Jenny holds up her arms like she's surrendering, then she sits at the kitchen table and holds her face in her hands. "No control over anything."

I know I'm supposed to feel bad for her. Part of me wants to sit and put my arms around her, tell her everything will be okay. I want to tell her I'm not mad, but I am. And that I don't hate her, which I don't. I could never. But right now I am so sick of always being the adult. I have nothing left to give her tonight, and all I can do is leave her like that and go to bed.

Chapter 11

I'm not sure what to expect when I walk into the kitchen to the smell of coffee. It's only 7:30 and I didn't think Jenny would be up this early after last night. She could be angry or still feeling sorry for herself or she could give me silence and expect me to read her mind. Anything is possible with Jenny. But she's sitting there as calm as anything, looking at her phone, a full cup of coffee in front of her, a plate with crumbs on it. She looks up at me and gives me a small smile. "I'm really sorry about last night." She doesn't even seem hungover.

"Okay." I open the refrigerator and take out the orange juice, glad there's no beer.

"Is that all you have to say? *Okay*?"

Here we go. "What do you want me to say?" I'm angrier than I thought I was. "I had to call Jack so you wouldn't get arrested. Do you remember that? If it weren't for him, you would probably be in jail right now. And I don't even know what they would have done with me."

"Maybe if it weren't for Jack I wouldn't have needed to drink in the first place."

I can't help laughing. "Oh my God. You're blaming your drinking on Jack?" It's so ridiculous. And typical.

"If he hadn't encouraged you to continue searching for this phantom mother of yours you want to know so badly, everything would be fine. You wouldn't be lying to me, sneaking around, listening to him instead of me. And I'm not blaming him for my drinking. I'm blaming him for stirring things up, bringing you to see a reporter. A *reporter*, for God's sake. You would never have done that on your own."

Jenny is right about that. I probably wouldn't have even known about Eric, and even if I did see his article, I don't think I would have ever contacted him or met with him if it weren't for Jack. But I'm thankful to him for that, for helping me get one step closer to finding my birth mother. Maybe. "You're right. Jack is helping me. Because I asked him to. Because he sees how important it is to me. Your drinking is all on you."

"Tell me you're not going through with this. Tell me you're not going to meet with that reporter and tell him about me. Unless you want me to be arrested for kidnapping, because that's what they will say I did. Is that what you want?"

What I want is a bowl of cereal and some quiet time to think about what I'm going to say to Eric. I sit across from her, my arms resting on the table. "You know it isn't. But what if there's a way I could do the interview and we're protected? He said he keeps his sources anonymous. Why don't you come with me? You can tell your side of the story, only if everything we tell him is confidential." I think of what Jack said about no guarantees, but what if there could be?

Jenny shakes her head slowly. She gets up and stays on the other side of the table and stares at me, into me, her eyes more sad than angry now. "If you can actually do this, after everything I've done for you, after you saw last night how much this upsets me, it's clear how little I mean to you. So go. You want to find this person so bad, this person who means more to you than I do, then go ahead. *Go*." She turns around and heads down the hall to her room.

I stand and take one step towards her, make my voice as strong and sure as I can. "What if she did exactly what you did? With the baby?"

Jenny stops but doesn't turn around.

"What if she gave me up so I'd have a better life? Isn't that what you did with your son? What if she wanted me but couldn't take care of me?"

She turns around but doesn't come any closer. "What are you talking about?" Her voice is weak and she sounds scared.

I swallow and keep going. "I remember that summer, when I was about five, and you told me you were having a baby. I remember you were so happy and I was so excited that I was going to be a big sister. You told me it was a secret, and that made me feel special too."

"What else do you remember?" Jenny's voice is barely a whisper.

"I remember you being pregnant, fighting with Gene a lot, more than usual. You were really angry, then so sad. It seemed like you were always crying and I wanted so much to make you feel better, but I was also scared. I remember Sam coming over and bringing food. Then I remember being with Darlene when you went to have the baby. I wanted to stay with you. I was scared you weren't coming back. Then I remember you coming home without the baby and telling me you gave him to a family who could give him a better life." All the time I'm telling her this, Jenny doesn't move. All the color seems to drain from her face.

"I didn't have a choice. And I did it for you too. I wanted you to have a better life too."

"I get it. But what if that's what my birth mother did? What if . . ."

"That's not what she did. You were in foster care. That's not giving you a better life. I made sure my son went to a good family, a family with money and a nice house. I made sure he would be taken care of. That's not what happened to you." Jenny has all her color back and then some. "You were in foster care, which means your precious *birth mother* either didn't want you or she wasn't taking care of you and they took you away. I wanted my baby more than anything. There's no way our situations are the same."

"You don't know that."

"Why are you trying so hard to believe this person who gave you up is better than me?"

"That's not—"

"Well you go find out. Go." Jenny starts to turn around again but stops and glares at me. "And don't you ever, ever compare me to that woman again."

I want to say I'm sorry. I want to go to her and put my arms around her and tell her how I know she did the best she could, but I just stand there and watch as she walks into her room and comes out a few seconds later with her sweatshirt in her hand and leaves. It's like a repeat of last night, except she doesn't slam the door and I don't think the bars are open yet.

I feel frozen and scared and am having second thoughts about meeting Eric. Jenny is right. How can I do this to her after all she has done for me? If doing this interview, even if it means finding my birth mother, somehow lands Jenny in jail, how could I?

"I can't do it." I'm standing outside the apartment next to Jack's car instead of sitting in the passenger seat where I thought I'd be right now, on our way to meet Eric. It's already warm, even though the sun hasn't quite come up over the buildings across the street. I'm in my bare feet and jeans and the tee-shirt I slept in. "I'm sorry. I just can't do it to Jenny. I'll wait until I'm older, or find another way, but right now she's too fragile. I'm sorry."

Jack opens his door and steps out, stands next to me. "Don't be sorry. It's okay. Do what you feel is right. If you're really sure, I'll call Eric. How was the rest of the night after you and Jenny got home?"

"She apologized and I went to bed. I hate seeing her like that."

"You shouldn't have to deal with that."

"I feel like I pushed her to it."

"You can't blame yourself. There's no excuse for that kind of behavior. I'm sorry. It's not my place to say. I just don't like seeing you hurt like this."

"I'm fine. Except this morning I made her upset again, and sad. I think she'll be better now that I'm home. I'm not going to even mention my birth mother anymore."

"And you're okay with that? With just giving up?"

"I think I'm kind of relieved. I wasn't sure what I'd say to Eric or what he would do, and I can't take that chance of getting Jenny in trouble when all she did was save me. Maybe someday Jenny will understand why I want to know where I came from, why it's so important, but right now she's not ready."

"If you're sure." Jack pulls out his phone and I listen to his side of the conversation with Eric. "I'm sorry we wasted your time. No. We're sure . . . yes, she's right here." He holds the phone out to me.

Eric asks if I'm okay, and if I'm sure. He doesn't sound happy about our cancelling, but I can't feel bad about that on top of everything else. "I'm sorry," I tell him, and I mean it. As soon as I hand Jack his phone I feel like such a loser. "I feel bad."

"I'm sure it's not the first time someone cancelled on him. The important thing is that you're okay. I have to say I'm a little worried about you after last night. Was that typical?"

"No. No. I haven't seen her like that in a really long time. I guess I didn't realize how upset all this made her. When she gets back, I'll tell her I cancelled the meeting with Eric and I'm not going to look for my birth mother. Jenny needs to know how important she is. Just saying it isn't enough."

Jack nods. "You're important too. Don't lose sight of that."

"I'll try. And thanks for everything. Thanks for being there for me." I want to say more, but I don't know what. I don't want to let him go, but I have to.

"Of course. You have my number. I'm only a phone call away if you need me, or if you just need a friend to talk to." I give him a quick hug and when he kisses the top of my head, it's the nicest feeling I've had in a long time.

I stand on the sidewalk and watch until he's out of sight, then I walk back into the apartment, back to Jenny and my old life, feeling like all this was for nothing.

Chapter 12

I'm walking fast, going nowhere. Nothing will ever change, except to get worse. I replay last night in my head, seeing Meggie looking so lost and scared when she walked into the kitchen, then the shock of her bringing that Jack home. *Aaahm just here to help.* I'm not falling for his good old boy act, not for a second. This stranger she's known for what? Two days? Now they're best friends? All so she can meet this person who didn't want her. How did this woman all of a sudden become more important than me?

The sunshine and warm breeze feel good. I take deep breaths, try not think too much. What's the point? I pass people without looking at their faces, and I'm sure they don't see me either. People walk their dogs that stop to pee on every fire hydrant and scrawny tree and fence and bush, trying to claim everything as theirs. The way of the world.

I'm getting into one of those nice, fancy neighborhoods. The houses are set way back from the street, the lawns already green. Yellow and red and purple flowers in front. Bigger trees for dogs to pee on. Everything is just so damn perfect.

In a couple of minutes I'll cross the street and turn around, go back the way I came. I don't want to be late for my appointment with Dr. Phillips. I finally have someone to listen to me and not judge.

All of a sudden, a little boy comes up from behind and rushes past me. He appears out of nowhere and looks about three, four at the most. When he turns to look over his shoulder, he has a huge smile on his dirty little face. His hair is so pale and fine it's almost white. Whoever he's running from either doesn't realize he's gone or is very slow.

I look around and walk a little faster, keeping my eyes on the little boy, his chubby legs going as fast as they can. No one is coming after him. There's only an old man with a cane walking on the other side of the street, then a skinny woman jogs past me. She gives me the smallest nod when we make eye contact, as if she's doing me a favor. I pick up my pace and watch the boy, glance behind me one more time to see if anyone is coming after him, but there's no one.

This kid is way too young to be alone. I wonder who's supposed to be taking care of him. When I'm only a few yards behind and he's almost to the corner, cars zipping by, he trips and falls. I rush up to him as if he's mine. Of course I know he isn't. My son would be older than this now, almost 11.

The boy is on his belly, his arms straight out, his hands and knees probably scraped pretty good. I crouch down next to him as he sits up. He's howling, enormous tears spilling out of his eyes. I'm careful not to touch him, not to do anything that might scare him any more than he already is. When he turns his hands over and sees the blood, he stops crying for a second until it registers, then starts in again. A woman walks by in tight pink capris and a white tank top and gives me a look as if I did something wrong instead of watching out for this kid. She stops at the curb to wait to cross the street, arms folded across her skinny chest, turns and stares at me one more time. I want to give her the finger, but she's not worth it.

"Are you okay, honey? Let me see." His right knee is scraped and bleeding too, and I wish I had a Band-Aid. The best I can do is take out a crumpled but clean tissue out of my purse and gently dab the blood. "It's okay. You're okay. Here, let's stand up. Who are you with, sweetheart?"

He stands up and looks down at his hands and knees again, then up at me. "I run fast." He wipes his eyes with his fingers, his nose with his sleeve.

"You sure do. But who's taking care of you, sweetheart?" Obviously, no one.

"Maddy." His eyes are the color of the sky, and what I thought was dirt on his face is chocolate.

"Maddy must be looking for you. What's your name?"

He sniffs and wipes his nose again, this time with the back of his hand. "Ben."

"Ben. That's a nice name. Were you running away from Maddy?" What if he was trying to get away from her?

"I run fast."

"I know you do, Ben. Where's Maddy?"

He stares at me, then looks around and his eyes fill again. "I don't know where she is."

"That's okay. How about we find her? I reach for his hand and he takes it as if I'm no stranger, and we turn and start back down the street.

"I run fast." At least he's back to smiling now.

"Do you live around here, Ben? Do you know where your house is?" I don't need this right now, but I can't just leave him alone. What the hell is wrong with people they can't watch their kids? Maybe I should call someone. The police? Sure. That's all I need. Questions and more questions. They'll take one look my Led Zeppelin tee-shirt, faded jeans and sneakers and know I don't belong in this neighborhood. But what if we can't find his house? What if someone just abandoned him and he's not even from around here? Am I meant to save another neglected kid?

"Excuse me." A young woman, out of breath, rushes up to us. She looks about 18, and she's all dressed up like a fitness commercial, complete with the terrycloth sweatband and make-up. After she studies my face for a second, she turns to Ben. "Hey, Buddy. Are you okay?" She reaches for him and he lets go of my hand as she lifts him up. He puts his arms around her neck and starts crying again. This must be Maddy. "You okay, Buddy?" She rubs his back while she glares at me like I'm some kind of monster. "Who are you? What are you doing?"

I glare right back at her. “I’m the person who helped him when he was all by himself and fell down and hurt himself. He was scared and alone and I was trying to find out where he lived. He’s pretty young to be left alone, don’t you think?” I won’t let this girl make me the bad guy here.

“He wasn’t alone. He ran away and I was looking for him.” She holds him close and rubs the back of his head and I can tell she cares about him. But still. She should never have taken her eyes off him. Maddy sets him down, crouches in front of him and puts her hands on his arms. “Don’t ever do that again, okay, Ben? I was really scared when I couldn’t find you.”

“I run rast.”

“I know you do, but you can’t run away from me when I’m not looking, okay? Next time you want to run fast tell me, and we can have a race, okay?”

Ben nods. “I’m thirsty.”

“Let’s go home and get you some water.” She takes his hand, the same hand I was holding just a minute ago. Before they walk away, she says, finally, “Thank you.” Ben doesn’t even turn around, doesn’t even say goodbye. I turn and walk back the way I came, out of this neighborhood, back to where I belong.

I used to believe in signs. For a long time, seeing signs was the only thing that gave me hope—a picture of Jesus, a church steeple, a song on the radio. All those things gave me false hope that things were going to get better. It’s probably crazy, but what if meeting Ben, being there just when he needed me, was a sign? Maybe a sign about my son, that he needs me? First Meg brings him up out of the blue, now I end up on a street I have never walked down before, just at the right moment this little boy needed me. When was the last time I even noticed a little boy? I was there when no one else was. Who knows what would have happened if I wasn’t there? What if some stranger came along in a car and snatched him? What if my son needs me and this was a sign? It doesn’t really matter now. After Meg talks to that reporter and sets everything in motion, it's just a matter of time until they come for me.

"She's home," I announce, before I sit, before we even say good morning.

Dr. Phillips raises both palms up to the ceiling like she's receiving grace, and a big smile lights up her face. "Your Meggie is home? Well, things are turning around, aren't they?" She offers me one of the swivel chairs in front of her desk and takes the other one. "Here, sit. Tell me all about it."

I have so much to tell her, but I don't know where to start, so I glance out the window as if there's something interesting out there. After a minute of silence, she jumps up. "I'll get us some coffee."

I watch the few cars passing by, listen to the clinking of the spoon as Dr. Phillips stirs cream and sugar into my coffee before she holds it out to me. I don't know how she can drink it black.

"Thanks." I take a small sip, grateful for her patience. "So, she came home last night. She showed up with this guy, Jack. She met him at the bus station of all places. I'm surprised she survived an hour out in the world by herself. She's so naïve. She trusts everyone. She's lucky he wasn't some serial killer or human trafficker." I sip my coffee, get up and add another spoonful of sugar.

"But she's okay?"

"She's fine. Stubborn as ever. She wants to be called *Meg* now, and she's still as hell-bent as ever on finding her so-called mother. And this Jack found a reporter she plans to talk to who might be able to help, but she has to tell him things that will probably land me in jail."

Dr. Phillips sets her mug down on the table between us, frowns, trying to figure out what the hell I'm talking about. She can't, though. She has no idea what I've done. "In jail for what, Jenny?"

"For something I did a long time ago, something people would think was wrong because they weren't there and they don't know the circumstances. Whatever I tell you, you have to keep it confidential, right?"

"Absolutely. Everything we say here is protected, Jenny. Doctor-patient confidentiality. It's real. No doubt about that."

"Even if what I did would be considered against the law? It was the right thing to do. I knew it then and I know it now. But the police wouldn't see it that way."

"Okay. Here's the thing. Unless you're about to threaten violence towards someone or bring harm to yourself, I have no obligation to disclose anything we talk about here. That being said, because your sessions are mandated, I do fill out a form each week to confirm you're fulfilling your obligation to the court. But, beyond that, what we talk about here is strictly confidential."

I nod, hold my coffee in both hands like it's some magic potion that will give me courage. "I haven't told you much about Gene, have I?"

Dr. Phillips tilts her head, leans forward. "This is the first time I'm hearing the name."

"Gene was my first and only boyfriend. My parents hated him because he was older than me, rode a motorcycle, had long hair. You know. My mother called him a thug and didn't want me near him. But I was in love. I really was."

"I believe you." There is no expression, no judgement in her eyes. Just patient listening.

"One day we were walking down the street and I saw this car. I didn't know at the time what drew me to it, then I saw a little girl, a baby really, all alone in the back, strapped into a car seat. The windows were up and there was no one around. Do you know how many kids are left alone in cars every year? And die? At least 40. I didn't think twice. I opened the door and unbuckled her, lifted her out. She didn't wake up or cry or anything, and I just held her close and started walking down the street with her. I remember how she felt in my arms, so tiny and helpless."

Dr. Phillips opens her eyes wide. "This was your Meggie?"

I nod.

"And what was Gene doing?"

"He was in the store buying beer, then he caught up with me. He was shocked to see me carrying a baby, and he wasn't happy about it. He asked me what the hell I was doing and I told him how she was left all alone in that car. He said we should bring her back, but how could I? All I wanted to do was get her away from that car and whoever left her there. I wanted to save her. I did save her."

Dr. Phillips nods, takes a sip of coffee and lets me talk.

"Gene didn't think it was our responsibility. I told him someone needed to be responsible. And we took her home."

Dr. Phillips sets her coffee down, rubs her face with both hands like she's trying to wake herself up. This must be where she tells me she can't keep this secret, that she's obligated to turn me in, that this isn't covered by doctor-patient confidentiality. But she doesn't.

"So just like that you brought this little girl home, this baby, and no one noticed? You just decided to raise her as your own daughter? It was really that easy?"

"Easy? No. God, no. It completely changed our lives. But I didn't care. I knew I had to take care of her. She was in foster care. The people who left her to die in that car only cared about the checks, so they never even reported her missing until we had already had her a couple months. By then it was too late to give her back, even if we wanted to. She was calling me *Mama* by then, and I named her after my grandmother, Margaret. As far as we were concerned, I was her mother."

"Okay. Give me a few seconds to process this. It's a lot. And when I say process, I don't mean any kind of judgment. You'll never get that from me." Dr. Phillips pushes her hair back and looks as serious as I've ever seen her. "I've heard a lot of stories, Jenny, but this is a first. You saw a child in danger and you rescued her. Did you call the police?"

I take a deep breath. "If I called the police, they would have put her right back in the system, maybe even with the people who left her alone. And who would be in trouble? Me."

"How did you know she was in foster care?"

I look down at my hands and tell the truth. "I didn't know then. I found out later, when it was finally on the news."

Dr. Phillips takes a few seconds. "Who else knows about this, Jenny?"

"All this time, it was just me and Gene, then Meg found out. Now her new friend Jack knows because she told him everything, and she's planning to tell a reporter."

After a deep breath and a long sigh, Dr. Phillips looks me in the eye. "I may have spoken too soon about confidentiality, Jenny, and I'm sorry."

"What do you mean? You said—never mind." *Here we go. I should have known.*

"How old is Meg, exactly?"

"She's 15. Around there. Almost 16. What does that have to do with it?"

"Here's the thing. Meg is still a minor. Technically, in the eyes of the law, you committed a Federal crime, as you probably already know. Actually, a state crime as well. And you also may already know there's no statute of limitations. Because Meg is still a minor, they—the FBI I would imagine—would consider her in danger, and I would have a duty to report it."

I bolt up from my chair, almost knocking it over. "Danger? I saved her from danger. And now you're going to report me? After you said I could tell you anything?"

"I said I would have a *duty* to report it."

I shake my head, cross my arms and hold onto myself. "I thought you were different. I thought I could trust you. You know what? It doesn't matter."

"Well, Jenny, it does matter. It matters a lot. Just because technically I would have a duty to report it, well, I have never believed things are black and white. There is definitely a lot of gray area here. Tell me more about Meg and how she feels about all this, how she felt when you told her what happened."

I sit back down. "Okay. There was a show a couple months ago about missing foster kids. There was this age-enhanced picture of a girl who looked just like her. That's how she found out. She saw herself on television and started asking questions." It hurts to think of this now. "I was so angry at the time because she wouldn't drop it, but then I thought it was okay that she knew, maybe even good. Until it wasn't. Now all she wants to do is find her *real* mother. I guess I'm not real enough for her." I finish my coffee, barely warm, but sweet. I think about having another cup, but what I really want is a cold beer.

"And now you think she's going to turn you in? Why would she do that?"

"Her new friend Jack brought her to a reporter she thinks can help her find her birth mother. She knows what this would mean for me, but she's going to do it anyway. She actually asked me to go with her, tell my side, whatever that means. I did what I did and I'm not sorry."

Dr. Phillips sighs, stands and puts her coffee mug on the counter. "I know there's a lot to this, from that day you found Meg and all the years you raised her. It had to have put a tremendous strain on you, having this hanging over your head all this time. I'm glad you're opening up to me about this."

"Well, I'm not, not if you're going to report me. But I guess it's going to get out there anyway, so, what difference does it make?"

"And you're sure Meg is going through with this?"

I nod. "She is. And once she tells this reporter everything, he can write his article, get her what she wants, then it's only a matter of time before the police will question her, then me. She knows this, and she's doing it anyway."

Dr. Phillips writes something on a card, holds it out to me. "Here's my cell number. Call me if anything happens. Will you do that? It could get very serious."

"Are you going to report me?"

"I have to do some thinking and some research, but I will let you know before I do anything. That's a promise."

I shake my head and stand. "Do whatever you have to do."

Chapter 13

As soon as I unlock the apartment door and open it a few inches, I hear footsteps and freeze, then there is Meg, opening the door all the way. Her eyes are wide and shiny as she pulls me in for a hug. I feel her take a deep breath and sigh it out. Did she think I wasn't coming home? Is any of this real? After a few seconds, I pull away, close the door. "I thought you'd be gone by now."

"I'm not going."

"What happened?"

"I decided not to do it."

I fold my arms and stare into her eyes, wait for more.

"I'm really sorry. I didn't think it would upset you so much. I mean, I knew you wouldn't like it, but I thought . . ."

"What?" I hear how sorry she is, but it doesn't seem possible she dropped it just like that. Is she still going ahead with it but just not telling me?

"I couldn't do it." She walks past me, into the kitchen. "I'm going back to school Monday, see what I need to make up. Can you write me a note that I was sick or had a family emergency or something?"

I follow her, watch her take a glass down and fill it at the sink. "So all of a sudden you just changed your mind? And after everything you put me through, you want to act like nothing happened?" I should be happy she's dropping it, but if she let it go this easy, she could just as easily change her mind again. I sit at the kitchen table and Meg sits across from me, and I wait for her to explain. She needs to convince me.

Meg folds her hands on top of the table and looks me in the eye. "I said I'm sorry. Seeing how upset you were last night, I don't want to be the reason you don't do what you're supposed to do and get better." She looks me in the eye. "I don't want to see you like that. If it makes you want to kill yourself drinking, it's not worth it."

"That's a little dramatic."

"Not really."

"I'm glad you're home where you belong, but I still don't understand how you dropped all this so fast. You already knew how upset I was about it, so it can't be just that. Are you going to change your mind and start looking for her again next week? Or if that reporter finds the information you want, are you going to talk to him, tell him our business? I don't want to be worrying all the time about what you might do."

"I told you I'm not doing it. I'm done, okay? And you're right. It's not just that you were upset. I also don't want you to go to jail."

"What about your friend Jack?"

"I told him I'm not going to look for her anymore. I told him I'm done. We called Eric and cancelled the interview. You don't have to worry." Meg goes to the refrigerator, takes out the eggs and milk, bread and margarine, and busies herself making breakfast while I make coffee.

In a minute, we have steaming plates of scrambled eggs in front of us, buttered toast cut in triangles. My girl.

"My father died." I just blurt it out like I'm telling her about a movie I saw.

Meg's eyes open wide, shocked and sad as if she had known him all her life, as if she lost a dear grandfather. "What happened?"

I shrug. "I guess he had a heart attack."

"You don't seem upset about it."

"I'm not. I don't even know why I said anything. Thinking about him only brings back bad memories."

Meg frowns, trying to understand, but she never, ever could. "Even if you didn't like him, he was still your father."

"It goes way beyond not liking him."

Meg's face gets dark and I'm sure her thoughts are going to the worst places now. "What did he do?"

I look past her, out the window just as two birds fly by like two kids having a race. "He was just a jerk."

Meg stares at me, wants me to tell her more, but I'm too ashamed to ever tell anyone. I would have to admit I was complicit, that he never forced me, that I actually felt special. She would never look at me the same again. What kind of father enjoys watching his daughter take off all her clothes to try on new things he bought, pretty lingerie more suited for a hooker than a barely 13-year old girl? His own daughter. Sick bastard.

"Is your mother still alive?"

"She's the one who called me, said I wasn't invited to the service and hung up on me. So no." I walk over to her, give her a quick hug. Her hair smells like strawberries. "I'm glad you're home." Now I wait for Dr. Phillips to tell me what she's going to do.

* * * * *

Sunshine pours through the windows of Dr. Phillips' office, lighting up the pale green walls and shiny laminate floors, bouncing off the glass tabletop. As soon as we sit and face each other, I start. "When I got home from our appointment last week, Meg was there. She was home. She cancelled her meeting with the reporter and decided to stop looking for her birth mother, at least for now."

"Wow." Dr. Phillips leans forward. "Just like that?" She stares at me and waits because she knows there's more. Of course there's more. "Did she explain why? From what you told me, it seems sudden. But sometimes people do things that seem sudden to us, when they actually gave it a lot of thought."

"She saw how much it hurt me, and she realized it was the right thing to do. So, now there's no reason to report me, right?"

The coffee maker beeps and Dr. Phillips pushes herself up and steps over to it. “Coffee?”

“I need to know what you’re going to do. There’s no point in me being here if you’re not going to keep anything confidential.”

Dr. Phillips pours two coffees, fixes mine with cream and sugar and brings the mugs over to the table. “I think I’m a pretty good judge of character, Jenny. I’m not perfect, but I have good instincts. I never believed Meg was in any danger from you. Just the opposite, in fact. I can tell how much you love her, all the sacrifices you made to keep her. I don’t think it would be in Meg’s best interest to put you both through hell after all this time. Nothing good would come of it if you went to jail and Meg went back into the foster care system, especially at her age. That’s where I stand. No need to worry.”

“That’s it then?”

“As far as I’m concerned. Everything you tell me in our sessions will remain confidential. Just as it should be.”

I nod. Take a deep breath. I’m safe. “Thank you.”

She waves my thanks away. “It’s only right. You trusted me, Jenny and I want that to continue. Do you want to tell me more about what happened with Meg?”

I look over at the picture behind her desk of a lake, a dock stretching over the water towards the mountains, the sun setting in an orange sky. “That’s nice.”

Dr. Phillips stares at it and smiles. “It’s beautiful, isn’t it? Peaceful. My brother took that picture.” She takes a sip of coffee, sets her mug down and leans back in her chair, moves her eyes from the picture to me.

“The night Meg showed up with Jack, I was so relieved, so glad to see her, but then there was Jack, this stranger she trusted with everything. I tried to get her to understand how I felt, but she was determined to meet with a reporter and tell him everything too. I went out and got drunk. I tried talking and I tried listening, but I couldn’t make her understand how much it hurt that she didn’t think of me as her real mother.”

Dr. Phillips nods and keeps her expression blank, calm.

"I kept ordering beers and shots and I knew I didn't have the money to pay for them. I didn't care. I just wanted the hurt and anger to go away."

"Do you think you did that for Meg? So she would see how upset you were about her decisions?"

That hurt. "I didn't want her to see me like that. God. Jesus. No. That's not what I was doing. I just wanted to feel better. I wanted the pain to go away. But she did see me. Not only did she find me, but she had to call her friend Jack to pay the tab or I'd probably be in jail right now."

Dr. Phillips is frowning a little, as much as she ever does. She's listening.

"It's nothing new. From the time Meg was little, she has always taken care of me. Should've been the other way around. I know that. I knew it then, but I still let her."

Dr. Phillips thinks about this for a few seconds. "It must have felt okay at the time, or, if not quite okay, just the way things were. It's not like we plan every minute of our lives, Jenny. Sometimes things just unfold in a certain way and become normal. People like Meg are natural caretakers. Whether by necessity or a sense of duty, or simply out of love, there are people in the world who instinctively care for others. Put others first."

That's my Meggie. "I should have taken better care of her. No wonder she wanted to find her birth mother."

"How do you see things changing now?" She leans forward, smiles like she's expecting the best news.

"I think things will be better now. We don't have any more secrets, so that's good. And now that she knows the truth and finally accepts that I'm her mother, I think we'll be closer."

Dr. Phillips nods slowly, looks at me then glances out the window at the blue sky.

"What?"

"She's still out there."

"I know."

Chapter 14

"Ah believe I have information about your biological mother."

I'm sitting on my bed with my geometry book open in front of me, trying to make sense of the numbers and letters and symbols. Hearing Jack's voice after almost a month gets my heart pounding and I stop breathing for a few seconds. He has information about my mother? I don't know what to say. I don't know if I want to know. Yes, I do. Of course I do. But Jenny.

"Meg?"

"I'm here."

"Did you hear what I said?"

I close my book and set it aside, swing my legs over the side of the bed. "I didn't want you to keep looking. I told you I wasn't doing that anymore."

Now there's silence on Jack's end, and I wonder what it means. "Jack?"

"I should have asked first how you are. How are things at home?"

Even though Jenny is working, I close my bedroom door before I sit back down on the bed. "I promised Jenny I wouldn't keep looking. I told you that."

"And I had every intention of following your wishes and dropping it. Then Eric contacted me."

"Was he looking for information about me? Does he know about Jenny? What did you tell him?" I thought this was over.

"I told him I couldn't divulge anything you told me in confidence, which is everything, really. He said he had information about you, and about your biological mother. Apparently, he did some digging of his own."

"What does that mean?"

"Do you think we can meet?"

"Did he find her? Does he know for sure? How did he—?"

"We really should do this in person. I have something for you, but only if you want it."

I try to breathe normally and am so glad Jenny isn't home. "I can meet you at the library. Do you know where it is?"

"I can be there in half an hour."

Jack is already there when I walk in five minutes early. He's sitting at a table in a corner, reading something on his phone, and when he looks up at me he stands and gives me that smile that lights up his eyes. I sit across from him, windows on our right letting in the hazy morning sunshine. Someone left a book there, a thick book, the edges of the hard cover worn and frayed a little. I push it aside without looking at the title, and we lean towards each other, our arms resting on the smooth, cool top.

He studies my face for a few seconds, my hair. Does he notice I curled it? "It's really good to see you." There's a thick manila envelope on the table by his elbow. Information about me? My birth mother?

"It's good to see you too." I hadn't realized until now how much I missed him. He's wearing that same blue shirt as the first day we met. "I didn't expect to hear from you again after I changed my mind about meeting with Eric. I felt like I disappointed you."

"It was absolutely your right to change your mind. And whatever you decide today, I will respect that."

"You said Eric called you?"

"Apparently he still wants to know your story, how you ended up missing from foster care to living with Jenny for 13 years. I think you piqued his curiosity. I know you said you wanted to drop it, but I felt you had the right to know the information is here, if you want it." He puts his hand on the envelope.

"If you still want to drop the whole thing, that's fine. I'm not here to judge or to pressure you, and I surely don't want to cause any more friction between you and Jenny."

I don't know what to say. I look down at the envelope and can't believe that the information I was so determined to find is right there, and he's asking me if I want it. It's what I've been searching for, what I've been obsessed with, ever since I found out Jenny wasn't my biological mother. "Can you tell me what Eric said?"

"He called and said he was following up on your story. He wanted to know if you changed your mind. Then he said he found information on your birth mother and would be happy to give it to you if you agreed to an interview. He said you would be protected as a source and anything you say would be confidential. I told him I would meet with you and ask. That's all."

"But why would he go to all the trouble when I told him I changed my mind? And how could he even get that information? I mean, isn't it confidential?"

Jack shrugs. "I assume he has his ways. Contacts. People can find a way when they want something bad enough."

I shake my head, rub my hand over the smooth table. There must be a hundred coats of polyurethane. "When you said you had information, you didn't tell me there were conditions." I think of Sam. *You didn't think it was free, did you little lady?*

Jack looks me in the eye. "If you want my opinion, it seems like a good deal to me. You get to know who your birth mother is, who you are, maybe get some questions answered. And Eric gets his story. It wouldn't be such a bad thing to expose the flaws in the foster care system. I believe you agree with that. Who knows how many foster children weren't as fortunate as you, who are still missing? I truly believe Eric's stories could bring real change. Maybe even beyond foster care to all missing children."

"Like your sister."

He reaches across the table, touches my hand for a couple of seconds, then folds his hands on the table. "I saw how desperate you were to find out where you come from. I thought this would be a good thing, a welcome surprise."

"It is a surprise."

"All I told him was that I would meet with you. I never guaranteed anything. You can always say no and I'll take this back to him and make sure he doesn't bother you again. I'm not here to pressure you."

It kind of feels like it. "How sure is he that this person he found is really my birth mother? I mean, does he know for sure?"

"Eric did a lot of digging." Jack looks at the envelope. "You gave him quite a bit of information to work with, probably without meaning to. He knows you were a foster child when you were a baby. He knows you went missing when you were around three. And of course there was the show. It's truly hard to miss the resemblance between you and Adeline Jenkins."

"So he really thinks I'm Adeline Jenkins? I mean, he's sure?"

"He didn't give me the details, but I am assuming that's who he believes you to be. And as far as him being sure, he's as sure as someone can be I suppose without a DNA test. I believe he pieced it together as best he could."

I stare at the envelope. "And he put this all together for me?"

Jack nods. "I do admire his investigative skills."

"He put all this together, but won't give it to me unless I agree to an interview, tell him about Jenny."

"Ideally, Jenny would agree to be part of the interview too. But if she refuses, Eric would do the interview with just you. Jenny would have details and insights and the firsthand experience, so his reasoning is, and I agree with this, that if your story is going to be told, Jenny should be the one to tell it."

"And he gave you the information. Eric was that sure I'd say yes?"

"I would call him optimistic. And of course he did all this in good faith. He saw how much you wanted the information, how much it meant to you. All he needs is your word and he will set up a time with you. He does want to do this fairly soon, while there's still interest in his stories about foster care."

"And if Jenny says no, I can still have the information?" I don't know how I could even ask her.

"As long as you tell Eric the whole story."

I stare at the envelope, reach over and put my hand on it, slide it towards me. My name is written in cursive on the front. "Have you looked at it? Did he tell you anything?"

"This is for your eyes only. I'm just the messenger, or facilitator, if you like. I agreed to do this for Eric, and for you, because I truly thought it was what you wanted. I thought it was important to you."

"It is, but I have to think about Jenny."

"You have a right to know who you are. You deserve that."

I nod. I do have a right to know. It crosses my mind just for a second that I don't have to tell Jenny. Not right now anyway. But I said no more secrets. And Jenny deserves to know. "Okay. I'll do it." I try to justify it by telling myself I might be saving other kids. I might make a difference. "It looks like there's a lot in here."

"I'm sure Eric was thorough."

I pick it up and stand. "Do you think Friday will be okay with Eric?" That will give me four days. "10:00? At that same diner?"

Jack stands too, pushes in his chair and turns to me. "I'm sure that will be fine. I'll call him today and set it up, pick you up at nine? Hopefully, both you and Jenny."

"No. That's okay. I'll figure out a way to get there. You've already done so much. Thank you." I start to walk away and Jack puts his hand on my arm to stop me.

"There's one more thing. When you do meet with Eric, whether it's alone or with Jenny, don't say anything about this information he found."

"Why not?"

"He may have used unconventional means to get it. He actually may have risked his career for you. That shows how important he believes your story is. If anyone, including you, mentions it at all, he will deny all knowledge."

I feel like I'm in a spy movie, but I guess it makes sense. I nod and walk away without another word.

Jenny is curled up on the living room couch watching Jeopardy. I'm sitting at the kitchen table pretending to do my homework. I slip out the papers, set them in front of me and look at the back of Jenny's head. There are two sets of papers, each held together with a black binder clip, yellow sticky notes on top, one that says *Becky (birth mother)* and one that says *Meg (Adeline).* My heart starts pounding and I feel so guilty, but I start scanning everything, starting with Becky.

Most of the paperwork is from her years in foster care. She had been there since she was six, when she was taken from her parents because of reports of abuse and neglect. Already I feel like I shouldn't be seeing this. How did Eric even get this? I'll read everything more slowly in my room when I'm alone, then find a place to hide it.

Becky was in four different foster homes, one for more than three years before she was finally sent to a group home when she turned 13. She ran away twice. The second time she made it all the way up to Maine, gave birth to me in a clinic, and was returned to the group home. She voluntarily signed me over and I was placed with my first foster family. My mother's whole life, and the beginning of mine, is right in front of me now. Everything in here is sad and awful. The final forms are an arrest report from last November when she was charged with Involuntary Manslaughter. I take a deep breath and take in as much as I can. Court appearances, guilty plea, sentencing hearing scheduled.

I take the sticky note off my paperwork, or Adeline's. I can't think of myself as Adeline. Not now, probably not ever.

I was born in Harmony, Maine when Becky was only 15, like me. I was put right in foster care as soon as Becky was returned to the group home. A family took me in when I was three months old, then I was with another family when I was two. Then there is the Missing Child Report filed by DCF when I was three. That's when Jenny got me. I glance through reports from Social Workers and Supervisors. No one and everyone was to blame for me disappearing. No one knew what happened to me, and even with all this paperwork, I still feel like just one of a million missing kids.

Jeopardy is almost over. They are on the final round, so I flip through the last few forms before I come to my birth certificate at the very bottom, as if it's the least important thing. Maybe it is. Becky Jenkins is listed as my mother, and the father is *Unknown*. When I look at the date I see my birthday is March 29. I'm already 16. I turned 16 months ago and didn't even know it. After I straighten the papers and slip them inside my school planner, I carry everything to my room.

I know who my birth mother is and I know who I am now, so why don't I feel different? All that time I thought I knew who I was, and now I know I'm someone else. At least I was born someone else. I really thought I wanted to know, but now that I do, I don't feel happy or different or better. And I still have questions only Becky can answer. I want to know how she felt about me when I was born, whether she wanted me, whether she loved me. All that paperwork might as well be about someone else.

* * * * *

The first time I saw my mother was in a courtroom three days after Jack gave me the envelope. When I had read it through again, I noticed Becky's sentencing hearing was on Thursday. Talk about timing.

There were 17 people in the courtroom that day, including me. Groups of one, two and three, heads close, whispering. I wonder if anyone else knew Becky, if anyone else was there for her. It was hard to tell, but I didn't think so. No one but me seemed to be paying attention when she was brought in.

Becky didn't wear a prison uniform. She wore skinny jeans and a white tee-shirt that was way too big for her. There was a chain around her waist that made her shirt bunch up. Her hands were cuffed close together in front, giving her a few inches of movement from the chain connected to leg irons that made an awful clanging sound when she walked. The way the chain tightened with each step, I could tell she wasn't used to taking baby steps.

She was thin and pale, like me, but her hair was short and spiky and died bright yellow. I watched as she held her head high and looked straight ahead, led in by two uniformed officers, one man and one woman. She took a seat at the table with a man in a pale blue suit who must have been her lawyer.

It wasn't a trial or anything, no jury, no witnesses or drama. Just Becky and her lawyer at one table, a young woman at the other one, probably someone from the D.A.'s office. Everyone stood when the judge came in, a large man with short gray hair and glasses with no rims that sat on the end of his nose.

The courtroom was silent as the judge read the charges: *Possession of a Class B Substance with intent to distribute. Involuntary manslaughter.* Involuntary is such a strange word. I didn't mean it? I couldn't help it? Becky said she understood the charges.

Becky and her boyfriend (my father?) had been selling pills laced with fentanyl. Her boyfriend took too much and died. The D.A. woman said Becky was with him at his time of death, that she was aware of both the contents of the drugs he ingested and the amount, and that she failed to call for medical assistance until it was too late. In addition, the D.A. had offered a generous plea deal if Ms. Jenkins would cooperate and provide information about the source of the drugs, an offer she refused.

Becky's lawyer said the deceased had a history of heavy drug and alcohol abuse and the state of his body made it unclear whether that particular dose was what killed him, and even if it was, he took it of his volition. Becky was sentenced to 15 years at the Massachusetts Correctional Institution in Framingham.

I sat alone in the back of the courtroom and didn't move, didn't go to her, didn't cry. As the two court officers led her out, she finally looked around the courtroom. She blinked a few times as if she was waking up or walking out into bright sunshine, not sure where she was or what had just happened. Her eyes slid right over me like I wasn't even there, and it felt like she had given me up a second time.

All the way home, I heard Jack's voice in my head asking, *So, now what?* Good question.

Chapter 15

After supper, Jenny and I sit outside. There's a concrete rectangle to the left of our door where we set out two folding chairs and a little glass-top table. We call it our patio, and it's the best thing about living on the first floor. We even found a fake palm tree someone had put out in the trash that gives us a little shade and a little privacy, not that anyone else sits outside besides us. Most of the other people in our building either work two jobs or are old and stay in and watch television, like Mrs. Reynolds next door. Whenever we do see her, she fills us in on General Hospital, and it reminds me of when I stayed with Darlene in her trailer.

I wait until Jenny finishes her ice cream before I start, keeping my voice as casual as I can. "I saw Jack the other day."

Jenny's eyes flash for a second. "Where?"

I imagine all the things going through her head—that I lied, that I'm going behind her back, that I'm starting this all up again, but she just scrapes up the rest of her ice cream and licks both sides of her spoon, giving me a chance to explain.

"I didn't call him. He called me. He wanted to check in to see how we're doing, then he asked if we could meet to talk. I didn't want to say anything until I knew what it was about. I met him at the library."

"Okay. So what was it about? What did he want?"

I look out towards the quiet street while I get my words straight, even though I practiced this conversation in my head a hundred times last night.

"Was it about your birth mother? Did he find her?"

"No." I hate lying, but technically I'm not. Eric is the one who found her. Jack was just the go-between. *The facilitator*. I wish I could tell her everything, but it feels like way too much right now. I don't think she would understand and be happy for me. More likely she would feel threatened or angry or upset, even with Becky in jail. I will tell her eventually, when the time is right and she's more secure, if that ever happens. I look her right in the eye and tell her some truth. "I told him not to look anymore. I told you that and I meant it."

"What did he want then?" Jenny's voice is strangely calm, as if she's asking what I want for dinner.

"That reporter called him. Eric Roberts? He still wants to do that story on me, on my disappearing from foster care, I mean. He's not really writing about me. He's writing about the foster care system and how so many kids go missing and seem to be forgotten. He thinks if we tell him what happened when I was in foster care, it would help change things for other kids who might be in danger, like I was."

"You told him no, right?"

I wonder now if I should have said anything to Jenny at all. "I told him I'd let him know."

Jenny turns away, shakes her head, then turns back to me, not quite as calm anymore. "One phone call from Jack and you go running off to meet him, and now you're going back on everything you said? Everything we agreed on?" She takes a deep breath and I see she's struggling to be calm again. "Why?" Her voice is soft and sounds like hurt. "Why would you even think about doing this to me? We're doing really good, right? *I'm* doing really good."

"I told you, it's not about me, and it's not about you. Not really. It's about the foster system. Eric is doing this series and there's a good chance that our story could make a difference. Remember that show? All those kids that are missing? They need to take better care of the kids they're supposed to be in charge of. I mean, I'm a perfect example, right? If you didn't save me that day, I might have died." I hope she believes me. It's not the whole truth, but it's still true. I owe

Eric an interview now and I really don't want to do it without Jenny, without at least telling her. It would feel like too much of a betrayal.

Jenny looks around, and even though there's no one near, she lowers her voice. "This is so important to you that you would risk me going to jail? You know the police wouldn't care about reasons or circumstances or the fact that I saved your life. All they would see is me as the bad guy, abducting a child, and they'd throw me in jail."

"But what if Eric guarantees he wouldn't reveal his source? That's what we would be, so we would be protected. He wouldn't use our real names or anything either. I would never ask you to do this if I thought you'd get in trouble."

"You actually want me to go with you? What makes you think you can trust this guy? What makes you think his motives are so pure, that he just wants to help these kids?"

"Jack believes him, and I guess I do too."

Jenny looks out across the street. "Jack. Oh well then." She takes a deep breath, sighs it out and turns to me, her face serious. "How can you be sure this Eric wouldn't turn me in?"

"Okay, how about this? How about we meet with him, then you can decide for yourself if you want to do the interview. Would you do that?"

Jenny picks up our bowls and spoons and napkins and walks inside. I listen through the screen door to Jenny washing the dishes. I picture her face, frowning into the sink. I close my eyes and think about Becky in a jail cell, behind bars like an animal. I think of her as a scared kid with a baby. Me.

Jenny comes back out with two glasses of ice water and sits. "I talked to my counselor about you. I told her everything. About that day I saved you and took you home, how I pretty quickly became your mother. I also admitted I wasn't always the best mother. Actually, I think I was a pretty lousy mother sometimes, but I also know I did my best. Considering."

"You were always a good mother." My words rush out and I hope Jenny believes it's the truth. I reach over and put my hand gently on her arm, wait until she looks me in the eye again. "I mean it. That's what I remember."

"You don't remember anything bad?"

"I remember you were upset when Gene was gone, but you did your best to get us through. I hated how sad you were, and angry. I tried to do everything I could to make things okay, to make you happy, but I figured out only Gene could do that."

Jenny lets out a long sigh as if she had been holding her breath. "It wasn't your job to make things okay. I was stupid to depend on him so much. I kept believing in him, even when I knew better. It killed me when you were hungry, when you didn't have decent clothes or shoes. I should have done better."

"You did the best you could. *We* did the best we could."

She tries to smile but doesn't quite pull it off, then she takes a deep breath and her voice is strong. "So, when does this guy want to meet?"

"You'll do the interview?" I thought I'd be relieved, happy even, but I'm not. I feel like I might be setting her up, and I'm scared.

"I'll do it for you. I don't see how this is going to help other kids, but if this is what you want."

* * * * *

"I protect my sources, Jenny. Absolutely. If I didn't, people would never trust me, never come forward. They would be too afraid of repercussions. I've been doing this for more than 25 years and have never revealed a source. I'm not about to start now."

Jenny and I are sitting on one side of a booth in the same diner Jack and I first met Eric, which feels like a lifetime ago. Eric sits across from me. I think about Jack. I'm sure he wanted to be here, be part of this. It wouldn't be happening if it weren't for him. When he called last night to check that I was still meeting Eric and whether I was sure about a ride, I told him Jenny was coming and it would be better if he wasn't there. The Uber was only $20, and it felt right for it just to be Jenny and me. I don't think she will ever like Jack or trust him like I do.

Eric takes out his notebook and sets it on the table, pulls a pen out of his pocket. "I want you to know I appreciate your meeting with me. I was pleasantly surprised when you called to set this up." He's really good at pretending it was all my idea, that I don't owe him this.

"Can we start by you telling me exactly what you already know about my daughter?" Jenny's voice is strong and clear.

Somehow I didn't expect Jenny to ask this. I expected Eric to ask questions, Jenny and I to answer, and that would be that. I stare at Eric and hold my breath.

"What I know is that Meg believes she is, or was, a foster child who went missing when she was about three. There was a foster child named Adeline Jenkins who disappeared at that time and she and Meg may be one and the same. I know she is looking for her biological parents and hopes to find the reason she was put into foster care. I know she has been well taken care of since she was abducted, and presumably adopted, by someone. Because you are here, I assume that someone is you, but I don't operate on assumptions. Honestly, Jenny, I have more questions than I have knowledge."

Jenny nods as she takes this all in. "So you know my daughter was in the foster system. And you must also know the people who were supposed to be taking care of her didn't, that they only cared about the checks. And you must know the system didn't seem to care at all about finding her or getting her back."

Eric's face stays calm, neutral. "It's no secret that DCF has been under scrutiny for years, with good reason. I'm looking for stories that will shine a spotlight on these foster kids, the ones who go missing from an agency formed and funded to protect them and what we, *we as a society*, are going to do about it."

"What do you want from me, exactly?"

"I'm looking for the truth, Jenny. I want to know if you were somehow involved in the disappearance of a child from foster care. I'm not accusing you of anything. I'm trying to connect the dots from how a child went missing from foster care to becoming your daughter."

"And you want a good story."

"That's the plan. And I happen to believe it's important. It's not an opinion piece, Jenny. I'm trying to get as many facts as I can."

"You want facts? Okay. Here are some facts."

I put my hand on Jenny's arm to calm her. She turns to me, takes a deep breath. "Thirteen years ago, I saved Meg's life. I saw her alone in the back seat of a car, no one around, and took her out of there. I raised her as my own daughter. No, it wasn't exactly a legal adoption, but I gave her a home and took care of her. I'm the only mother she has ever known." She reaches for her ice water and drinks down half of it.

Eric looks at his notes, scribbles something. He frowns at Jenny, then at me. "Meg. The first time we met, you said you thought you were one of the missing children portrayed on television. Do you believe you're Adeline Jenkins?" He knows I am, but he doesn't know how much Jenny knows. Is he trying to confirm what he already knows?

I turn to Jenny, but she holds her eyes on Eric. "I think I might be. Did you see that age-enhanced picture they did on that show? It looks like me, right?"

"I definitely see a resemblance, but you can't rely on that as the only evidence. There are probably a hundred girls who resemble that photo. Do you have more than that?"

"I just told you what happened," Jenny says, almost angry now. "I would think you could figure it out. This Adeline Jenkins disappeared from the back seat of a car. I took Meg from the back seat of a car. Was there more than one foster child this happened to?"

"Are you ready to go on the record with your whole story?" Eric asks.

Jenny looks at me, nods. "Let's do this."

Eric sets a little tape recorder in the middle of the table. "Do you mind if I record this?" Before we have a chance to answer, he presses a button and says he is with *two people who have come forward with their experience involving the Department of Children and Families and a missing foster child in Massachusetts. They have agreed to give their stories on the condition of anonymity.*

We sit there for almost an hour, the waitress keeping our drinks full—ice water for Jenny, ginger-ale for me, coffee for Eric. I watch Jenny, her back straight and chin up, as she tells Eric everything about that morning she saved me, filling in some of the blanks for me too, about taking me to a house up in New Hampshire so I would be safe, buying me everything I needed, taking good care of me. She said it wasn't long before I started calling her *Mama*, and it wasn't until at least two months that I was reported missing and people finally started looking for me. Too late.

"Can you verify any of this, Jenny? Were there any witnesses? Anyone to corroborate your story?"

"My *story*? Are you saying I'm making all this up?"

"I'm saying I can't bring this to my editor without some kind of verification. Were there any witnesses? Anyone you might have confided in at the time?"

"The only other person involved was my boyfriend at the time, but he's in the wind. I have no idea where he is or if he's even alive, and even if you did find him, he's not the most reliable *witness*. Do you actually think I would tell you this if it wasn't true? Something that could get me arrested and thrown in jail?"

Eric frowns, looks at his notes and taps his pen on the table. "Okay, look, Adeline Jenkins' foster parents were charged with neglect and fraud. They don't dispute the facts that they left Adeline alone in their car, except to say they were only gone a minute and the windows were down enough to provide fresh air. What I'm looking for is perhaps any contact you may have had with DCF or the police or a social worker that would provide evidence of negligence on their part."

"I gave you everything I have. I thought their negligence was clear."

"Bottom line is their story has already been told, more than once in fact, and corroborated. What you gave me is your recollection. And an obviously good outcome for Meg."

Jenny looks both shocked and relieved. "So you're not going to report me for kidnapping?"

"Honestly, Jenny, I don't see what purpose it would serve, either for the story or for DCF, or for you and Meg, for me to report this. However, because this would be a Federal crime, the rules can be a bit hazy and my editor may not be too happy about it, but I am going to keep my word and protect you as my source. And, to put it bluntly, Jenny, your part in this story is not really relevant as far as bringing any change to the foster care system. I'm glad you had a happy ending, but I want to focus on the kids who weren't so lucky and what DCF is doing to make positive changes."

Eric turns to me. "Is there anything you remember that would suggest your situation is different than what Jenny described? Anything you want to add?"

"I was too little to remember living with that foster family, but obviously they didn't take good care of me." I tell him my earliest memories are living in the trailer, how Jenny made sure I went to school, took good care of me. "I wasn't hungry or deprived or anything. Mostly what I remember was feeling safe and loved." I know I am stretching the truth, but I need to make

Jenny look and feel as good as I can. What difference does it make now how things were then?

Jenny drinks down the last of her water, sets the glass down hard. “So, we’re all set? Did you get everything you need?”

Eric nods, turns off the tape recorder, starts putting his stuff into his briefcase. “Thank you both for meeting with me. I have a deadline of tomorrow to get it in the Sunday edition, so if there’s anything else you remember or want to say, give me a call by this afternoon.” He takes two cards out of his pocket, hands one to each of us and it’s over. I feel like he went to a lot of trouble for me, putting together all that information, and didn’t get much in return.

Chapter 16

It's only been a couple of days since the interview with Eric, but it feels like forever ago. It's finally Sunday, and his article should be coming out today. Jenny and I haven't mentioned it, both of us pretending to be so busy—me with school work, her with work and appointments. We eat dinner in front of the television. I feel like we're not so much watching as waiting, but I'm not sure for what. I pretty much stay in my room, trying to study for finals with my mind more on Eric's article and what it might bring than geometry and U.S. history. It won't be long now and our waiting and worrying will be over, one way or the other.

After days of dark skies and showers, the sun comes out. Finally. Is this a good sign?

"Let's go for a walk," Jenny says.

"Good idea." We grab our purses and head out without another word. It's humid and getting warmer, and it's nice to be outside, feel the sun on my face. I want to tell Jenny not to worry, that Eric will protect his sources just like he said, but I'm not completely sure about anything, and I'm worried too.

I turn to her and she has a haunted look in her eyes. "Are you okay?"

Jenny takes a deep breath. "When you told Eric you were never hungry, that you always felt safe, is that what you really remember, or did you just say that to make me look good?"

Her question takes me by surprise and I think about it for a few seconds. "I guess I do remember not having enough to eat sometimes, but I was okay, and I knew it wasn't your fault. I don't remember leaving the trailer much except for going to school, like we were stuck in our own little world. Maybe that's why I felt safe, because we were so isolated from the outside world. I think the only time I didn't feel safe was when Sam came over. He scared me. Not that I felt like he was going to hurt me, it was because he always made you upset or sad. I could tell you didn't like him, so I didn't like him either."

"You got that right. What else do you remember?"

"I remember Gene was gone a lot. It's funny; I don't remember him leaving, but I remember him being gone and how different it felt. Quiet and empty. It seemed like he was gone a long time and as soon as I started getting really afraid he wasn't coming back, he would show up with food. Buckets of fried chicken or pizza, canned food and bread. Beer. And even though you were mad at him, it didn't take long for you to make up and we were all happy again. For a while at least. That was our life and I guess I was used to it. It's all I ever knew."

"Some life, huh? I made a huge mistake being with Gene for so long, believing in him, depending on him so much. Way too much."

"You were young, and you loved him."

Jenny shakes her head slowly and smiles a sad smile. "I did. I really did. But I was blind. And stupid." She turns to me and laughs. "I kept thinking he was going to change, especially after we got you, that we would settle down, be a family. Ha. And I call *you* too trusting."

"He wasn't all bad, right? Didn't he used to bring us home presents sometimes?" I remember soap shaped like a heart, little boxes of crayons.

"That was supposed to make up for leaving us for weeks at a time with no money, not much food. Yeah, he was quite a guy."

"I don't know how you did it." I never realized until now how much Jenny put up with and gave up, for me.

"I had no choice. I had to take care of you. I was responsible for you. But I'll be honest, sometimes I resented you a little. I'm sorry to say it, but sometimes I thought how much easier my life would be if I never found you that day and brought you home." Jenny slows down, takes my arm. "But, then you would look at me with those big needy eyes of yours and call me mama and I couldn't imagine not having you."

I think about this for a few seconds and feel such an overwhelming sense of love for Jenny. If anything happens because I talked her into doing that stupid interview I'll never forgive myself. "Do you still resent me sometimes? You're right. Your life would have been easier. Maybe you and Gene would have been happier. Maybe it's because of me it didn't work out."

"If it is, then thank you. If I had stayed with Gene, we'd be living in some crappy apartment, still doing drugs and drinking our life away. If we still had a life. No. I don't resent you, not for one second. I think you saved me as much as I saved you."

Up ahead we see a white van pull up next to the machine that holds the newspapers and watch as a kid gets out, his Red Sox cap on backwards, jeans and tee-shirt at least two sizes too big for him. He moves fast as he carries a stack of newspapers, fills the machine, locks it and drives away. I pull 50 cents from my pocket, buy a paper, fold it in thirds and carry it under my arm as Jenny and I walk home.

The article begins on the bottom of the first page, continues and finishes on the third. The title is, *Saving Our Children.* Jenny and I sit at the kitchen table with the paper in front of us, both reading silently.

There are currently more than 9,000 foster children in Massachusetts. At any given time, approximately 800 of those children are reported missing. According to the Department of Children and Families, there are protocols in place to identify and report missing children. Federal law requires state social service agencies to submit a report to the National Center for Missing and Exploited Children. They are also required to notify local law enforcement. In addition, DCF does everything within its power to search for a missing child. Unfortunately, what happens after the initial reporting leaves us with more questions than answers: What happens after a child is reported missing? Who is ultimately responsible for finding these children, and what happens after they are found? It is easy to put the blame solely on DCF, but the underlying responsibility rests with us all.

The article goes on about legislation passed in the last 20 years, the cycle of funding increasing, then decreasing. *The fact is that unless you are directly involved in foster care, either as a foster parent or someone in the system, there is little attention paid to the agency tasked with taking care of our most precious and undervalued population, our children.*

There are interviews with teenagers reported missing who ran away from their foster home, either because they were abused in some way or wanted to reunite with their families or were lured away with promises of a better life, only to be trafficked. One boy who lived in a group home says, *We were always sneaking out at night, getting some bum to buy us beer. We didn't cause any trouble because we didn't want to get caught and get sent somewhere else. I liked the freedom, but I missed having a home. I guess I even kind of missed having some rules, having someone who cared enough to know where I was and what I was doing. In two years I'll age out of the system and I'm not sure what I'll do then.*

A 14-year-old girl said she was approached by a couple who said they would take care of her but didn't want to go through all the red tape. *They seemed really nice and said I could bring a friend, so I wasn't really nervous. It seemed like a chance to have a home, but then they had these parties and asked us to be "nice" to some of their friends, which meant having sex with them. My friend and I ran away from that, back to the group home that didn't seem so bad anymore.*

The article goes on about three teenage girls found dead a month after running away from a foster family, a 5-year-old missing and presumed dead after not being seen for more than six months, then finally, me, *a 3-year-old girl still missing after being left in the back seat of a car by her foster parents and not checked on or reported missing for months. And by that time, the child simply joined the ranks of the missing.* That's all he wrote about me and my story. I'm not missing, and he knows it.

Eric finishes the article saying, *How many more children will it take who are hurt, missing or dead to make real, lasting changes at what should be one of the most important agencies in the state, the one that looks after children who have no one else? It's up to all of us to demand change now.*

"Wow," Jenny says, her voice soft. "All that worrying for nothing. What the hell did he want the interview for if he wasn't going to use any of it?"

"I know. I thought there would be more. About us." I'm relieved. Mostly relieved, but I actually feel a little let down too. "I mean, I guess we're safe though, right?"

"I guess we are," Jenny sounds a little skeptical.

"It was a good article," I say. "I mean, I guess it wasn't supposed to be about us anyway. I hope it makes a difference for all the missing kids out there." I want to believe our secret is buried forever, that Eric either doesn't believe what Jenny did or it's just not worth reporting. Old news? Not relevant, he said. He gave me all that information about Becky and me for nothing? Nothing for him at least. I don't get it.

After school on Monday, as soon as Jenny goes to work, I call Jack. He answers on the first ring like he was expecting my call. "Did you see the article? What did you think?"

"I was going to call you. It wasn't exactly what I was expecting. I thought there would be more about you and Jenny."

"Me too, but I'm also relieved."

Jack is silent for a few seconds. "Do you want to meet and talk about it?"

I was hoping he would want to see me again. "I can meet you at the library."

"I'll be there in a half hour if that's okay."

I curl my hair, put on a little mascara, lip gloss. I don't want to look like I got ready for him, but I want to look good. I walk right to the same shiny table in the corner, sit in the same chair I sat in last time. The table is clear and clean. I look up to see Jack, and as soon as he sits across from me, he says, "Well, Jenny must be relieved. And you."

"We are. I thought for sure there would be more. I mean, he wanted that interview so much he called you, got all that information on my birth mother and me just so we would agree to the interview, but then he didn't seem that interested in what we had to say. He did record it, but then he didn't use it."

"He recorded it?"

"He had this little tape recorder in the middle of the table."

Jack thinks about this, a serious look on his face. "I really expected more."

"Me too, but I guess the article—"

"You and Jenny both met with Eric?" Jack interrupts. "Did she tell him everything? Did she tell him how she abducted you?"

I don't like that word, or his tone, but I let it go. "She told him everything. I was really proud of her. It took a lot of courage. But he said he already knew I was taken from the back of a car, that I wasn't reported missing right away, all that. He said Jenny's part in it wasn't relevant for his story. And I'm glad he didn't write about what Jenny did. I mean, who knows what would happen if, well, anyway, it's over now, I guess, and Jenny is safe."

Jack shakes his head and frowns. "I will admit I was more than a little disappointed with the article. I was expecting more," he says again.

"Like what?" I ask. Did he want Jenny to get arrested?

"Like the truth." Jack's voice has an edge now.

"He did tell the truth. He wrote about all the missing kids, the ones who disappeared and the ones who ran away. I think it might make a difference, make people more aware of the kids in foster care, about how the system needs to do better."

"But he didn't tell the truth about Jenny. Not about what she did."

"That's not what the article was supposed to be about though. I guess he didn't want to write about anything positive."

"Since when is kidnapping positive?"

All I can do is stare at him for a few seconds. "Where is all this coming from?" As soon as my words are out, I realize exactly where it's coming from. It's about his sister. "Are you upset because Jenny didn't get in trouble? Because you think she got away with it?"

"She did get away with it. Just like the people who took my sister."

"It's not the same. Jenny isn't anything like those people." I want to defend Jenny and what she did, and even though I believe what I'm saying, my words sound hollow. I see Jack's point in a way, but Jenny saved me. She took care of me, raised me as her own daughter. Who knows what those people did to his sister. It's definitely not the same, and I'm sure Jack knows this. He's just hurting. Grieving his sister.

Jack sighs and looks away, stares out the window. It's cloudy now, gray. "It's the anniversary of the day Alicia was taken."

"I'm really sorry." I wish I knew what else to say.

Jack turns back to me, takes a deep breath and his voice is calm again. "Have you contacted your mother yet?"

"Not yet." I tell him everything I learned about Becky, how she spent her whole life in foster care, about having me when she was barely16, about her arrest and how she's serving 15 years for involuntary manslaughter. I watch Jack's face and see no surprise, no judgement. "I went to her sentencing hearing. I wanted to see her, see what she was like. Part of me stupidly thought she would recognize me."

"But she didn't."

"She looked right through me."

"Well, I'm not surprised. She hasn't seen you since you were just a baby. And it surely sounds like she has some problems."

I let out a laugh, then feel bad about it. "You could say that."

"But she is still your mother. She gave birth to you."

I almost tell him what Jenny has been saying all along, that giving birth to someone doesn't make them a mother, but the words won't come out. "I know."

Jack nods, focuses outside the window again. "It surely looks like rain." He sounds so disappointed, like he was planning an outdoor event. Then he looks at me. "I can't believe you haven't contacted her, now that you know who she is, after all you went through to find her. If only to put her mind at ease that you're okay." The same words he used when he made me call Jenny.

"I'm planning to write to her when I get home." Not true, but maybe I will.

"And have you told Jenny yet?"

"Not yet. I wanted to wait until after the interview."

"How do you think she'll react?"

"It's hard to tell. She's been so much better lately. I think the therapy and the not drinking has been really good for her. And I think she's trying to make up for my childhood."

Jack frowns. "What do you mean? She wasn't good to you? She didn't harm you or neglect you, did she?"

"No. No. She tried her best, she really did. It's just that we didn't have much and she feels bad about that." I don't want to share with him, with anyone, how I tried so hard to take care of Jenny, even when I was just a little girl. That's between me and Jenny. "As far as how she'll react about Becky, I think she'll be okay with it. Especially when I tell her Becky is in jail. Jenny might feel a little vindicated in a way, I guess."

"Even when you tell her about Becky's life? I hope Jenny is a better person than that."

"Jenny is a good person. She's just really insecure. You saw that when you met her, right? And as far as giving Becky peace of mind, I don't think she ever gives me a thought."

"You don't know that."

"No, but why should I set myself up for disappointment? What if she doesn't want to know me?"

"What if she does?"

Chapter 17

It's not like I didn't plan to reach out to Becky, eventually, but after talking to Jack I feel like I should have done it already. What am I waiting for? I can't stop thinking about how vulnerable and pathetic she looked in the courtroom, the chains holding her like she's some kind of dangerous monster.

After everything Jack did for me to help find her, I want him to know it wasn't for nothing. And I also want to keep our connection. Right now this is all we have.

I try to put the right words together in a letter, but it's hard because I don't even know Becky. All I know is what I read in the reports and forms, all written by strangers about someone who was just another statistic, another unfit mother who couldn't take care of her baby. I feel sorry for her, but I don't know how to write that or how she would feel about it. Is Jack right that it would give her peace of mind to hear from me? Does she ever think about me, wonder or worry about me?

I write to her in my room with the door closed, telling Jenny I'm doing my homework. Sometimes I wish lying didn't come so easily, but sometimes it's for the best. My letter ends up being pretty short.

Dear Becky,

My name is Meg (It was Margaret, but now I go by Meg). I found out recently I'm your biological daughter, the one you gave up to foster care. I want you to know I'm doing fine. I'm almost finished my junior year of high school. I get good grades and I would be on the honor roll if it wasn't for geometry.

I saw you in court the day you were sentenced to prison, but I don't think you saw me. At least you didn't recognize me. I guess I'm not surprised, though, since you haven't seen me since I was a baby. I'm sorry for all you have gone through. I know you didn't have an easy life, and I want you to know I don't blame you for anything. I was in foster care, until I was adopted when I was three. They have always treated me like their own daughter, and I feel really lucky.

I hope you're going to be okay. If you want to write back, I would like that so we could get to know each other a little. I would also like to know who my father is.

Sincerely,

Meg

I fold it and slip it into an envelope, then take it out and add, *P.S. Would it be okay if I came to visit you?*

I drop it in the mailbox on my way to school the next morning. I need to tell Jenny soon about Becky. If she does write back to me, and I'm not getting my hopes up, Jenny will see it and wonder who's writing to me from prison. And I'm ready to tell Jenny anyway. No more secrets, no more lies. As soon as I find the right moment.

Eleven days later, there's a letter addressed to me from MCI Framingham. I'm glad it's still in our mail box and not on the kitchen table. Jenny left me a note that she had gotten another cleaning job and would be home a little after four. I take the letter to my room, sit on my bed and rip it open.

The handwriting is spiky cursive.

Dear "Meg,"

I was surprised to get your letter. I guess I was surprised to get any letter. It sounds like you are one of the lucky ones that made it out and I'm glad for you. Now let me set you straight on some things. First of all, you were born into the system. It isn't that I didn't want you (which I'm not even sure about) or that I made a choice to give you up. Choices were something I never had and never will. I was always a foster kid, ever since

I can remember, handed off from one family to another, then group homes, until I finally had it and ran away with my boyfriend. After a month on the run we made it to Maine, where you were born. I was still a minor, so they threw me back in the system. You being a foster kid is just a fact of life and not a pretty one, but there it is. And like I said, you're one of the lucky ones who got out.

She sounds so angry.

If you are my daughter, your name is Madeline. I named you Madeline because I liked it. It's soft, not like Becky. It came from a book I liked when I was a kid. I could read it when I was only four. I remember someone saying oh what a bright little girl, but if I was so bright, I wouldn't be here. I don't know who changed your name to Adeline, but I don't like it. And Margaret? I like that even less. It sounds like an old lady's name. You're right to change it to Meg, but I still like Madeline better. See what I mean about having no choices? Can't even name my own kid.

As for your father, you're better off not knowing his name. We were young and stupid and it doesn't matter anyway because he's dead. If you were in court that day I was sentenced, then you know they blamed me. It's not like I forced him to take anything. I guess they had no one else to pin it on and someone had to pay. If you still want to visit, I'll get you on the visitor's list. Don't worry about it if you change your mind.

Becky

I read her letter twice before I fold it and put it back in the envelope, slip it under my sweaters in the bottom drawer of my dresser. I want to see her now, close up and not in chains. I want her to see that I'm good. I want to hear her voice and hear her say my name. I want her to see me.

It's easy to find information about visiting inmates at MCI Framingham, but I find out I need to be accompanied by a parent or guardian because I'm a minor. I'm so sick of being called that. *Minor: Lesser, not important.*

Now that I found Becky, I'm not about to wait two more years to meet her. Who knows if she'll still be alive by then? You hear so many awful stories about prison fights and people getting killed. Before I talk to Jenny, I decide to call Jack. I haven't talked to him since that day after the article came out. Hopefully he's not still upset about it. I want him to know that I'm following through, that I wrote to Becky and she wrote back, and that I want to see her. All that will make him happy.

"I wanted to let you know I wrote to Becky," I tell him.

I can feel his smile through the phone. "I am glad to hear that. It makes everything worthwhile now, doesn't it?"

"And I got a letter back from her today."

"Well I imagine she was glad to hear from you."

"She sounded kind of angry. She said it wasn't her fault that I was in foster care. She said she was in foster care all her life and I was born into the system and it wasn't her choice to give me up. It was kind of good to hear that, I guess. It sounds like she's had a pretty hard life, in and out of foster homes. She said I was one of the lucky ones who got out. And she doesn't like my name. She said she named me Madeline, but I don't like that. I'm sticking with Meg."

"I think that's a good choice. I like your name. I do feel sorry for her and her life. I'm sure she wanted better for you. How much did you tell her about yourself?"

"Just basic stuff. That I found out I'm her daughter, that I'm doing well in school. Not much. Mostly I wanted her to know I'm okay in case she ever thought about me and felt bad about giving me up."

"Did she ask how you found her?"

"Nope."

Jack takes a few seconds to respond. "Interesting."

"I want to visit her, but I need a parent or guardian."

"I imagine prison rules are pretty strict. Will Jenny take you?"

"I haven't told her about Becky."

"I thought you were done with secrets."

"I'm waiting for the right time."

"Maybe Jenny's stronger than you think. Maybe she would think it's a good thing, a way to make up for . . . things."

"What things?" As soon as I ask, I'm not sure I want to know. Does he mean Jenny taking me from that car? Her drinking? Does he think she's a bad mother?

"I'm sorry. Don't mind me. I'm speaking out of turn. I'm just saying Jenny might surprise you."

"Maybe you're right."

"Maybe so."

As soon as we hang up, Jenny is standing in the doorway to my room. "Doing your homework?"

Everything seems so normal. I'm sitting at my desk, my computer open in front of me, my mother asking about my homework. She's so calm and peaceful. I hate to ruin that, but it's time she knows about Becky. "I don't have any."

"Facebook?"

"I was actually searching how to visit someone in prison."

Jenny freezes. "For school?"

I shake my head. "I want to visit someone."

"Who do you know in prison? Is it Gene?" She shakes her head. "I'm surprised it took this long. What's he in for?"

"Not Gene."

Jenny comes in and sits on the side of my bed. "Who?"

I decide to just blurt it all out. "My birth mother. I found out who she is. Her name is Becky and she's in prison. I want to go see her, but I need a parent or guardian because I'm a minor. I was wondering if you would take me."

Jenny blinks a few times. "You're serious. Okay. Back up. How did you even find out about her? When?"

"Eric found out, as a thank you for the interview." That's true enough. "I guess he has contacts and he did some research and gave me the information. I wrote to her and she wrote back and now I want to meet her. Maybe you do too?" I know that's a stretch, but I blurt that out too.

"No. Actually I don't. So you've known this for a while now and didn't say anything?"

"I'm sorry. I didn't want to upset you. I was waiting for the right time."

"The only thing that upsets me is that you felt you couldn't tell me, that you didn't trust me enough."

"I'm really sorry."

Jenny puts her arm around my shoulders. "I'm sorry too. It's mostly my fault you didn't feel you could tell me. You probably thought I couldn't handle it, right? That I'd fall apart, start drinking again? I need you to believe in me. Can you do that? Can you trust me?"

I hug her back. "I will. I do. I promise. But what I found out about Becky, it's a lot."

"So, what's she in for?"

"Manslaughter."

Jenny's eyes open wide. "She killed someone? Who?"

"Her boyfriend. My father, I think. She didn't actually kill him. They were both doing drugs and he overdosed and died and they blamed her."

"And you want to see this woman?"

I stare at her and feel a little angry. "*This woman* had a really hard life. She was in foster care ever since she can remember. I want to meet her. And I want her to see me, see I'm okay."

Jenny takes a few seconds to stare at me, into me, and all I see is caring.

"What else do you know about her?"

I open my dresser drawer and pull out the envelope, hand it to Jenny. "This is all the information Eric got for me. Plus the letter I wrote to her and the letter she wrote back."

Jenny hesitates, then takes it. "Are you sure?"

"I should have shown you this already. I'm really—"

She puts her hand up to stop me. "I get it. Just trust me now, okay?"

"I will. I do."

"I'll take you, if that's what you want." She sets the envelope down, reaches over and tucks both sides of my hair behind my ears. "I don't want her to hurt you, but I don't think I can save you from that."

Jenny and I take the 45-minute bus ride to Framingham. There aren't many people on the bus, maybe 10 or so, and no one is paying any attention to us. I'm nervous and excited and can't believe I'm actually going to meet my birth mother. I wonder if she's excited to meet me too.

Jenny has been pretty quiet all morning. She must be thinking about everything she read about Becky, about me. "I appreciate you doing this," I say. "I know it must be hard."

"Harder for you." Jenny pats my leg. "Do you know what you'll say to her?"

"I guess I'll ask a little about her life, where she's from, if she has any other family."

Jenny nods, looks out the window.

After a minute, I have to ask. "Are you glad she's in jail?"

"You think I want to see you hurt?"

"I'm not hurt. I'm disappointed I guess. I feel sorry for her that she had such a hard life and now half her life will be gone by the time she gets out of prison. And I don't think she has anyone."

"Maybe she has you now." Jenny doesn't look at me when she says this, and I can't tell if she's upset or proud of me. Then she turns and looks me in the eye. "I don't think she deserves you, but that's who you are. You have a good heart. Just don't expect too much, okay?"

It takes a long time to go through all the security before I can see Becky. Processing at the Outer Control Lobby, going through the metal detector, the paperwork, showing identification, the questions, the search, turning my pockets inside-out, opening my mouth, the stamp on my hand, the waiting, then, finally, the visiting room. There are windows on one side with bars on them, letting in a little sunshine, cinderblock walls and about a dozen tables with chairs.

Becky struts in like a normal person without a care in the world—no bright orange jumpsuit or handcuffs. She glances at the Corrections Officer who tilts his head towards me. Close up, she looks older than I thought, older than Jenny, even though they are just about the same age. Her yellow hair isn't as bright as it was in court and not spiky. Her eyes are the same color as mine. I wonder if she hates the color too. She wears a light gray sweatshirt and matching sweatpants, white sneakers.

She drops into the chair across from me, folds her arms across her chest. "How do I know you're really her?"

I open my mouth, close it when nothing comes out. She stares at me, takes in my face, my hair, my arms. I didn't expect her to ask this and I have no real answer ready. All I came with are questions. "I have a friend who found out for me."

She narrows her eyes and stares into me a few seconds. "Why?"

I can't believe she's asking me why. "When I found out I was adopted from foster care, I wanted to know where I came from, who my parents were. I guess I wanted to know who I was."

Becky laughs. At me. "If you don't know who you are by now, I can't help you."

I feel my face get hot and try to think of what to say next.

"Look, I get you wanting to know who your parents are. But now you know. I'm asking why exactly you wanted to see me. The letter wasn't enough for you?"

"You're my mother." It feels like the worst lie I have ever told.

"I thought you went missing. I figured you were dead." Her expression doesn't change. It's like she's talking about a pet hamster or goldfish she flushed down the toilet.

"I thought you'd want to meet me. I thought you'd want to know I'm doing well."

She laughs and checks me out one more time. "I used to wonder sometimes how you turned out. Now I know." She keeps her eyes on my face, my hair. "I used to be plain too. You should think about dying your hair or at least getting some highlights. And try wearing some makeup." She stands and starts to leave, then turns back to me. "In case you were thinking about it, don't come back. I don't need this shit." She turns and walks away, followed by the guard.

I sit there and stare at the door even after it clicks shut and try to breathe.

"Ready, miss?" Another guard stands next to me and we walk out to the waiting area.

Jenny stands when she sees me, her face full of concern, like I might be sick or hurt. I'm both. She opens her arms and it's so clear at that moment who my mother is.

Chapter 18

"You must be relieved." Dr. Phillips has the newspaper open on her desk when I walk in, a smile on her face that disappears when she sees I'm anything but.

On the ride home from the prison, Meg told me every detail about her conversation with that horrible woman who doesn't deserve one more second of thought, one more tiny space in Meg's head. I have never felt so bad for anyone in my life. My sweet girl who wanted nothing more than to make that woman feel a little better about giving up her child.

I sit and glance at the newspaper, open to the article I have given so little thought to. All I care about now is helping my Meggie get over this disappointment. I knew she'd only get hurt. But I also knew I couldn't stop her from following through with this, and now she's devastated. I pace to the window and back, stop in front of the lake picture and stare at it, wishing I could be there right now with my Meggie.

Dr. Phillips doesn't ask me any questions yet, gives me the time I need while she pours us coffee. Once we are sitting in our chairs in front of her desk, I take a deep breath and tell her all about Meg finding out about her birth mother from Eric, everything we know about her now and her hard life in foster care, taking Meg to that prison to see her and how horribly she treated my Meggie. "I've never seen anyone so crushed."

"Wow." Dr. Phillips shakes her head. "That poor kid. After everything she went through to find her, after everything you went through to come to terms with this. I honestly don't know what to say."

"I thought I would feel good somehow, feel at least a little vindicated if she turned out to be someone awful, but I didn't want her to be this awful. I had a bad feeling that Meg would only get hurt. I told her this, but she had to see it through and find out for herself."

"We learn a lot of lessons in life the hard way, don't we? Sometimes it's the only way. It's awfully difficult, though, when you see someone you love hurt like that. She's lucky to have you for support."

"I never expected the person who gave birth to such a special kid could turn out to be so evil. God how I hate that woman. Becky. Her name is Becky."

"Hate is a strong emotion, Jenny, isn't it? It's a powerful one, and sometimes we can be consumed by it if we're not careful. Now I'm not telling you how to feel. I would never do that, but I will say that in my experience, it hurts the hater much more that the person on the receiving end. I hope you can move on from that, just as you want to help Meg move on. Becky doesn't deserve to take anything else away from you or Meg."

"She won't. She was way more important when we didn't know who she was. Now that we do, she's not someone we want to know. I let the thought of her scare me. I gave her too much power and I didn't even know who she was. And she won't come between Meg and me anymore."

"If you think Meg would ever want to talk to someone, I can recommend some therapists who specialize in treating young people Meg's age."

"I know she'll be fine." I would take Meg to a therapist if she wanted, but in my heart I want to be the one she turns to. I want to be the one to make her whole again.

"Just a thought." Dr. Phillips takes a sip of coffee, sets her mug down on the edge of her desk. "You've had a lot going on. Do you want to talk about the article? When you came in I said you must be relieved. Worst thing a therapist can do, put words in your mouth. I'm supposed to *ask* how you feel."

"I was glad I did it, but I was surprised he didn't think what happened was important enough for his story. You know what he said? That basically it's old news that Meg was taken. The fact that I rescued her and raised her and made sure she had a good life isn't *relevant*. It makes me angry, all that running, all those years hiding and scared, so afraid of someone finding out. And now I don't think anyone gives a damn. It doesn't even matter."

Dr. Phillips nods and says, "People can be funny. But I do think it would matter to the authorities, so this reporter, Eric, did you a real favor. He could have run with it, sensationalized it. We've all seen that. So I think you're lucky there." She picks up the newspaper, scans the article. "He does write about Meg going missing from foster care, how she was left alone and taken. And, more importantly, how DCF hadn't checked on the foster family, on her, in more than a month. It seems that was the point of the article, the missing kids and the fact that there needs to be something done about it."

"Do you really think anyone actually cares about these kids?"

"I think a lot of people do. And if these articles get enough attention, there could be more funding, more people working at DCF, more safeguards in place. And at the very least, I think it might make people think twice about leaving their kids in a car, foster kid or not. What about you? Are you glad you did the interview?"

"I did it for Meg, so yes. And you're right. I am relieved."

Dr. Phillips brings our empty coffee mugs to the counter, opens her little refrigerator and pulls out two bottles of flavored waters. She hands one to me and sits. "For what it's worth, I think you did an incredible thing raising Meg like you did. Something most people wouldn't even consider. And it all worked out."

"That day I found Meg, I had no idea what I was doing. I mean, I don't know what was driving me, but something was. Something brought me right up to that car, to that sweet baby all alone and helpless. I can't honestly say I thought about it. I just knew I was doing something good, maybe for the first time in my life."

Dr. Phillips starts to say something when her phone buzzes. She frowns, picks it up and listens for a couple of seconds. "I'm with a patient." She mouths the word *sorry* to me, listens some more, says she will be right out. "I'm really sorry about this. Can you hang on just a minute?"

I swivel my chair towards the door, and when Dr. Phillips opens it I see two men in dark suits standing there, holding up their badges, just like in the movies. I can't breathe as she steps out and closes the door behind her. I go to the door to listen, then back away when I realize I can't hear anything through the thick door. A million thoughts and questions run through my head and I look around for a way out, but there's only the window. It has to be about Meg. The article. Did Eric report me? So much for protecting his sources. Just because he didn't print anything about me doesn't mean he didn't report me. I told him everything. How could I be so stupid to trust him?

Dr. Phillips comes back in alone, closes the door behind her. "Okay." She takes a deep breath and sighs it out. Her eyes dart around the room, then focus on me. "Those guys are from the FBI. They want to question you, but since this is *my* office and you are *my* patient, I told them they would have to come back with a warrant. I wasn't sure about that, but I held my ground. They acted innocent and nice, said they were following up on an anonymous tip and just had a few questions and they would wait. I asked what it was about and they said they would wait until we were finished. I also told them you would want a lawyer present for any questioning they wanted to do."

"It has to be the article, right? But the article didn't say anything about me. Do you think Eric reported me anyway? I knew I never should have done it. I never should have trusted him." I'm sweating now even though it's cold in here.

"Let's back up a minute. I don't see how it could be the article, Jenny. No names were used and nothing points to you, or

Meg for that matter. How about this? What if we call your lawyer? Justin, right? We can ask him to be here while they question you. At least then we'll know what this is about. Maybe it's not even related to Meg. And you don't have to answer anything that might incriminate you. It's better not to say anything right away."

I get up and start pacing. Hopefully she's right. Maybe it's not even about Meg. Maybe it's Gene. Maybe he's in some kind of trouble. But why would they want to talk to me about it? "Why would they come here? Why not my apartment? How would they even know I was here?" My voice is getting higher and higher. I sound like a scared, guilty kid. *Stop it.*

Dr. Phillips shrugs, holds her hands out. "I have no idea. It's certainly a first for me. But you know what? I'm glad I'm with you. We'll sort this out, okay? Let's call Justin."

Justin is there in 45 minutes, telling us his last case was dismissed and he wasn't far. He wears only slightly wrinkled chinos with a white shirt and dark blue blazer, a tie that looks like it has tiny horses on it. "You know I'm not a criminal lawyer, right?"

"And I'm not a criminal. I don't even know what this is about, but it's the FBI so it must be serious, right? Dr. Phillips thought I should have a lawyer when they questioned me."

Justin narrows his eyes. "You have no idea why the FBI would want to talk to you? Not even a guess?"

I shake my head, close my lips tight. While we waited for Justin, Dr. Phillips and I had decided the best thing to do would be to play dumb and let the FBI do all the talking. It seems like a good plan, but still, I'm so scared.

"Okay," Justin says, "if you're ready, let them in, if that's okay with you, Dr. Phillips."

The two men introduce themselves, agent this and agent that, one tall, one short, uniforms of dark suits, white shirts, striped ties. They show their badges again, thank us so politely for seeing them. The tall one says, "We just have a few questions."

"Let's sit down," Dr. Phillips leads us to a round table in the corner with four chairs, pulls another chair over and sits close to me. They don't seem surprised I have a lawyer.

"Can you tell me what this is about?" I ask. Staying calm.

"We received an anonymous tip about a possible kidnapping." The short one takes out a small notebook. "Are you familiar with . . ." He flips through a couple of pages like he doesn't know what's in there, then stares at me. "Adeline Jenkins?"

"No." This can't be happening. Not now. "Why?"

"We're investigating a kidnapping from approximately 13 years ago. Adeline Jenkins was kidnapped while in foster care."

"And you're just investigating this now? What does it have to do with me?"

"We're following up on new information we received recently. It's our understanding you have a daughter." He looks at his notebook again. Prick. "Margaret? The same age as Adeline Jenkins."

"Are you questioning everyone with a 16-year-old daughter?" That comes out angrier than I intended and the two men glance at each other.

Finally Justin speaks up. "I'm advising my client not to answer any more questions until you clarify exactly what you think her involvement is."

They glance at each other again, then the short one pulls a folder out of his briefcase. He opens the folder and I see that age-enhanced picture of Meg, clearer than the one we saw on television. He pushes it in front of me. "Is this your daughter?"

"Again," Justin interrupts, "I'm advising my client—"

"No." I push the picture away from me.

The tall one sighs as if he wants this to be over as much as I do. "Adeline Jenkins was abducted from foster care 13 years ago and never found. We have reason to believe she and your daughter may be the same person."

"So someone calls in a tip and you come here accusing me of kidnapping?"

"We're not accusing you of anything. We're simply trying to ascertain whether the information we received has any merit."

"Well it doesn't."

"Can you tell us your whereabouts 13 years ago? Specifically . . ." Again the notebook. "May 14, 2003?"

"You're kidding, right? Can you tell me yours?"

The two agents raise their eyebrows and almost smile.

"I think we're done here," Justin says, but no one moves.

I'm more angry than scared now. At myself. I knew better. I knew we should have left it alone, kept the past in the past. But no. I had to tell all about it. To a reporter. I'm so screwed.

A phone buzzes and the tall guy pulls it out of his inside pocket, glances at it and shows his partner, who reads it and nods.

"I'm afraid not. Jennifer Carson, you're under arrest for the kidnapping and unlawful imprisonment of Adeline Jenkins. You have the right to remain silent . . ."

I listen to his words, but they don't get through. This can't be real. All I can think about is Meg. My Meggie. What will they do with her? She's too young to be alone. They'll put her in some awful place or with some foster family. I'll lose her. After all this, I'll lose her. Do they have her already?

"I'll meet you there." It's Justin. I forgot he was there. This can't be happening.

"I'll come too, if that's all right," Dr. Phillips says.

Before they can put handcuffs on me, I fish my keys out of my purse and hold them out to Dr. Phillips. "Can you check on Meg for me please? I need to know she's okay. I need someone to watch out for her."

Dr. Phillips hesitates just a second, then nods and takes them. "Of course. I'll call first, tell her what happened and that I'm on my way. I'll make sure she's okay. Try not to worry."

Right.

Chapter 19

My life is ruined. Jenny's life is ruined. All because of my stupid obsession with finding my birth mother. I had to find her no matter what. I had to keep pushing and pushing, and now Jenny was arrested and will probably go to jail. Because of me.

I don't have anyone else to call except Jack. I know I depend on him too much, but he's all I have right now. He'll help me. I know he will.

He answers on the second ring and I don't even say hello. "They arrested Jenny. They arrested her and took her somewhere. I don't even know where she is. I don't know what to do. I tried to call her, but it went to voice mail. It's all my fault."

"Whoa. Slow down. Tell me what happened."

I stand between shelves of history books and keep my voice barely above a whisper. "The FBI arrested her. It's all my fault. Eric must have turned her in. We should never have done that interview. I should never have trusted him. It was so not worth it. And now they arrested Jenny. I don't know what to do."

"But I thought Eric promised to protect her."

"I guess he lied."

"Okay. Take a deep breath and tell me exactly what happened." Jack's voice is so calm it makes me a little calmer.

"All I know is they arrested her. This woman called and told me. She said she was Jenny's counselor, but how do I know it wasn't the FBI or DCF or something? She said not to worry and that she was coming over. I don't trust anyone anymore. Except you. I'm really scared. They would take me, right? Put me in foster care? Some group home or something? I mean I don't have any family they could put me with, so I threw some things in my backpack and took off. I didn't know what else to do. I'm sorry. I didn't have anyone else to call."

"Don't be sorry. You did the right thing. Where are you?"

"At the library. I was going to the bus station, but I only got as far as the library. Because what if they're looking for me? What if they're at the bus station waiting? That's the first place they'll look, right? I don't know what to do."

Jack takes a deep breath, sighs. "I'm afraid you're right. If they arrested Jenny, they will most likely come looking for you, question you. And I'm afraid you may also be right that because you're a minor they would take you into custody, find a suitable placement for you. You shouldn't be alone at a time like this. I'll come there and we can talk about your options."

I feel like I can breathe again. "Thank you." A minute ago I was so lost and scared with no idea what to do, no idea I even had options, but I feel stronger now, a little better. I feel bad that I'm always asking Jack for something. He's always there for me and never asks for anything in return. Someday I'll find a way to pay him back.

In less than 20 minutes, a long 20 minutes, Jack is here. I'm sitting at a table in the corner where I can see the main door, a book open in front of me, my head down. There are only a couple of older men, alone, reading newspapers. Then Jack is standing over me like my protector. He's a little out of breath but doesn't sit down.

He looks around, looks over his shoulder. "I don't think it's wise to stay here. They are most likely looking for you and this could very well be one of the places they look."

I don't ask questions. I don't want to waste any time. I nod, pick up my backpack and stand.

"You might want to leave your phone behind. They can track your whereabouts."

I hate leaving my phone, my only connection to Jenny, but Jack is right. I pull it out of my pocket, turn it off and drop it into the trash can next to the door before I follow him out. His car is parked a block away and we don't say anything as we walk quickly. I keep my hood up and my head down and feel like a fugitive in a movie, an innocent person running from the bad guys.

Once we're in his car, I feel better. Just being with Jack makes me feel safe. I keep my hood up, lean back and close my eyes, take a deep breath and sigh it out. What a mess. "I don't know what I'd do without you."

"That's what friends are for." Jack starts the car, checks his mirrors and pulls out.

"You said we'd talk about my options?" Will he tell me I can stay with him again, or is that too much? I don't want to get him in trouble, but I'm pretty sure, for whatever reason, he would do anything for me. "Do I actually have options?"

"Not many at the moment I'm afraid." Jack keeps checking his mirrors. Does he think someone is following us? "Not with the authorities most surely searching for you. You don't deserve to go back into the system, I know that. The only real option I see at the moment is to get as far away from here as we can."

We? "You're coming with me? I can't ask you to do that. I don't want you to get in trouble too."

"Don't worry, okay? Let's focus on getting you somewhere safe."

"But where can we go?" The sudden thought of Darlene comes to me. "What about the trailer park where I lived when I was little? There's a friend there who would help me."

Jack frowns and shakes his head. "Too risky. They will surely look to places you've lived before."

Of course he's right, plus I wouldn't want to get Darlene in trouble. "Then where?"

He glances at me for a second. "What about Georgia? No one will look for you there. I thought of it on the way to the library after you called. It seems like the safest and easiest option. Unless you have another idea?" He turns onto Main Street and I see the sign for the highway up ahead.

I don't say anything right away. Georgia? It seems like another country, and so far away from Jenny. "I don't know."

Jack slows down, puts on his directional and pulls over in front of a bakery. He turns to me, his face serious and kind, his voice soft. "I don't want to make this decision for you. Just say the word and I'll turn around and take you home, or to the police station, or wherever you want to go. Maybe foster care won't be so bad. There surely must be one good foster family out there willing to take in a teenage girl, or, if not, I have every confidence you can hold your own if they place you in a girl's home."

"I don't want to live with some strangers. Remember all those kids Eric interviewed? How bad it was? Especially for the girls? I guess I don't have a lot of choices right now, do I? I can't go back to the apartment. They're probably waiting for me right now. Oh, God, here I am thinking about me, poor me, and Jenny is probably sitting in a jail cell right now. And it's all my fault."

"Listen to me. None of this is your fault. You didn't ask to be taken from that car. And you certainly didn't force Jenny to keep you, or to do that interview for that matter. Whatever happens now is all on her." Jack sounds a little angry, or maybe he's just being protective of me, as usual.

"But if I hadn't pushed it, if I hadn't been so obsessed with finding Becky, none of this would be happening."

"If Jenny hadn't done what she did, none of this would be happening. You need to stop blaming yourself."

"I know you're just trying to protect me, and I appreciate everything you've done. It's a big decision. Running away, going so far. Jenny will be frantic again, worrying about me."

"I'm sure she knows by now you can take care of yourself. I'm sure she will know you'll be okay. And I'm pretty sure she doesn't want to see you back in foster care."

"No. She would want me to be safe. But she doesn't think I'm safe with you."

"I know. And I get that." Jack glances into his side mirror, then back to me. "It will all work out just the way it's supposed to. You'll see." He reaches into a canvas bag in the back, pulls out a thermos. "Here. It's iced tea. Peach. It will help calm you."

I unscrew the top, take a sip. It's cold and sweet. "It's good." I hold it out to him, but he shakes his head. I take another long swallow, the liquid cool on my throat. I trust Jack. Even if Jenny doesn't. "Are you sure you want to do this? You could get in big trouble."

"I am more than willing to take that chance."

In just a minute, we are on 495 South towards Worcester. It is so bizarre how things happen so fast. How life changes so fast. I am actually running away, and I'm not exactly sure what I'm running from except trouble. How long can you run from trouble before it catches up to you? I don't know anything right now except it feels like I have no choice.

"Why don't you try to sleep for a bit? We have a long way to go. It will take about 15 hours or so, depending on traffic. Put your seat back and relax."

I find the lever and put my seat back, close my eyes. There's no way I can sleep, but the quiet inside the car, the humming of the tires on the road, the comfort I feel being with Jack . . .

My neck is stiff when I wake up. It's dark. I look at the clock on the dashboard and see it's almost ten. How could I have slept so long? My mouth is dry and I take a sip of tea, not as cold now, but still cool, still good. "Where are we?"

"Almost to Lynchburg, Virginia. We still have a ways to go, but we're making good time. There's a rest stop coming up where we can take a break, use the restroom, get a bite to eat. All I need is some coffee and to stretch a bit."

My throat is so dry and I'm starving, but that's nothing compared with what Jenny must be going through. I should be there with her, but here I am running away with Jack. She must be so worried. When she thinks about it, she will know I'm with Jack. Who else would I call? I hope she believes Jack cares about me and will take care of me, even though that will be hard for her. Maybe impossible.

We're back on the road in less than an hour. Jack insists I stretch out on the back seat where I see the blanket and pillow from the couch in his office.

"I can't believe how tired I still am," I tell him. "I never sleep this much."

"Stress takes a lot out of you. Sleep is exactly what you need right now."

I climb in the back and lie down and it reminds me of being a little girl in the back of a car, Jenny and Gene in front. Going on an adventure in a big blue car.

I have no idea how long I was asleep, but when I sit up and rub my eyes, it's just starting to get light. Jack must have driven all night. "Where are we?"

"Pretty close, actually. Sleep okay? I know it's not the most comfortable, but I thought it best not to stop."

"I wouldn't mind stopping for a bathroom," I say. I'm stiff and my mouth is dry and I try not to think about how dirty I feel and how awful I must look.

Jack and I make eye contact in his rearview mirror and he smiles, and again I think of Gene. "We're almost there."

I turn and look out the window at the silent street, trees and houses and yards of normal people living normal lives. I feel so lost and out of control, and all I can do is hope I'm doing the right thing. I don't know what else to do. We are in a pretty nice neighborhood, a narrow street with houses close together, mostly small with porches out front, some with flower boxes.

Jack pulls up in front of a house set back from the street a little more than the others. It's pale green and narrow, and the front door is shiny black. There's no number on the door, just a wreath made of twigs. "Here we are," he says.

He turns off the engine and we sit, staring at the house. "You must be exhausted." I'm amazed how Jack can function on no sleep. I know he drank a bunch of coffee, but still.

"I'm fine. I'm not much of a sleeper anyway. I'll catch up on sleep tonight. The important thing is you're safe."

"Are we in Savannah?" I ask. "Is this where you grew up?"

Jack doesn't seem to hear me. He stares at the house and a small smile comes to his lips. He nods, his eyes still on the house. "You'll be safe here."

Chapter 20

It takes a minute to climb out of the back of Jack's car. I was curled in a tight ball, sleeping and dreaming dreams I can't remember. I stretch my arms up, shake my legs, take a deep breath. The air feels thick and smells like grass.

"We can get our things later." Jack doesn't wait for me to catch up as he walks up to the house, pulls out a key and opens the door. "Mama? Mama, it's me. Come see who's here." He makes it sound like I'm an old friend. Or maybe he told her about me?

I follow him into a small, clean kitchen and look up as a woman leaning on a cane fills the doorway leading to a dark hallway. She's about my height, but must weigh at least twice as much as me. Jack steps aside and the woman looks at me with no expression, then her face lights up like she recognizes me. Her eyes get watery and she lets her cane drop onto the floor as she takes a step towards me, her arms out wide. A hugger. Great.

I go in for a quick hug to be polite, but she holds on and calls me Alicia. *My Alicia.* When she finally lets go, I step back, ready to tell her I'm not Alicia, that I'm Jack's friend Meg, but she takes my hand and leads me down the hall into the living room. The television is on, some game show with screaming and buzzers. She sits on the couch and pulls me down next to her and shuts off the television. Jack stands in the doorway staring at me and his mother, a small, satisfied smile on his face.

"Where in the world have you been? I knew you'd come home. I told Johnny you would be home any day now." She looks over at Jack, beaming now. "Didn't I tell you, Johnny? Didn't I say?"

"That you did, Mama. That you did."

What is going on?

She turns to me now. "I want to know where you've been all this time. You didn't call. You didn't write. Why didn't you call me? I was worried sick."

I open my mouth to speak, but I can't find my voice. *This isn't happening.*

"She's here now, Mama." Jack's voice is soothing. "That's what counts, right?"

Jack's mother pats my leg. "You are right. She's home. Wait til your father sees you. He has missed you so. His little princess."

"Can I use your bathroom?" I stand. I have to get out of here.

"You don't have to ask permission, silly," his mother says.

I lock eyes with Jack and hope he sees the panic, the confusion, but I don't want to insult him, or his mother. She's obviously sick. This is too weird.

"I'll get us some iced tea." Jack turns and goes back into the kitchen and I follow, watch as he opens the refrigerator door. I wait for him to say something, but he doesn't look at me.

"She thinks I'm your sister," I whisper. "And why is she calling you Johnny?"

"My given name is John. She used to call me Johnny when I was little. I go by Jack, as you know. Just as you go by Meg."

"But she really thinks I'm your sister."

"She gets a little confused sometimes. She means no harm," Jack whispers. "Surely you can give her a few minutes? The powder room is down the hall on the left."

The bathroom is tiny, barely fitting the pink sink and toilet, so clean and shiny, like no one ever uses it. I look in the mirror over the sink. My hair is a mess and my eyes are bloodshot and I have a red line on my cheek from sleeping on my side. I would love a shower and clean clothes, but what I really want is to be home with Jenny. I'll ask Jack to help me get home, take me to the bus station. I should have enough money for a bus back. I don't know what I was thinking, running away like a coward. I need to be there for Jenny.

We sit and have iced tea and his mother talks about when Alicia was a little girl. She asks me if I remember the pink dress she made me when I was in first grade.

I glance at Jack, who smiles and nods. Clearly he wants me to go along with this, and surely I owe him that much. What harm will it do? "I loved that dress," I say, going deeper into whatever this is.

His mother looks at me with such love. I see how much it means to her to think her daughter is back, but I'm not her. I don't belong here. She goes on and on about spelling bees and science fairs, as if no time at all has passed since Alicia was seven, but then she comes back and seems to remember Alicia has been gone a long time. The one thing that doesn't change is how much she truly loves her. I hope Alicia's alright. Maybe she will come home someday.

"Do you have any homework?" She asks. "You want to keep getting those straight A's. Just because you won that spelling bee doesn't mean you get a pass on your homework."

I don't want to play this game anymore. Why didn't Jack warn me his mother was like this? This was a huge, stupid mistake.

Just when I thought things couldn't get worse, Jack says, "Mama has your room all ready, right Mama? She kept it nice for your all this time. I'll get your things." *Oh my God, has Jack lost it too?*

"I'll come with you."

I start to get up, but his mother puts her hand on my arm, pulls me back down to the couch. "You need to take these glasses to the sink and wash them, young lady. You still have chores to do."

I look past her and hear Jack open the door we came in and all I want to do is run. I have the same trapped feeling as when I was in that sandwich place. Tito's. Trapped. But Jack saved me that day, didn't he? He did. He definitely did. And he saved

Jenny from getting arrested. He gave me a place to stay and he helped me find my birth mother. He has always been there for me. So what is this?

"My" room obviously belongs to a seven-year-old. Pink frilly curtains, a fluffy pink comforter with unicorns and rainbows and puffy white clouds. Pink letters in cursive say *Sweet Dreams* over her bed. There are dolls and stuffed animals on the shelves, all lined up, some leaning on each other, a dollhouse in the corner of the room, a little white desk and matching chair. I sit on the side of the bed and try to imagine this little girl sitting at her desk, playing with her dolls. She must have been happy here. It looks like something little girls dream about. I never even imagined a room like this when I was a kid. But I did have a doll.

I hate to imagine what could have happened to Alicia, what kidnappers might have done to her. Poor kid. And now poor me. I close my eyes and pray to Jesus and Mary to get me out of this crazy mess.

"Here you go." Jack has my backpack in one hand, a glass of iced tea in the other, a slice of lemon on the rim like they do in restaurants. He stays in the doorway for a minute, studying my face. I'm not sure what it shows. Sadness? Fear? Anger?

"You should have told me." I keep my voice low so his mother won't hear. She doesn't deserve to be any more upset.

Jack sets my backpack down next to the desk and sits with me on the bed. "I didn't know how." His eyes get shiny, and I feel worse for him right now than I do for myself. "Mama hasn't been the same since Alicia was taken." His voice is soft.

"What about your father? Where's he? You said they bought a trailer and were travelling around looking for her."

"They did. For years. Then last year my father was diagnosed with prostate cancer and wanted to come home. That's what broke Mama even more, that they would never find Alicia. Since he passed last January, she just carries on pretending both of them are coming back. Your being here is making such a difference. I hope you know how much I appreciate this."

I stare at him. Surely he doesn't mean me to stay. "I need to go back. You know that, right? I can't stay here and pretend to be your sister. I never should have come. I panicked."

"You called me."

"I know."

"And I came."

"But I can't stay here. I need to go home." My voice is a whisper.

"I know that's what you want. And at some point it will be the right decision. But truth be told, you have no home to go back to right now. I would imagine Jenny has already been arraigned. They tend to do those things quickly. And I would assume they wouldn't grant bail for such a crime, but even if they did, and she was able to pay it, they surely wouldn't return you to the person charged with your abduction. Do you think she would feel better knowing you're back in the foster system, or knowing you're with a friend?"

"She doesn't think of you as a friend. She doesn't like you, and she doesn't trust you."

"Do you?"

"You know I do."

"That's all I care about. I don't want you to end up in some foster home, and I'm sure it's the last thing Jenny wants. You don't deserve to be in a place like that."

"Jenny doesn't deserve to be in jail either."

"Doesn't she?"

"No—she—wait—you sound like you're glad she was arrested."

Jack turns to me, touches my cheek, pushes my hair back behind my ear like Jenny does sometimes. But it feels different. "This was always going to happen, one way or another, you know that, right? I think maybe Jenny has been waiting for this for a long time."

"What? To get arrested?"

"Justice."

My breath catches in my throat and I can hardly get my words out. "It was you? You turned Jenny in?"

"It was the right thing to do. You may not see it now, but it was. No one has the right to just take another person off the street. You can't kidnap a child and expect no consequences, no matter what the intention or the outcome."

I stare at him and shake my head. "I thought you were my friend."

"I believe I'm your only friend, which is a shame. I'm sorry if you're hurt by this, but in your heart, don't you agree it was the right thing to do?"

"It's not going to bring your sister back."

Jack raises his eyebrows, smiles. "Actually, it did. For Mama it did."

"Oh my God. That's why you brought me here. It wasn't to save me. You wanted me to take your sister's place. Was that your plan all along?"

"No. Not all along. Not until recently, when I saw your life, when I saw Jenny's erratic behavior, her drinking, her anger. It was no wonder you wanted to find your biological mother."

"You saw Jenny once. And she happened to be at her worst, but that's not who she is. She's a good person."

"I'm not judging."

"I trusted you." My voice is getting louder and I don't care. "I need to get back to Jenny."

"Who's Jenny?" Jack's mother stands in the doorway, leaning on her cane, looking from me to Jack, waiting.

"A friend from school," I say. *What am I doing? I'm acting as crazy as they are.*

"Well. You'll be late for school if you don't hurry."

"There's no school today," I tell her. "Teacher conferences."

"Again? Those teachers. They hardly work if you ask me. Seems like they have every other day off, and they only work half the year as it is." She turns and heads back down the hall.

"Jenny had no right to take you," Jack continues. "But let's for a minute say she did save you from the danger of a hot car, or worse. She had no right to keep you. She should have called the police if she thought you were in danger."

"I *was* in danger. And if she called the police I would've ended up right back in the system."

"Jenny didn't know you were in the system when she abducted you, did she?"

God I hate that word. "So what? That doesn't make it less true."

"Interfering in someone's life like that isn't right."

It doesn't matter what I say. Jack isn't going to change his feelings about Jenny, but this isn't right either. "This is about your sister."

"Maybe so. But it's also about you. And justice."

"What happened to me is nothing like what happened to your sister, and Jenny isn't anything like the people who took her. You must see that."

"Same crime. Different people." Jack stands and starts walking away as if we're finished.

"Then what do you call this?"

He stops, turns around. "You came here of your own free will. You have been pretending to be my sister since we arrived. No one forced you. You're making your own choices. It's not so different from pretending to be Jenny's daughter, is it?"

There are so many things wrong with this. "I wasn't pretending anything. I am Jenny's daughter. I am not Alicia. I pretended a little for you. I could see that's what you wanted, and I wanted to do something for you after everything you did for me. But I can't just stay here and pretend to be your sister. I have to go home."

"I care about you. I hope you know that. I truly do. I have tried to show you that since the day we met. Every time you called, I came. When you were in trouble, I rescued you. When Jenny was in trouble, I was there."

"I know."

"I am asking you for a favor now. I'm not expecting you to stay forever, but it would mean a lot to me, and to Mama, if you stayed just a few days. Would you do that for me? Going back now wouldn't do Jenny any good. There's nothing you can do for her right now, and all they would do is put you in foster care. Take a few days to rest and think and be ready for whatever happens when you do go home."

I feel frozen. I don't know what else to say. It's true Jack has always been there for me. From the day I met him. And I'm just now beginning to understand why. He didn't protect his sister, and he wants to protect me. From Jenny. And it's a way to make his mother feel better, to make up for losing Alicia. I feel bad for him and his mother and his sister, but I feel worse for Jenny. I owe Jenny more. I owe her my life.

Chapter 21

I can't believe this is happening now. For years I waited for someone to come get me. I worried, I lost sleep over it, and when I finally felt safe, like no one on earth cared about what happened 13 years ago, they come and arrest me. It's almost funny. But it's not.

I'm pacing back and forth in what they call a detention cell. When I glance out between the bars all I see is an empty hallway and gray walls. I don't know what the difference is between this and a jail cell. Probably nothing.

After I was fingerprinted and photographed, Justin and I met in a small room and I told him everything. I thought he might walk out when I told him what I had done, or at least have been angry, but he stayed calm and professional, nodded as he made notes. I explained how the only reason I met with Eric was that he promised to keep everything confidential.

"It must have been him who told the FBI," I said. "So much for protecting his sources."

"Confidentiality can get murky when it comes to Federal crimes."

"What will happen now?"

"You'll have your arraignment where they'll read the charges and take your plea. You'll plead not guilty and we'll try and get bail."

"Do you think I'll get bail?"

"Depends on the judge. I'll do the best I can. I'll be back when your arraignment is set."

The only things in here are a bench, a toilet and a tiny sink. I don't even want to sit on the bench, much less use the toilet.

There's no bed or blanket. I guess that's the difference between this and an actual jail cell. Temporary. At least I'm alone.

Not long after Justin leaves, Dr. Phillips rushes in, I go over and hold onto the bars like in the movies. I understand now why prisoners shake them. Dr. Phillips puts her hand on one of mine, and it's the first time I have ever seen her look afraid or nervous, or maybe it's pity I see in her eyes.

"I'm sorry to say, Jenny, I don't know where Meg is."

"What do you mean? They already took her?"

"No. I checked with DCF. They don't move quite that fast."

"Oh my God. Did you even talk to her?"

"I called, told her what happened and that I would be right over, but when I got to your apartment, she was gone. I knocked a few times, and when there was no answer, I let myself in with your key. There was no note, no sign of her. I couldn't tell if she had taken anything. I mean, nothing looked out of place."

"What did she say on the phone? She must have said something." She can't be gone again. She can't be.

"First she asked if you were okay and what was going to happen to you. I told her you would be arraigned and hopefully released until trial. She asked what was going to happen to her, if she was going to get to stay with you when you come home. I told her I didn't know, but not to worry, that we would figure everything out together."

"I'm sure she already figured it out, that they were going to throw her back in foster care. She's not stupid."

"I'm sorry, Jenny. Maybe I shouldn't have called first. I probably scared her. She doesn't know me. I told her I was your therapist and that you had asked me to check on her, make sure she was okay. Maybe she didn't believe me. She might have thought I was the police."

"I never should have done that interview, telling him everything. Now I'm in here and my Meg is gone. Again."

"From everything you told me, Jenny, Meg is smart and resilient. I'm sure she was scared, and in my experience, when people are scared, they either freeze or run. I'm sure when she's had a chance to think this through, she'll come back to be here for you. She won't want you to go through this alone."

"She probably called Jack. Her savior."

"I know you don't trust Jack, but—"

"I don't even know him. And neither does Meg."

"Bur she considers him a friend, right?"

"She's 16. She thinks because he helped her find that biological mother of hers and gave her rides that he's her friend. What if he was just waiting for her to be alone and vulnerable?"

"I know this is difficult, Jenny. It's awful that there are so many things unknown right now. Have you told the police about Jack?"

"I didn't know she was gone til now. I'll tell them as soon as they get me the hell out of here."

"I'm sure the police and the FBI will do everything they can to find her."

I try to go over everything in my mind that Meg told me about Jack, but it's not much. Not much at all. Then Justin walks in with a man in a suit. "Your arraignment is in two hours," Justin says. "This is Agent Peters with the FBI. He wants to question you about Meg."

"About time." I watch as the guard unlocks my cell and I follow Agent Peters down the hall, with Justin right behind me.

"What are you doing to find my daughter?" Justin and I are sitting on one side of a gray metal table across from Agent Peters. He's a little older than me, maybe late thirties, with hair as thin and fine as a baby's that he hasn't bothered to comb.

"We were notified less than an hour ago of Adeline's disappearance. We're doing everything we can at the moment."

"Which is?" I say, glaring at him.

"We're monitoring the bus terminals, train station, airport. Do you know if she has the resources to leave the country?" He makes it sound like she's a criminal on the run.

"She's 16. You do know that, right? She's a kid. She has no resources. And her name is Meg."

Agent Peters stares at me like I should know exactly where Meg is, or as if I'm responsible for her being gone. "You have no idea at all where she could be?"

God how I wish I did. How I wish I knew she was safe. "I have no idea where she could be, but I know someone she would call—this guy Jack. She trusts him. God help her. She thinks he's her friend, but I don't trust him. I never did. I wish I could, especially knowing he would be the first one she called. He could be a predator. A trafficker. We need to find her."

"We're doing our best, but to be honest, Jenny, it's usually challenging to find a runaway. When someone doesn't want to be found, especially if they have help, they can usually hide themselves pretty well."

"She's not a runaway. She probably panicked when she found out I was arrested, but I'm telling you, we need to find Jack."

"Boyfriend?"

"He's almost twice her age."

Agent Peters sets down his mug, his face calm, no expression. Are they trained to show nothing? It must come in handy when they play poker. He pulls out a pad of paper and a pen and I think of Eric and my stupidity. "Okay. Does Jack have a last name?"

"I don't know his last name." I can't believe I never asked Meg his last name. Talk about being all wrapped up in myself. "He's from the south somewhere. Wait. Georgia. Savannah, I think. At least that's what he said. He has a southern accent. His sister was kidnapped, so there must be a report on that, right? He said she was seven. I think he said it was about 12 years ago. From a park. He said they were in a park and he was supposed to be watching her." This all comes out in a rush, and I'm grateful I can give him that much.

Agent Peters doesn't interrupt, his eyes going from me to his notes, a serious expression on his face. Finally.

I try to remember anything else Meg might have told me about him, but like an idiot I didn't want to hear it. I should have asked more questions, found out more about him. What the hell is wrong with me? "He's about 30, a little taller than me, light brown hair, thin. His nose is a little crooked. And he has a southern accent. I already told you that."

"Jack from Savannah." Agent Peters stares at me, as if I'm holding something back. "It's not much to go on."

"It's more than you had a minute ago."

He stares at me again. He's good at that. "I'll see what we can find, but as I said, it's not much to go on."

While Agent Peters is gone, Justin tells me what to expect at the arraignment, about reading the charges, pleading not guilty, hopefully setting bail, but I'm only half-listening. I'm praying to no one in particular, over and over in my mind. *Please keep her safe.*

Agent Peters is back in about a half hour, carrying a green folder. "We checked for a story of a kidnapping of a seven-year-old girl in Savannah and the surrounding area 12 years ago and we had a hit on a little girl named Alicia Evans." He sits across from us again, opens the file and pulls out some papers.

"Her brother John reported her missing from Haddon Park in Savannah. He didn't have a lot of details except there was a woman and a gray van. He didn't actually see the abduction and was pretty sketchy on a description of the van. Gave a fairly good description of the woman, but the local police came up empty, as did we." Agent Peters flips through the pages of police reports, witness statements.

I reach over and pick up a copy of a newspaper article from the *Savannah Sun*, and there is Jack. He's younger and his hair is longer, but it's him. "That's Jack. That's him." My heart is pounding and I'm sweating now, almost like I'm the one guilty of something. "Now that you know who he is, you need to find him. I'm sure he has my Meg. Do you think he would have taken her to Savannah?"

Agent Peters frowns. "Jenny, you said earlier Ad—Meg and Jack are friends. Do you have any reason to believe he may harm her in any way? Do you believe she would leave willingly with him?"

"You make it sound like my daughter is some kind of fugitive that ran away with this guy. She's 16. I don't know how many times I need to remind you of that. If she did leave willingly, it's because he has her convinced he's her friend and that it was her only choice. What kind of a friend, a man nearly twice her age, would do that?"

Agent Peters looks down at his papers, then back at me as if he doesn't know what he should do. What's wrong with him? "Based on this information, there may be sufficient cause to issue a multi-state Amber Alert, and we'll contact the local police in Savannah." He frowns again, finally serious about all this, then he stands. "Is there anything else you can tell me? A local address? What kind of car he has?"

"I didn't even know his last name and you expect me to know what kind of car he has? Just do your job. Please. I need to know my daughter is safe." I want so much to believe Jack is the good friend Meg believes he is.

My arraignment is quick and straightforward and unreal. A man from the State's Attorney's office is at one table, alone with his folders and papers, and Justin and I sit at the other table. I glance over at him once. He has short salt and pepper hair, looks a little like he's in the army. He stares down at his papers, but I'm sure he already knows exactly what he's going to say. We stand when the judge walks in and stay standing while he reads the charge: Kidnapping in the Second Degree. He asks me if I understand the charge. I say I do, even though I don't. Then he asks how I plead.

In my strongest voice, with confidence I try to feel, I answer, "Not guilty, Your Honor."

Justin asks that I be released on my own recognizance, explaining that I'm not a danger to the community, I'm gainfully employed, but I lack the resources to flee. As if I would *flee* and leave Meg on her own, or in the so-called care of the foster system again.

The State's Attorney asks for bail, says because of the seriousness of the charges he believes bail should be set at $50,000. It might as well be 50 million. The judge sets bail at $10,000, tells us the pre-trial conference will be in five weeks. And it's done. We walk out of the courtroom and I have images of being locked up until the hearing, then Dr. Phillips comes up to me and tells me not to worry. I owe her way too much.

Agent Peters is waiting in the hallway, and when Justin asks if we could have a few minutes, he nods. We sit on a bench opposite the courtroom while Agent Peters stands near us, his hands folded in front of him. I look at Justin and hope he has this. He is so young and innocent looking with his pretty blue eyes. "So what happens next?"

"Before the pre-trial conference each side provides the other with what evidence they have, witness statements and such."

I shake my head. "There were no witnesses. Just Gene, but I don't want him anywhere near this, anywhere near Meg. He wouldn't be reliable anyway."

"Okay. Well, we'll see what they have and go from there. You can also have people write letters on your behalf which we will submit to the judge attesting to your character. Friends, employers, anyone you can think of."

I nod, but the only person I can think of right now is Dr. Phillips.

"Jenny, I want you to know I'm willing to represent you in this, and I'll do my best, but you might want someone with more experience with criminal law."

"I don't think it matters who I have. No offense, but I think I'm pretty much screwed."

Justin takes a deep breath, sighs. “Let’s meet tomorrow and go over everything, okay?”

I thank him, knowing how lucky I am to have anyone on my side. When Justin walks to the elevator, Agent Peters steps towards me and I expect him to take me back to my cell, but he takes me downstairs to the room they brought me to when we got here. On the way he tells me my bail was posted and they’re processing my paperwork.

“Dr. Phillips?”

“I don’t have that information. Your lawyer may know.”

It has to be her. Who else? I stand at the window and sign some papers for my release, take my stuff and head for the door.

“Jenny.”

I stop but I don’t turn around. I don’t like the sound of his voice. Agent Peters doesn’t say anything else until I turn and look at him. I’m not expecting him to say anything good.

“If and when we find her, you do know she’s not going back to live with you.”

I glare at him. I have no words.

His voice is softer now, but controlled. “You have no rights when it comes to the girl.”

“*The girl* is my daughter.”

“Not in the eyes of the law, Jenny. If she does prove to be Adeline Jenkins, she will have to be returned to DCF, where they will determine a proper placement.”

“A proper placement? You want to pull her from the only home she’s ever known and throw her back in the system? And you wonder why she took off.”

“It’s not my call, Jenny. It’s the law.”

“Well it’s a shitty law.” I storm out of there before he can say anything else.

Dr. Phillips is waiting for me by the front doors and gives me a ride home.

“Thank you. For everything.” It’s all I can manage right now.

She nods and doesn't say a word, doesn't ask me any questions or tell me not to worry, that everything will be fine. She glances over and pats my knee for a second. That's plenty. I'm all talked out and I need to think. I need to believe Meg is okay and coming home. And even if she'll be in a foster home until she's 18, I can live with that if it means she's safe. But only if it means she's safe.

When we get to my apartment, I don't get out right away. I dread walking into the empty rooms, but maybe there's a clue. Maybe Meg left me something, a sign, that she's okay, but that's probably wishful thinking. I'm sure she was too panicked to think straight.

Dr. Phillips shuts off the car and we sit for a minute, listen to the ticking of the engine. "Will you be okay?"

"Once I know Meg is safe. And if you're wondering if I'm going to drink, I'm not. I have to be here for her. I have to be strong. Thanks again for everything. I owe you big time. I don't think I'll ever be able to repay you." No one has ever done this much for me in my life.

"No need. Really. Let me know if you hear anything, will you do that? Or if you need anything?"

I don't trust myself to speak. I nod and go inside to wait.

Chapter 22

"I have never asked you for anything," Jack says. His tone is even, just stating a fact. We're standing in the hall outside Alicia's room, our voices barely a whisper.

"You are now."

"You're free to say no." Jack touches my cheek and looks into my eyes. Is he thinking of his sister? Or does he still think I'm pretty? "I thought this would be a safe place for you to have some space, some time to think about everything before you're thrown back into the system."

I take a step back and we lock eyes for a few seconds. He looks away first. "A few days," I say. "That's what you're asking me for?" I feel like I don't have many choices. Stay here, safe, or go who-knows-where when they get me back in the system. I think about what I have learned about the foster care system, how broken it is, how much it has failed the children it's supposed to take care of. I think of the stories Eric wrote about. And I think of what it did to Becky, how it broke her.

"Three days. If you would do that for me, it would mean a lot."

I take a deep breath and wonder how I could possibly do this. How can I not? "I need to call Jenny and tell her I'm okay. I need to give her some peace of mind. You cared about that before. Isn't that what you want for your mother? Please, just let me call her." I sound like a little kid begging for a toy.

"Of course you can call Jenny. I'm going to the store to get some groceries, and I'll also get you a phone so you can call Jenny and let her know you're okay. Would you mind keeping Mama company while I'm gone? Maybe fix her something to eat? She'd like that. I won't be long." He turns and I follow him into the kitchen, where his mother is slipping two slices of bread into the toaster.

"I'll be right back, mama. I'm going to get some groceries."

"Don't forget chips," she says.

"I wouldn't think of it."

When the door closes behind him, I hear a lock turn, go to the door and try the knob. Locked. There are no buttons, no way to unlock it from the inside. What did he say about not being a prisoner? I rush down the hall to the back door. Locked.

I walk back to the kitchen just as the toast pops up. "The doors are locked," I say.

Jack's mother smiles. "He always locks the doors when he leaves. It's to keep us safe. You know that. There are dangerous people out there. He's a good boy." His mother sits down heavily at the kitchen table. I take out the toast, cool and crispy now. There's a stick of soft butter on the counter. I wonder how long it's been there, but when I smell it, it smells okay. I spread it thick on her toast, cut it in half, set it on the table in front of her, like I used to do for Jenny. She likes toast too.

"Aren't you going to eat something? I hope Johnny remembers that cereal you like, and chips. Do you still like those ripple chips? Maybe we can watch a movie tonight." Jack's mother picks up a piece of toast, crunches a big bite.

"I'm not hungry. I'm going to take a shower." As soon as Jack gets back I'll go outside and call Jenny, tell her I'm okay so she won't worry. Of course she'll still worry, but maybe less. I hope hearing my voice will help.

I take a quick shower and change my clothes, feel a little better, a little calmer I think. As soon as I step out of the bathroom, I notice how quiet it is. No television blaring. Did Jack's mother go back to bed? I walk to the living room and stand in the doorway, see his mother staring at the dark television screen. "I'm waiting for it to go back on. Right after Johnny left, it just went dead. He'll fix it when he comes home. That boy is so handy."

The refrigerator and clock over the stove are working, so it's not the electricity. It does look like an old television, but the timing is weird. I hate being locked in like this. I think of Jenny in jail and feel sick to my stomach. I clean the kitchen, even though it doesn't need much cleaning, and in less than an hour I hear the lock turn. The door opens and Jack walks in with two plastic grocery bags in each hand, sets them on the counter. "Sorry I was gone so long."

How do guys time things like that? Gene did the same thing to Jenny and me for years. As soon as we were on the verge of giving up hope that he would ever come home, he appeared like magic. It never seemed right or fair that he would wait until we were down to our last piece of bread, the last scrape of peanut butter, but we were so relieved and happy to see him it didn't matter.

"The television is on the fritz again," his mother says. "Can you fix it? My shows start in an hour."

"I'll try," Jack says, unpacking groceries, putting cans on shelves, milk in the refrigerator.

"Did you get chips?" His mother reaches into one of the bags, pulls out a huge bag of wavy potato chips. She smiles and pats Jack's shoulder. "You're a good boy."

As soon as Jack's mother heads back to the living room to wait for the television to come back on and her shows to start, Jack pulls a phone out of an inside pocket of his jacket. "It's all pre-paid and set up."

"Thank you." I take the phone and hold it tight, finally connected to the world again, connected to reality. "I'll call from outside so your mother won't hear me." I take one step towards the door before Jack puts his hand on my arm.

"Can we speak for a minute before you call Jenny?"

I stop and wait. Please don't let him change his mind about getting me home.

"I know you're anxious to speak to Jenny, set her mind at ease. Maybe you're even anxious to go home, even knowing you wouldn't exactly be going home. It says a lot about your relationship that you want to make sure she's okay, even after everything."

"After everything, she's still my mother."

"Did you think about what I asked? About giving me three days, giving Mama three days with Alicia?"

"I thought about it. And I thought about how Jenny must be going crazy worrying about me. She doesn't need that on top of everything else."

Jack nods. "I know. And I know you might never forgive me for Jenny getting arrested, but I hope in time you'll understand."

I don't know what happened to my anger, but all I feel now is sorry for Jack, sorry for his mother, and mostly sorry for poor Alicia. "What happens in three days?"

"It should be all I need."

"For what?"

"To disappear and arrange for your rescue." He gives me a tired smile. "And to save you from the likes of me. You know I can't be here when they come. I took you across state lines."

Even after what he did to Jenny, I don't want to let him go. "But you said you'd take me home."

Jack takes my face in his hands, kisses my forehead. "I said I'd see to it you got home safe. And I will. Thank you, for giving Mama such a gift. Even if it's a short time, she has her Alicia back. You take care now."

"What about your mother? You're just leaving her?"

"Don't you worry about Mama. Her day care provider will be back on Saturday. She has been taking care of Mama since I moved away. And her sister lives not too far, comes down about once a month. You are very sweet to worry about her."

I turn and walk away, step into the bathroom so he won't see me cry, listen as he calls out, "Bye, Mama!" Then I hear the door close behind him and he's gone.

He left me. With his mother. "It's still not working, Johnny!" she calls out from the living room. I squeeze the phone in my hand. He asked me for three days. To disappear, to escape from the police who would arrest him because he was trying to help me.

When I left home before, I was gone almost four days before I called Jenny, and it was only because Jack made me. I promised I wouldn't do it again, wouldn't leave like that. But here I am. Will she understand why? The last thing she wants is to see me in foster care, exactly what she saved me from in the first place. She knows I have no one else to call but Jack. I'll wait until Jack's mother is sleeping, then I'll call Jenny from the bathroom. I can't let Jack's mother hear me call someone else *Mama.*

"Meg?" Jenny sounds frantic. "Are you okay? Where are you?"

"I'm fine. What about you? Are you okay? Are you home?"

"Where are you?"

"I'm safe. I'm okay. I got really scared when some lady called and said you were arrested. She said she was your counselor, but I didn't trust her. I thought maybe she was from DCF or something and was coming to take me. I'm sorry I left like that, but I was really scared and I panicked."

"Where are you? Are you with Jack?"

"No." *Not anymore.* "I wanted you to know I'm okay, and I'll be home in a few days. But they're probably going to take me away from you, right? And put me in foster care?"

"You're not going to tell me where you are? Who you're with?"

"Can we talk about you? What happened?"

"The FBI got some tip from an anonymous source, which I think must be Eric. They questioned me, then they arrested me. I had my arraignment and someone paid my bail, most likely Dr. Phillips. We have our pre-trial conference in five weeks. That's it. So I don't want you to worry about me, okay? Please, you need to come home. I need to see you and know you're safe. I know they'll most likely put you in foster care, but hopefully it won't be bad and I'll do everything I can to make sure we can see each other. At least I'll know where you are."

"I'm safe, mama. I promise. Can you trust me that I'm safe for three days? Think of it as three less days of me in foster care." I have to trust that Jack will keep his word.

Jenny is silent for a minute. "Will you call me again so I know you're—"

"Mama?"

By the third day, Jack's mother and I have a quiet routine going and I'm going crazy being trapped here, especially with no way to contact Jenny. Jack must have only put a couple of minutes on that phone, just enough for me to let Jenny know I'm okay. Even though I feel trapped and a little used, there is a small part of me that feels like I'm doing a good thing here, a kindness for a woman who thought she lost everything and now has it back. For three days. After all Jack has done for me, I can do three days.

The television doesn't work, so I keep his mother entertained with cards. We play rummy for hours, keeping score to 500, then 1,000. I teach her how to play scat and we play that for hours too. She takes a nap from two to three and I wander around the house, look through closets and only find old wool coats, a fishing rod, a road atlas. I look through the atlas, find Georgia. I trace the roads with my finger and wonder where I am.

I make supper while she's sleeping, tuna casserole one day, grilled cheese and chips the next. On the third day, Jack's mother makes us fried bologna sandwiches for lunch and I'm surprised how good it tastes. While we eat, his mother talks about how much I've grown, how proud she is of me, and I learn about Alicia's short life, how smart she was, how she loved pink.

The banging on the door makes both of us jump. "Police!"

"Oh Lord," his mother says, both hands on her heart, her eyes wide and her face drained of color. "Something's happened."

I go to the door, turn the knob and open it. It wasn't locked. All this time, it wasn't locked. There are three police cars out front, lights flashing, two policemen standing right outside the door, their hands on their guns. Are they here to save me or arrest me?

"Are you Adeline Jenkins?" one of them asks. He looks about 20, has a southern accent like Jack, and still has his hand on his gun, ready to pull it out if he has to. A gun.

"No," I answer automatically. "My name is Meg."

He hesitates a minute. "Is there a John Evans on the premises?"

"No," I say again.

"Put your hands on your head and walk out slowly. Are you alone, miss?" He tries to see past me and looks almost as nervous as me.

"No," I say. "But it's just us." I put my hands on my head so he won't shoot me, turn and see Jack's mother come up behind me.

"Oh Lord," she says over and over while the policeman screams at her to put her hands on top of her head. She puts them over her eyes instead, and I feel so bad for her.

Chapter 23

I have only heard from Meg once, for about two minutes, until her phone cut out. I hope it was just her phone dying and not someone cutting off the call or ripping the phone out of her hand. I knew when I tried calling back I would get the message about the number not available, but I tried anyway.

She sounded pretty calm, I think. But she was anxious. Concerned about me of course, and what was going to happen. As much as I hate to think she's with Jack, I have to believe he won't hurt her. And as far as asking me to wait three days? Like hell. I'm pushing the FBI as hard as I can to do their damn job and find her. What the hell could she be doing for three days that's so important? Maybe she's just putting off coming home, not knowing for sure what she's in for, what they would do with her. I can't blame her.

Every time I call Agent Peters, he says they are doing everything in their power to find her. It feels like nothing. He reminds me he's under no obligation to tell me anything, but he does anyway, not that it's much. Mostly he asks questions—whether I remember anything else Jack might have said about where he lived, either here in Massachusetts or in Georgia. He tells me the last known address of Jack, or John as he went by before he met Meg, was his parents' house in Savannah, which was sold more than nine years ago. No forwarding address. No kidding. He tells me they are in the process of obtaining credit card records, bank account statements, goes on about databases and searches, but the bottom line is they have no idea where Meg is. How can it be so easy to disappear without leaving some trace?

I walk quickly to my appointment with Dr. Phillips, even though I'm early. I had to get out of that empty apartment. It's cloudy and windy and I should have brought an umbrella. I keep my head down, my jacket collar up against the wind. No matter which way I turn, the wind hits me in the face.

Dr. Phillips stands when I walk in, offers me my usual chair and we both swivel to face each other. "How are you holding up?"

"I'm okay. As good as I can be. It's Meg I'm worried about." I hesitate before telling her about Meg's call, not sure if it would be something she would need to report. But she hasn't reported anything before, and she said it would have to be something like me being a threat to myself or others, so I go ahead. "I heard from Meg."

Her face lights up. "That's great news. She's okay then? Is she coming home?"

"She said she's fine, that she's safe, and I want to believe her. She wouldn't say where she was or who she was with, but it has to be Jack, even though she said she's not with him. I'm sure she doesn't want to get her good friend in trouble. She said she'll be home in three days. You were right. She panicked and ran, and I don't blame her. It was so good to hear her voice, and she does sound okay. A little stressed, of course, worried about me, but she doesn't sound hurt or anything, or afraid, except for me."

"Three days? Did she say why three days?"

"She just asked me to trust her. I want to. I do. It's Jack I don't trust."

"Did you tell the police she contacted you?"

"I thought about it, but there's nothing to tell them, really. I still have no idea where she is. And if they know she was able to call and sounded fine, how hard would they look for her?"

"That's true. Maybe not with the same urgency."

"I don't know how urgently they're looking as it is. It doesn't feel like it."

For the first time since I've been seeing her, Dr. Phillips seems distracted. Is she worried about me? About Meg? She stares out the window and whatever is bothering her can't be good. When she finally turns back to me she says, "Jenny, I'm sorry to say I won't be able to treat you anymore."

I open my mouth, but it takes a few seconds to find my voice. "What do you mean? Why not? Because I got arrested?" She wouldn't just abandon me. She can't.

"As soon as I took your keys when you asked me to check on Meg for you, the line between therapist and patient blurred, big time. Now don't get me wrong, I was glad to do it and I'd do it again. In my book that was a genuine emergency and I didn't hesitate. I'm too involved in your life now to be objective in your treatment. I know that sounds awful, like something right out of a textbook, but it's real. I have a colleague who I think would be a good fit for you. She's been practicing for—"

"Wait. You're dropping me because I asked you to check on Meg? That doesn't make any sense. I know it was a lot to ask, but I don't have anyone else. You know that."

"That's what makes this so hard. Now here's the thing. It's a clear conflict of interest to have a personal relationship with a patient. Not only does it violate the ethical codes of conduct, it wouldn't be in your best interest for me to continue being your therapist."

"I thought that just applied to dating, or being *with* your therapist."

Dr. Phillips shakes her head. "I'm afraid not."

Doesn't she know she's all I have now? "You're saying you can't be my therapist and my friend too?"

"The rules are very clear about patient relationships."

I can't believe this. I try to think of something to say that will change her mind, but I have nothing. She wouldn't be doing this if she didn't have to. "So I messed up. Again."

"Jenny, it's not unusual for a patient and therapist to build a bond that seems as close as a friendship, and there's nothing wrong with wanting to be friends. And it certainly isn't because I don't like you or care about you. I do. But being a therapist means there are boundaries and a certain distance we need to maintain in order for me to help you."

"But you want to hand me off to some stranger, just when I need you the most." It's not a new feeling for me, being rejected, but coming from Dr. Phillips feels worse than any rejection I ever had, even from my parents.

"I'm referring you to a well-respected colleague, someone I know and trust, and someone who I think will be a good fit for you. Her name is Judy Denning. Would you give her a chance? I know you're going through a lot right now, and that's all the more reason to continue to talk to someone. I would never do anything that would hurt you or the progress you've made. I hope you know that."

I shake my head. I know I should feel thankful for everything she's done for me, inside our sessions and out. I am thankful. But I also feel abandoned.

Dr. Phillips picks up a card from her desk and holds it out to me. "I have so much faith in you, Jenny. And I want you to know I'll be there for you while you go through all these legal challenges. I'll write to the judge on your behalf as your therapist and can speak volumes about your character and your intentions, your hard work and your love for your daughter. And if it goes to trial, I will be happy to testify."

All I can do is nod. I don't trust myself to speak.

"I wish we could continue, Jenny, I really do."

"So that's it?"

"I do need you to sign this release, if you want me to be able to speak freely with the court on your behalf. It's pretty standard, but if you want Justin to look it over before you sign it, that's fine."

Of course I want her to speak for me. Who else do I have? I sign the form without reading it, take the card, and stand. I know she wouldn't do this unless she had to, but it still feels like I've been punched in the stomach. I put my hand out. "Thank you for everything."

Dr. Phillips takes my hand, then pulls me in for a hug. I glance at our chairs, the coffee machine and mugs, the pictures on the wall. It feels like leaving home. Worse.

"I'm proud of you, Jenny. You've come a long way. And I know you'll continue to get stronger, for yourself and for Meg."

Walking home in the rain feels exactly right.

The third day Meg has been gone, the sun comes out. A good sign? *Please come home today*. I look at my phone every 15 minutes while I scrub the tile in the bathroom, wash the kitchen floor, polish the furniture. Finally, at a few minutes past two, the phone rings.

"Meg?"

"We located her and she's on her way back. She's fine. I wanted to let you know right away." Agent Peters' voice has a tiny bit of feeling. Not much.

"Where is she? Is she okay?"

"She appears to be fine. They found her in Tennessee. An anonymous tip led us to a house in a little town outside Memphis. When they arrive in Boston, she'll be processed at DCF. They'll do an interview, probably a medical exam."

"Tennessee? What the hell is in Tennessee? Was she with Jack?"

"She was with an older woman we haven't identified yet. Meg was upset, of course, but cooperative. The woman was very distraught and pretty incoherent. As I said, it was an anonymous tip that only gave the location. It doesn't appear she was being held against her will or harmed in any way."

An older woman? Another anonymous tip? "What will they do with her? When can I see her?"

"Once she's processed, they will find a suitable placement. As far as seeing her, you'll need to speak to your attorney about that."

"Speak to my attorney about seeing my own daughter?"

Silence for a few seconds, then, "We shouldn't even be having this conversation. There's a case pending against you for kidnapping her, so in the eyes of the law, you have no legal rights when it comes to Meg. But I know how worried you've been about her. I just wanted you to know she's home and she's safe."

"She's not home. Home is with me." At least he calls her Meg now.

I thank him for letting me know and end the call. She's safe. Pretty much. Even though she's with DCF, at least I know where she is. Now I need to start getting her back.

Justin sounds tired when I call. I tell him about Meg, how they found her and she's on her way home, then back with DCF. "Can you find out when I can see her?"

"Jenny, I'm glad she's back and she's safe, but they may not think it's in her best interests to see you. You're facing serious charges concerning Meg, and they can and will use that when making their decision."

"I know what I've been charged with. I haven't been convicted. I haven't even had my hearing yet, so they shouldn't be able to use anything. The last I heard, people are innocent until proven guilty." They have to let me see her.

"You need to understand that you have no legal rights when it comes to Meg. I'm sorry, but that's the law."

The same words Agent Peters used. I want to scream *I'm her mother*, but it wouldn't do any good. I'm finished banging my head against the wall. Saying I'm her mother doesn't make it so when it comes to these lawyers and judges and agencies that are supposed to look after kids like Meg. I know who I am and I know what I am to Meg. I'll do whatever it takes to get her back, and when I do, I'll make sure it's by the book so I won't ever lose her again. "Okay. Then tell me what I need to do to see her. Tell me there's something we can do. Please."

After a few seconds of silence, Justin says, “I’ll contact DCF, find out who her case worker is and see if I can set up an appointment.”

It’s a start. It’s something. “Thank you.”

“I wouldn’t get my hopes up, Jenny.”

“Too late. Hope is all I have right now. You said they do what’s in the best interests of the child. Tell them it’s in Meg’s best interests to see the person she considers her mother, the person who raised her for 13 years. All I’m asking for right now is to see her. And I’m sure she wants to see me too.”

Chapter 24

When we get back to Massachusetts, the police bring me to a clinic and hand me over to a woman who says she's Mrs. James from the Department of Children and Families. She asks if I'm okay. How could I be?

"I'm fine."

She takes my blood pressure, my temperature, looks into my eyes with a light. I follow her directions like a good little girl. I don't ask any questions she probably wouldn't answer anyway. I'm not handcuffed or anything, but I still feel like a criminal. Definitely a prisoner. Mrs. James sets a paper johnny on the exam table and tells me to have it open in the front and the doctor will be right in.

A woman in a white coat examines me and asks me all kinds of questions, mostly about whether I was coerced, abused, physically assaulted, touched inappropriately in any way. I feel like saying that's exactly what she's doing now, but I say nothing. She has straight, shiny black hair with bangs and her skin is almost as white as her coat. Her nametag says Dr. Shaefer. She has a stethoscope around her neck and a clipboard with forms on it and looks like she could be in a television series. As she checks off boxes and scribbles notes, she mostly keeps her eyes on the forms. When she does look at me, she narrows her eyes as if she's trying to look inside my head, trying to catch me in a lie.

Finally, I'm able to get dressed again and one more woman interviews me. She wears a light blue pantsuit that's a little tight and she smells like cigarettes. Her nametag says E. Roberts, and she doesn't even pretend to be friendly. She asks why I ran away, who I was with, what happened. A lot of the same questions everyone else asked me. Was I sexually assaulted in any way? Forced to do anything against my will? Some of the questions are fair, I guess, but a lot of them are ridiculous.

Everyone acts like I've been gone for years instead of a few days, but it does feel like a long time since I've been home, living a normal life with Jenny. How did everything get so messed up so fast?

E. Roberts doesn't want to believe I'm fine. "The FBI has been searching for you for days. We need to know exactly what happened and who you were with."

"When I heard my mother got arrested, I got scared and called a friend. I don't have anyone else, and I didn't know what to do."

"Does this friend have a name?"

"I'm not going to get my friend in trouble for helping me," I tell her. "I'm back, and I'm fine and it doesn't matter now what his name is, right?"

"Actually, it does matter. This friend of yours took you over state lines. You're a minor, and that's considered a felony."

"It was my choice to leave. No one forced me. No one took advantage of me. No one hurt me. I told everyone a million times I panicked when my mother got arrested because I have no other family. I was afraid I was going to be put into foster care, which is exactly what happened."

"As a minor, you're not legally capable of making such a decision." She's obviously not interested in the truth and not all that interested in how I am. All she wants is for me to give up Jack, and that's not going to happen.

"Can I please see my mother?"

"Your mother is currently incarcerated. We can see about making arrangements to visit her at a future date. In the meantime, I just need—"

"Wait. My mother, Jenny, is in jail?" Did Jenny tell me she was out on bail just to make me feel better?

"Your real mother. Becky Jenkins."

I let out my breath. "She's not my mother. Jenny is my mother."

She tilts her head and frowns like I'm some stupid kid. "We need you to confirm it was John Evans who brought you out of the state and cooperate with us in determining his whereabouts."

I shake my head slowly and give her a frown right back. She's not even listening to me. "I don't know anyone by that name. Can I ask, though, about the lady I was with when you found me? She was really scared, and she's not well. I think she has Alzheimer's or something. Can you tell me if she's okay?" I won't tell her about pretending to be her long-lost daughter for Jack, then for his mother too. There's no reason.

E. Roberts hesitates, then says, "Someone made arrangements for her care. That's all I know."

I knew Jack would take care of her. "Thanks for telling me."

* * * * *

"My name is Susan, and I've been assigned as your caseworker." The way she says it makes it sound like a punishment. Her brown hair, the same color as her eyes, is pulled back into a low ponytail. She wears a navy blue skirt and a white blouse, no makeup, no jewelry, not even a watch, and I wonder if maybe it's not allowed.

We're sitting in her office at DCF, a small room with a gray metal desk with thick files stacked on one side, a file cabinet, two chairs in front of the desk, which is about all that will fit. There are no pictures on the walls, no view out the window except for the side of the brick building next door. I feel a little sorry for Susan now, coming here every day.

After we talk a little about how I'm doing, how she knows this must be a challenging time for me, blah, blah, blah, she tells me there is a family that has agreed to take me in on an emergency basis.

"Miguel and Maria Cruz. They're from Mexico, and they are already fostering three other children, all boys, all under the age of ten. They're brothers who lost their parents, and the Cruz's took in all three so they wouldn't be split up. That's the kind of people they are. Good people. I trust you're going to be on your best behavior."

She doesn't know me, and she already thinks I'm going to cause trouble? "I'm not a bad person, or a troublemaker."

"I didn't say you were. I just want to make sure you know how lucky you are to be placed with a family like the Cruz's and promise you won't run away again."

"I won't. I promise. I ran away because I panicked. Now that I'm home, I'm going to do everything I can to be here for my mother." I have to remember to always call her my mother, not Jenny.

Susan stares at me for a long minute, and thankfully she doesn't mention Becky. "That's good. Especially for you. If you did, you would most likely go right into a juvenile detention facility for girls. You don't want that. You have a really good chance here for a fresh start."

Is she actually threatening me? Maybe I deserve it. I give her a smile I don't mean. "I'm going to be on my best behavior. I promise." I know she's just doing her job, but I decide I don't like Susan very much.

"Glad to hear it." She straightens the papers in front of her, slips them into a bright blue folder. "Let's go then. Unless you have any questions?"

I have a million questions that Susan probably couldn't or wouldn't answer anyway. I shake my head.

Susan doesn't stop talking the whole way to her car. "So usually we have a pre-placement visit, but the Cruz's agreed to take you on an emergency basis. Normally you would be placed in a group facility until we could find a suitable foster family, but when I was made aware of your circumstances, I called the Cruz's, explained your situation, and they signed the placement agreement this morning. Since they already foster three children, we didn't need to go through the usual time-consuming red tape."

She buckles her seatbelt, slides the key into the ignition and starts the car, then she turns to me. "Seatbelt, please?"

"Why?"

"It's common sense, plus it's the law."

"No, I mean it sounds like you went out of your way to help me, to keep me out of a group home or whatever, put me with a good family. Why?"

"First of all, I do the very best I can for everyone I'm assigned to. It's not always easy, given our limited resources and the number of families willing to take on foster children. Teens are especially difficult to place. But from what I understand about your case, your biological mother is in prison, the woman who raised you, who I know you consider to be your mother, may very well go to prison as well. I thought you deserved a stable, loving environment until things are sorted out."

I nod, buckle my seat belt. "Thank you."

"We're not the bad guys people make us out to be."

"I know." Maybe I do like Susan after all.

Chapter 25

It takes about 45 minutes from Susan's office to my new home. "It's a nice little neighborhood," Susan says. "And there's a school bus stop not far, so you don't need to change schools."

The last thing I have been thinking about is school, but I know I need to stick to my routine, keep my grades up, do everything I can to show Jenny and everyone else I'm more than okay. Susan stops in front of a small yellow house with blue shutters and a front door to match. There's a pot of red geraniums on the front step and a mat that says *Welcome*. Even though I'm worried about Jenny, I feel like I can breathe now.

It's weird to be living in a stranger's house, but Maria and Miguel are really nice. They look like they're in their 40's, and when they introduce me to the boys, Antony, Mateo, and Jorge, they all hang back, keeping their hands attached to some part of Maria—her leg, her arm, her side. The boys all have shiny black hair and dark skin and beautiful, watchful eyes. They are shy with me. Whatever room I'm in, they stare at me from the doorway and watch me. They probably don't trust me, a strange white girl suddenly moving into their house. I don't blame them.

It's nothing like what I thought a foster family would be, nothing like Becky must have experienced or where I must have lived as a baby. Miguel's English isn't very good, so Maria does most of the talking. She tells me a little about their life in Mexico, vague details about what she calls "truly evil" people who have no respect for other people or the laws. I don't ask questions, especially in front of the boys, but I've seen enough on the news to know how bad it is in some parts of Mexico and I'm glad they got out.

Maria asks about my school schedule, if I'm in any after-school activities or sports. I tell her I will be home right after school and will help with anything she needs. All she asks is that I keep my room clean, go to school every day and let her know if I'm not coming home right after school. "It is all right," she says, "if you go to a friend's home or stop somewhere, just please let me know so I don't worry."

I fall into an easy routine and almost feel guilty about feeling so normal, so settled. On the weekends, Maria shows me how to make rice and beans, empanadas, tamales. I never had Mexican food before, except once when Jenny and I went to Tim's Taco's in Hayville. It was awful, and nothing like this. Maria doesn't follow a recipe, explaining each step like she is on the cooking channel. I chop onions and carrots and celery, set the table. Miguel comes home from his job at the garage at 5:15, washes up and we all eat dinner together at 5:30. At 6:30, Maria goes to her job cleaning the office building around the corner.

The first time I offered to clean up after dinner, Miguel said, "We did not take you in to be our housekeeper." I told him I didn't mind, that I liked cleaning. That made him smile and shake his head and he told me I was a good girl.

I've been here almost two weeks now, and I'm still waiting to hear if I can see Jenny. We talk on the phone every day, but it's almost like we're strangers, just checking in. *How are you doing? How was your day? Any news?* It's so strange not being able to see my own mother, even though I know in everyone else's eyes she's not my mother. People who don't even know her think she's nothing but a criminal.

After I do my homework, I take out a sheet of paper to write to Becky. Again. I've written her two letters so far, and even though she hasn't written back, I want her to know I forgive her. I want to believe she cares, and sometimes I tell myself she pushed me away for my own good, that she feels guilty and thinks I'm better off without her. She must have some feelings for me, but maybe she has buried them so deep she can't reach them.

I write the date, then, *Dear Becky, Maybe you don't want to hear from me anymore, but I want to* . . . what? I realize there really isn't anything I want or want to say, nothing I want to tell her, nothing she deserves or even wants to know. Nothing. All my searching, all the dreams and wonder and worry about finding my birth mother, finding out who I am and where I come from, was all for nothing. Nothing good anyway. Now I know who my biological mother is and she made it clear she wants nothing to do with me. So why do I keep writing to her?

I crumple the paper into a tight ball, throw it into the trash can next to the desk and take out a fresh piece of paper. *Dear Mama, I hope you are doing okay. I'm sorry I made such a mess of everything. I know taking off like that was wrong, but I was just so scared I wasn't thinking straight. But I am now. I promise I'll do everything I can to make sure everyone knows you're my mother. Not Becky. You. I have been asking my case worker when I can see you, and all she says is to be patient and to be good. Being good is easy, patient not so much.*

Even though I can't see you yet, I'm lucky to be with Maria and Miguel and the boys. They're really good people and they're really good to me. So you don't have to worry about me being in some horrible place. I hope I get to see you soon. Love, Meg. Then I make it *Meggie.* That will make her smile.

It takes almost another week for Jenny and I to finally see each other. It's a supervised visit, as if they need someone to watch us, as if I'm in danger. We meet in a room down the hall from Susan's office at DCF, and we only have an hour. As soon as I walk in, Jenny jumps up and rushes to me, holds me tight. She feels thin and I hold on.

We sit across from each other at a small round table while Susan quietly sits in a chair in the corner pretending not to watch us. I don't care. The room is painted yellow and has bookshelves on two walls full of stuffed animals, books, blocks, obviously used for visits with little kids and parents. How sad. We reach our arms across the table and hold hands and don't let go the whole time.

"I'm so sorry," I start. "This is all my fault. If I hadn't—"

"Stop. None of this is your fault. If I hadn't fought you so hard about finding your birth mother, or if I hadn't told you anything in the first place . . . Listen. I don't blame you. We are where we are because of what I did 13 years ago. And I would do it again in a heartbeat because it meant saving your life and becoming your mother. I have no regrets."

"But they arrested you. You might go to jail."

"They did. And I might. But you know what? I'm actually kind of relieved in a way. I've been waiting for that knock on the door pretty much ever since that day I brought you home."

"But you saved me. You don't deserve to go to jail."

"In the eyes of the law I do. That's what my lawyer keeps saying. *The eyes of the law*. And they are in charge. But who knows?" Jenny squeezes my hand. "Let's not talk about that right now. We don't have much time. Tell me about you, how you're doing. Tell me about this foster family. They better be good to you."

I tell her about Maria and Miguel and the boys, how they are really good people. "They came from Mexico about 11 years ago. They lost their son there. I'm not sure what happened, but they wanted to get away from the violence. After they moved here and became citizens, they started taking in foster kids, usually Mexican. And now me. I have my own room. They said I could paint it any color I want, but I'm not doing that. It's just temporary until I can live with you again."

"Two years is a long time."

"Less." I squeeze her hands now. "It's not forever. It will go fast. What about you? Will there be a trial? Do you have a good lawyer?"

"I have Justin. He's doing the best he can. I think he'll do as good as anyone. I'm pleading guilty. Justin says it's my best chance to avoid jail time. So there won't be a trial, just a sentencing hearing. No reason to go through all that. It's not like I'll be found innocent."

"But they have no proof, right?"

"Actually, they do. They have proof of who you were then, and they have proof of the false paperwork Gene and I had Sam make. After they got an anonymous tip, which I'm guessing was Eric, they did a lot of investigating about your disappearance. About time, right? Anyway, it turns out they had Becky's DNA on file, and yours, if you can believe that one. Apparently Becky accused a counselor at the group home of being the one who got her pregnant and they did a DNA test. It wasn't him. She thought it was funny, or payback or something. There's more, but I don't want to go into that now."

"So they know for sure I'm Becky's biological daughter."

Jenny nods and stares at me. "So. Now I just have to show up and plead guilty and show remorse. I told Justin I don't feel remorse, but that's what I need to do to come out of this okay. I don't want you to worry." I can't believe how strong she sounds, how calm about everything.

"What can I do? There must be something. Can I testify or anything? Tell them what a good mother you are?"

"The only people who get to speak at the sentencing hearing are the lawyers and me. Justin is asking people to write letters on my behalf to give to the judge. Dr. Phillips is writing one, and I think he even got in touch with Darlene. And I think Mr. Stevens who owns our building will write something. I don't have many friends. Never did."

"I'll write one. I'll write a really good one."

Chapter 26

When Justin and I first talked about my trial, I told him I was pleading not guilty.

All he said was, "Jenny."

I've been hearing people say my name like that ever since I can remember, full of judgment and disappointment. "But we pled not guilty at the arraignment," I argued.

"You always plead not guilty at the arraignment," he said. "But then when they presented their evidence at the pre-trial hearing, it became clear they had a lot of ammunition that didn't exactly scream *not guilty*."

"So what you're saying is, I'm screwed."

"That's not what I'm saying. If you plead guilty to kidnapping and you show remorse, and we show you feared for her safety, raised Meg in a stable environment and always had her best interests at heart, there is a chance of little or no jail time. And there was no pre-meditation, no intent to harm."

I took this all in and it felt like he was talking about a stranger or someone on a television show. I didn't know what else to say. I knew I needed to follow his advice and I knew he was right. After all these years telling myself I saved Meg and that's all there was to it, I truly, deeply believed that, but it's also true I kidnapped a child.

"Jenny, look at me. By pleading guilty, you're basically acknowledging you broke the law. Admitting your guilt and showing remorse is our best way forward. Our only way, really."

"What if I don't feel remorse?"

Justin stared into my eyes. "I think you should. Actually, I think if you're being honest with yourself, maybe you do." I opened my mouth, but before I could say anything, Justin added, "Not for being Meg's mother, but for the way you became her mother."

"It's not that simple."

Justin stared at me again like he was waiting for me to figure it out.

"I thought you were on my side."

"You don't think I'm on your side? Then why am I here?"

"I'm sorry. I just." Just what? Feel like giving up? Feel like crying? Those aren't options. "I want them to hear my side, to know I'm not some criminal."

"Listen, Jenny." Justin's voice was gentle, like he was talking down someone ready to jump off a building. "You can make a statement at your sentencing hearing."

"So I need to tell them I'm guilty, show remorse I don't feel, and they tell me what my punishment will be for saving a little girl."

Justin sighed, rubbed his face. "Jenny."

"I know."

I walk into the courtroom for the sentencing hearing without looking around too much, head to the front where I'll sit next to Justin, facing a judge who will decide my future. This can't be real. But it is. Almost every seat is taken. Who are all these people? Don't they have anything better to do? The only empty seats are directly behind where I will sit. Reserved for family and friends. I am so glad to see Dr. Phillips already there. I glance over to my right for just a second and see Eric towards the back, talking to a young woman with a computer on her lap. The vultures are out. I feel everyone's eyes on me. I face forward and don't look around again. Screw them.

The courtroom gets quiet for a moment and I turn to see Meg walk in. I am so proud of the way she holds her head high, looks straight ahead then sees me and smiles. Her hair is pulled back into a low ponytail and she's wearing a gray dress. Not her best color, but she has a little makeup on and looks beautiful. She's with Susan of course, who hangs back and slides into the bench across from us. Meggie hugs me tight before she sits right behind me. Dr. Phillips puts her hand on my arm and nods. No one seems to have any words.

I look around again at the faces. A lot of eyes are on me, the rest on their phones. Justin had told me my story is getting a lot of press and not to pay attention to any of the stories. I didn't get the newspaper and I didn't watch the news. Whatever people said about me can't be good because they have no idea about my life. As scared as I am, I am determined to stay positive. I turn as a woman in a police uniform walks in and looks around before we make eye contact. Riley. I haven't seen her since my last AA meeting. Our eyes lock, then she's wrapping me in a hug, whispers, "You'll be okay. You got this."

"I can't believe you're here."

Riley frowns, shakes her head. "Of course I'm here."

Before I sit again, I see an old woman holding onto a walker as she takes small steps down the aisle. Meg gets up and hugs her, helps her to sit right next to her. Once she's settled, she looks up at me and smiles. "Hey, neighbor."

I can't speak right away. Darlene. She came all this way for me. Meg was right—she does look old. She looks like she lost a hundred pounds and her face is thin and wrinkled, but she has the same bright blue eyes that don't miss a thing. "Thank you for being here." We squeeze hands, then Justin is here, the State's Attorney is here, and the clerk tells everyone to rise.

The State's Attorney seems to dislike me personally right from the start. His name is attorney Kevin Joseph and all he wants is to put me behind bars and throw away the key. He never says my name. I'm *The Defendant.* I'm nothing in his eyes but a criminal. Attorney Joseph goes over all the evidence that Justin has already gone over with me. He says that by abducting Adeline Jenkins, by removing her from the care of DCF, from the family she was entrusted to, I endangered the child's life. It takes all my willpower not to jump out of my seat.

Justin puts his hand on my arm and whispers, "We'll have our turn."

Attorney Joseph doesn't look at me once, but goes on and on about my history with alcohol, my conviction for shoplifting. He talks about not only perpetrating the crime of kidnapping, but the attempts to hide it with false documents and lies. He makes me sound so awful. He says my only excuse is that I was saving her from the foster care system, but the fact is that I didn't know at the time she was a foster child. So what? He says I had total disregard for the law. Not true.

"If she truly thought the child was in danger, Your Honor, she should have contacted the police. We are a country founded on the rule of law, something for which the defendant clearly has no regard." Wow.

"Due to the seriousness of the crime, Your Honor, the state recommends incarceration for a minimum of five years."

Justin does a good job when he's up. He tells my side, how I saw a helpless infant in the back seat of a car all alone and my only intention was to save her. He says that far from being in danger while in my care, Meg was raised as my own daughter and well taken care of. He talks about the bond we share as mother and daughter. He also talks about me turning my life around, attending regular counselling sessions, an alcohol treatment program, working multiple jobs in order to maintain good living conditions for Meg. I love how he calls her Meg.

"And, Your Honor, even though she didn't know at the time that the child was in foster care, the fact that the child was left alone at the very least shows she was in harm's way. Leaving her there was not an option at the time, nor was alerting the police, as she believed the child would conceivably be returned to the same people who put her in danger."

"In addition, Your Honor, the foster parents did not report the child missing in order to continue receiving checks from DCF, which further establishes the fact that the child was not properly being cared for by her foster family. There was no criminal intent here, Your Honor. Her only intent was to remove a child from an inherently dangerous situation. We are asking the court for leniency, and believe justice would not be served by incarceration."

After a minute, the judge asks, "And Adeline Jenkins is currently back in the custody of the Department of Children and Families?"

"Yes, Your Honor. She is living with a foster family on an emergency basis."

The judge frowns. "So this child was placed in foster care as an infant, left unattended in a car when she was three by her foster family, where she was abducted by the defendant, raised as her own daughter for the past 13 years, and is now back in the custody of DCF?"

"Yes, Your Honor."

"There are no living relatives?"

"No, Your Honor. Her biological mother is currently incarcerated at MCI Framingham on manslaughter charges. Her biological father is deceased, and there are no other known relatives."

The judge looks at the papers in his hand, sets them down and looks at me. "Does The Defendant wish to make a statement?"

Justin and I have talked about this, not so much what I will say, but what I shouldn't say—that I have no regrets (which I don't) and that looking back I would do it all again (which I would). I promised I would just tell the facts as I know them and I will tell the truth. He strongly suggested I write down what I plan to say so he could look it over, but I didn't want to do that. I want the judge and everyone here to know what I have to say is the truth and what's in my heart.

"Yes, Your Honor."

I start at the beginning and go all the way back to that day, give them as many details as I clearly remember and some I'm pretty sure of. I tell them I was with my boyfriend, and that we had been up all night. I told them I partied a lot back then and that I used to steal things, small things, and that's why I looked in that car. I never told Justin this and I don't look at him. I look at Meg the whole time.

"When I saw that little baby strapped in all alone, I just reacted and pulled her out of there. I remember looking around and there was no one in sight. I didn't know if whoever left her there would be gone five minutes or five hours, but I knew she wasn't safe. It was just instinct, I guess. I didn't give it a lot of thought. I certainly didn't think of it as kidnapping her or abducting her. I thought of it as saving her. I do realize, though, that in the eyes of the law, it is considered kidnapping."

"I know there's been a lot said about how I should have called the police, but, honestly, it didn't seem like an option at the time. I thought the police would just give her back to the people who left her there and she'd be put right back in danger. We brought her somewhere safe so we could figure out what to do. When we finally saw something on the news, we found out she was in foster care and that her foster parents didn't even report her missing so they could keep getting the checks. We knew she'd be better off with us instead of sending her back into the system. I just wanted to keep her safe. We didn't have much, but she was always safe. And loved."

I pull my eyes from Meg and look up at the judge. "Your Honor, my lawyer says it's all about what's in the best interests of the child. I truly believed at the time that by taking her, I was saving her. I believed that raising her and loving her as my own daughter was in her best interests. And to be honest, throughout the years, I came to believe she saved me as much as I saved her."

When I look back at Meg, her eyes are shining, tears about to spill over, but she nods and I see a look of pride, definitely love. I walk back to my seat, ready for whatever the judge decides.

The Judge calls a recess, says we will reconvene at 2:00 and bangs his gavel. We all stand while he walks out of the courtroom, his robes flowing behind him. I turn to Meg and we hug. She tells me not to worry, that she will be with me no matter what happens. "We're probably not finished saving each other."

During the recess, I stay right where I am, while a lot of people either leave the courtroom or stand around chatting. I glance at Eric and our eyes meet for a few seconds. He starts making his way towards me and I shake my head and turn away.

"You did well," Justin tells me.

"Even about the partying and stealing? Do you think that was okay to say?"

"I think it showed you were being honest, and I also think it shows how much you have changed. I don't think it hurt in any way."

I thank Darlene and Riley and Dr. Phillips for being here, tell them I read the letters they wrote on my behalf and how much I appreciate it.

"I haven't been in a courtroom in 40 years," Darlene says. "Since my divorce." She turns to Meg, then back to me. "You have a good girl here. You brought her up right, even with all you went through."

"Thanks for saying that."

"I'll second it," Dr. Phillips says.

I still can't believe I have people who care about me, who care what happens to me and don't think I'm a bad person.

People start filing back in, and in a couple of minutes, the clerk is there. "All rise."

The judge clears his throat and looks over the crowd in the courtroom. His eyes linger on me for a few seconds, then on Meg, then back to me. "In all my 27 years on the bench, I have never presided over a matter quite like this. I have reviewed the letters written on your behalf, all attesting to your moral character and your devotion to this child, as well as a testimonial from Adeline herself. Clearly, there is a bond that has been established over the past 13 years."

"While there is no doubt of your love for this child, and of hers for you, there is also no doubt you broke the law. There are few crimes I can think of that are more heinous than to kidnap a child. I am convinced of your devotion to this child; however, I am not convinced of your understanding and acceptance that what you did was wrong, not only in the eyes of the law, but in a decent, law-abiding society. We cannot take it upon ourselves to decide what's right or wrong. We have laws in place that we all must abide by."

"That being said, I see no benefit to society to incarcerate you. And while I don't believe your actions 13 years ago were by any means justified, I do believe you provided a home for a child who was not being served by our clearly flawed foster care system."

"I hereby sentence you to five years' probation, during which you will continue your alcohol treatment as well as counselling as long as is deemed necessary. And, as a condition of your probation, you will serve one year of home confinement, followed by three years of community service. Court is adjourned." He bangs his gavel and I watch him walk away.

I can't breathe for a minute. My eyes fill with tears I must have been holding in for a long time and I just let them flow. I feel hands on my shoulders, Meg's arms around me, voices in the courtroom, all blurring together. It's over. I'm not going to jail. All those years, all that worry. It's really over. I know I'm not exactly free yet, but I'm going home.

Reporters are shouting questions at me as I walk out of the courtroom: *How do you feel about the verdict? Do you think you got a fair trial? What are your plans now?* I look straight ahead and brush past them, even the ones who stand in front of me and put their microphones in my face. How could I possibly tell them how I feel when I feel so many different emotions? It's none of their business anyway.

Mostly I'm relieved, but I also feel a strange sense of emptiness. I'm going home to an empty apartment, to a life without Meg until she turns 18. It seems crazy that I'm not happier than this, but I feel like some part of me is missing. Meggie? My son? Maybe I'm just tired. Tomorrow I can focus on piecing my life back together.

Chapter 27

Four sharp knocks on the door make me jump. It's Monday morning, and I'm on my second cup of coffee before I head out to my counselling appointment, thinking about what jacket to wear. The thick dark clouds are getting ready to open up and pour.

I can't imagine who it could be, glad I have a peephole to look through. It takes a second to recognize Gene, staring straight at me with bloodshot eyes. His hair is greasy and damp, his shoulders darkened from the rain, so it must have started already. He needs a shave and probably a shower. It's been more than a year, since that night Gene found me walking down the street, and how many years before that? At least seven. Meg was gone, I had just been arrested for shoplifting and waiting for a court date, and I was so low. Gene was obviously on his last dime, though he always somehow found money for drugs and booze. We sat in his car and drank rum and did a few lines and used each other one last time.

I open the door halfway. "What are you doing here? How did you find me?" I hadn't realized how much anger I had stored up. But there's also that stupid tug at my heart that has been there since the first time I saw him. The only difference is now I don't give in to it and let it take over. I won't.

He gives me that lazy smile that used to make me believe all is right with the world. "Easy. You just go on the internet, type in a name and poof! How ya doin', Jenny girl?" It's not even nine and he sounds drunk. He's probably been up all night. Thank God those days are long gone for me.

I smell the whiskey and cigarettes, look into his glassy eyes. This is the last thing I need, this junkie back in my life.

This man I loved so much for too long. "You can't be here. I'm on probation and I don't need you messing things up."

Gene sways a little, holds on to the door jamb and keeps that stupid grin on his face like we're having a good time. "Can I come in?"

"No. You need to go away. I mean it." I start to close the door in his face, but not fast enough.

Gene puts his arm out and stops it from closing. "Come on, Jenny girl, aren't you glad to see me? It's been a long time. I've been looking for you a long time."

"No. I'm not glad to see you, especially like this. You're wasted. And if you've been looking for me you must want something. You need to go now." I try to close the door again, and again he puts his hand out to stop it.

"You don't mean that."

"Yes. I do."

"Okay. If that's what you really want, I'll go. I just wanted to see how you're doing. And Margaret. How's she?" He looks past me, bounces a little. "Do you think I could use your bathroom?"

"I told you, you can't come in. My probation officer will be here any minute." For the first time ever I wish that were true.

"Please? I promise I'll be quick." Gene holds three fingers up like he's making a Boy Scout pledge and bounces a little more. "Please?"

I take a deep breath, step back and let him in, even though everything inside me screams not to.

Gene smiles like a little kid who won a prize and walks in. I was right. He does need a shower. He smells like he slept in his clothes for a couple of days at least. I wonder if he's homeless, looking for a place to crash. It won't be here.

"So, how ya doin'? I heard about the trial. Couldn't believe it when I read about you in the newspaper. That brought back some memories, hey, Jenny girl?"

"Bathroom is right there." I point down the short hallway. "On your right."

Gene looks down at my ankle, stares at the monitor for a few seconds, frowns. “That must suck.”

“You said you needed to use the bathroom.”

After he closes the door, I hear the water running, the toilet flushing, water running again. He’s probably washing up. I’ll have to disinfect everything when he leaves. Before he finally comes out I hear the medicine cabinet open, then close after just a minute. *Sorry to disappoint you.* Finally he comes out. It looks like he ran my comb through his hair.

“All set?” I ask. “You need to leave now.”

Gene moves closer, looks into my eyes. “Just as beautiful as always.” He reaches out and touches my hair, as if any of that is going to work now.

I step back and cross my arms, then he’s standing in front of the door so I can’t open it. What the hell was I thinking letting him in?

“I came to see if there’s anything I can do, anything you need.” As he talks, he looks around the kitchen. “Nice place, by the way.”

“The only thing I need is for you to leave. I’ve been fine without you all these years, and I don’t want anything from you now. I’m doing fine.” I keep my voice strong, even though I’m starting to feel a little afraid he won’t leave. Then what?

“I saw Sam the other day. We talked about you.” Gene laughs and coughs at the same time.

“I’m sure you had a good laugh. Did you talk about what a fool I was all those years?”

“Jenny.” His face gets serious. “We talked about what a good mother you would have been.”

“I *am* a good mother.”

“You know what I mean. To *our* kid.”

My heart feels like it’s being squeezed. “Why would you bring that up now? Do you really think I want to talk about the most painful day of my life? The worst thing I’ve ever done? Leave.” I reach past him for the doorknob, but he walks into the kitchen like he lives here, opens the refrigerator, disappointed again I'm sure, then pulls out the carton of orange juice, opens it and drinks some down. I watch and don't know what to do. He puts it back, opens cabinets, slams them shut.

"What are you looking for?"

"I thought we could have a drink, talk a little." He's looking more and more desperate and pathetic and maybe dangerous as his eyes dart around the kitchen.

"I don't have anything. I don't drink anymore."

That makes him laugh. "Come on." He shoves his hands in his pockets, but his eyes are everywhere. And nowhere.

"I'm telling you I don't have anything. Please go."

"You don't want to hear what Sam and I talked about?"

"You already told me." I put my hand over my nose for a few seconds.

"Yeah, I know. I could use a shower, and some clean clothes."

I stare at him and shake my head, wonder where the guy is I knew so long ago, the guy I couldn't live without. He could be a complete jerk, a self-centered prick who didn't care when he left me and Meg practically destitute while he was out having a good time for himself. Now he's the one with nothing. Karma? At least Meg and I have always had each other.

"Do you have anything to eat? My boss stiffed me on the last job and I haven't eaten in a couple days. Or maybe just a few bucks?" He pulls out a kitchen chair and sits. "I've been walking for a while. Looking for you. You can give me a few minutes, can't you?"

I can't help it. I feel bad. "If I make you a sandwich, will you promise to leave? I have an appointment at 10:30."

"Ah, caught you, Jenny Girl. First it was your probation officer coming any minute, now you have an appointment?"

"I do. I'll give you 10 minutes and a sandwich. Then if you don't leave I'll call the police. I mean it."

Gene holds his hands up in surrender. "Got it."

I fill a glass with ice water and set it on the table in front of him. "Well? What did you want to tell me?"

"Okay. So. Maybe it's nothing, but when I saw Sam about a week ago, there were these pictures in a frame. You know those double ones that fold? He has a really shitty office, not even a desk, just a table and chairs, boxes. But I noticed these pictures. One was a woman holding a baby, all smiles and shit, and then another one, just a little kid. A boy."

"How old?"

"I'm not good with ages. Maybe nine or ten? I asked him who it was and he just grabbed it and closed it up. Acted all sketchy, you know?"

You would know all about that. "So what? You think it's our son? Is that what you're telling me?"

Gene shrugs, drinks down his water. "The kid reminded me of you, that's what I'm trying to say. Same beautiful brown eyes, same nose."

I cross my arms and hold onto myself. "You're a liar."

Gene shrugs again. "Just sayin'. If you have a few bucks you can lend me, I can go back and try to find out for sure."

I finish making two sandwiches, using the last of the ham, wrap them up and put them in a plastic grocery bag. I walk to the door and open it, hold the bag out to him without a word. My heart is beating fast and I wish so much I had never opened the door.

Gene looks over at me, pushes himself up from the table and surprises me when he takes the bag and walks out. Before I close the door, he turns and smiles that Gene smile that used to get me. "You're a good person, Jenny girl. Always were. Too good for me."

I lock the door after him, open the window over the sink for a little fresh air. All I smell now is my own sweat mixed with his lingering stench. I go to the bathroom and turn on the exhaust, throw the towels in the hamper, wipe down the sink and think about how far Gene has fallen. He must have made all that up about the pictures in Sam's office.

I shouldn't have been so nice to him, shouldn't have let him in or given him food. Now he'll be back for more. Why am I so stupid when it comes to Gene? I can't let him anywhere near here again, not while I'm serving probation and on home confinement. I need to be beyond reproach. There's only one person I can think of to call who might be able to help me.

"Jenny?" Agent Peters sounds surprised to hear from me, but not bothered. Almost glad? Definitely concerned.

"Agent Peters," I say.

"Is everything okay?"

I tell him about Gene appearing out of the blue, how I'm afraid now that he knows where I live, he's going to come around again, show up whenever he feels like it. "I'm almost four months into this home confinement, and I'm not about to let him ruin everything. He's a drunk and a druggie and seemed really desperate. I don't want him anywhere near me, and I definitely don't want him anywhere near Meg."

"I assume you made that clear to him."

"He wasn't listening. I thought he might listen to you. That's why I'm calling. If you tell him to leave me alone, it might scare him enough to make him slither back under his rock."

He doesn't say anything right away and I remember how good he was at waiting me out, waiting for more with his poker face. Or maybe I overstepped.

"I'm sorry. You're the only person I could think of to call."

"I'm glad you did. He is definitely a shady character."

"How do you know?"

"I talked to him. Not long after they arrested you, I located and questioned him. You're right about the drugs and alcohol."

"You talked to Gene? How come I didn't know this? How come my lawyer didn't know this? In court they said they couldn't locate him."

"At the beginning of the investigation, we of course did a background check, contacted everyone you were associated with at the time of the abduction. You lived a pretty isolated life back then. After a few minutes of questioning Gene, I could see he wasn't reliable. First he said he couldn't remember anything from that long ago and had no idea what I was talking about, then when he saw I wasn't there to arrest him, he said he might be able to recall something. He wanted to know how much he would be paid, told me he would say whatever we wanted for a price. I told him that's not how we do things."

"Sounds like him. So even though he was involved in everything, you just let him go."

"Your case was already complicated, and I thought putting Gene in the mix wouldn't exactly help clarify anything. I thought it would only shine an even more negative light on you."

"It almost sounds like you were trying to help me."

After a few seconds, he says, "I did everything by the book, gave my honest evaluation of not only Gene's reliability, but his motives if he did testify. Honestly, after talking to you, and after my interview with Gene, I was convinced he would only be detrimental to your case."

I think about this for a minute. "Thank you." He's right. Who knows what Gene would have said, what he would have lied about. He would say whatever would make him look like the good guy, and expect to be rewarded for it.

"Just doing my job."

"I feel like I gave you a really hard time. I know I did. I was just so worried about Meg. I'm surprised you want anything to do with me."

"I know we met under less than ideal circumstances, but, well, the people I usually deal with are true criminals with no regard for right and wrong, truth or lies, and, more often than not, no regard for life. I'm not saying I condone what you did, but you're paying your debt to society and I'm a firm believer in second chances. And I want you to know I always saw the good in you. I saw your true love and commitment to Meg. And despite giving me a really hard time, I guess I saw your truth."

"No one has ever said anything like this to me before. Not even close."

"Maybe no one has ever looked below the surface. That's what I try to do. So, back to Gene. Tell me exactly what happened. Did he threaten you in any way?"

"In his own way, yeah. I mean, the way he wormed his way in here, started walking around like he owned the place, going in the refrigerator, opening cabinets, looking for something to drink, which I don't have. He's strung out and desperate and I don't want him anywhere near Meg. Or me. But mostly Meg."

"Do you think he would harm her?"

"Not physically, no. Gene isn't violent or anything like that. At least he never was. But he's really good at messing with people's heads, making people feel sorry for him. He blames everything on other people, on not getting breaks like everyone else. You know the type."

"Unfortunately I do, only too well. I'm glad you reached out. I'll see what I can do. It will have to be unofficial, though. Unless you want to file a formal complaint, which would go through the local police first of course."

"I really don't want the police involved. I want to stay under the radar, keep my head down, do what I'm supposed to do so Meg can come home."

"I'll have a talk with him."

"You'll probably find him in a shelter somewhere, or on the street."

"I'll find him."

"Thank you so much, Agent Peters."

"Charlie."

"Charlie?"

"My name."

"Thank you, Charlie."

Chapter 28

"How was school today?" Maria glances away from the steaming pot on the stove and looks at me for just a couple of seconds. She never stares at me, but I feel like she sees me.

"It was fine." I can't complain. Not to Maria.

She puts the lid on the pot, turns the radio down. "You got a letter in the mail today. I put it on your bed."

A letter? Who would write me a letter? Did Becky write back? I doubt it. Jack? "Thanks." I rush to my room, and on my bed is an envelope addressed to me in Jenny's handwriting. The return address is our apartment. I rip it open, and inside is another envelope addressed to me, care of Jenny, still sealed. There's no return address, and the postmark is San Diego, California. I rip that one open and pull out two sheets of plain white paper, folded in thirds.

Dear Meg,

The first thing I want to say is I'm sorry if I hurt you in any way. It was never my intention, and I hope you are doing well. You most likely are. As I told you once before, you are the strongest person I know. Jenny's arrest and all that followed must have been a huge ordeal for both of you, and while I believe it was the right thing to do, to hold her accountable, maybe I was wrong about Jenny needing to be punished. I have always tended to see things in black or white, good or bad. I learned from you there is another way of seeing things, a more human way. Empathy? Maybe so.

When I first saw you at the bus station, I felt a strong connection. It wasn't as simple as your making me think of my sister.

That was part of it, but there was more. I could see you needed help, and I wanted to be the one to help you. Then as I got to know you, I came to realize that one day I would bring you home to Mama. I never would have forced you. I hope you know that. I just knew it would happen and it would be my one chance to make up to Mama for not taking better care of Alicia. I meant no harm. And I want you to know you gave Mama more happiness and contentment than she has had since Alicia was taken from us.

Mama passed away three days ago, and I believe she is at peace now.

I also want you to know how grateful I am for our friendship. Even though we only knew each other a short time, I will always believe we were meant to meet and help each other.

This will most likely be the last time you hear from me, and I didn't want to disappear without saying goodbye. I hope you and Jenny are doing well and that you both have a long and happy life. I also hope you remember our brief friendship with fondness, and please remember I always had the best of intentions.

Warmly,

Jack

I read it twice more, then I stare at the handwriting, rub my thumbs over the words he wrote before I fold it back into thirds, then in half, in half again, then again, until it fits in the palm of my hand. I lie down on my side and close my eyes, squeezing his letter as if I can make his words, his essence, become part of me. I think about seeing him the first time in the bus station, not trusting him, but wanting to. I think about how good it felt when he called me pretty. And smart. I think about him bursting into Tito's and saving me. Every time I called him, he was there for me. I thought all he wanted was to help me. I don't want to believe he used me to make amends with his mother, but I guess maybe he did. I owe him so much. Maybe giving his mother some happiness was the only way to pay him back.

I feel a tear spill out and drip over my nose onto the pillow, then another one. I'm not sure what I'm so sad about. His mother, for losing her daughter like that, then her mind, now her life? That and maybe knowing I will never see Jack again. I shouldn't want to, but I do.

"Meg?" Maria stands in the doorway, drying her hands on a kitchen towel. Her long black hair is tied back with a bright blue bandana that matches the flowers in her blouse. She's always so colorful, just like her personality. "Are you okay? Did you get bad news?"

I sit up and wipe my face. "I'm fine. A friend of mine moved away. I'll miss him."

Maria sits next to me on the bed, puts her arm around my shoulders. "Losing a friend is hard. We don't make many true friends in this life. If we have even one good friend, we are very lucky."

Maria must have left behind friends in Mexico when she escaped. Sometimes I forget what a bad situation she came from, everything she went through, how strong she is. I nod, take a deep breath.

"It is good he wrote to you, yes? And you can write back?"

"I don't know where he is, and I won't hear from him again." It sounds so final when I say it out loud.

Maria nods and doesn't ask questions, just keeps her arm around me, pulls me a little closer. We hear the front door open, Miguel and the boys rushing in, the thump of their backpacks hitting the floor. Laughing and talking and footsteps running into the kitchen. "Mama? We're home!"

We get up at the same time but Maria stops before she reaches the doorway, turns to me. "I want you to know something, Meg. Since you have been with us, I have come to love you like a daughter. I know you won't be here forever, that you will be going home to Jenny when you are able, and that is how it should be. It's not easy to let go of someone, but the people we care about will always live in our hearts, yes?"

I nod, afraid I'll start crying again, then we both look out the door towards the noise, her boys, our home.

I shove Jack's letter in the back pocket of my jeans and we head to the kitchen. Miguel is lifting a spoonful of rice from the pot on the stove, glances over at us with a smile before he puts it in his mouth. The boys are climbing onto the chairs around the table, so beautiful and excited to be home and share their day. I pour glasses of apple juice, put out bowls of sliced apples and grapes, cheese sticks and crackers. While they devour their snacks, they talk about school, art class and recess, a science project, a field trip to a farm. I wonder how my life would be different, how Jenny and I would be different, if she hadn't been forced to give up her baby. My little brother. It's strange how you can love someone so much you never met.

"Why don't you all go out and play until supper is ready," Maria says. She turns to me and asks, "Would you mind watching them?"

We go outside where there is a little concrete area with a basketball hoop too high for Mateo, but Antony carries him on his shoulders which makes me nervous, but they love it too much to say anything except to be careful.

"Dinner is ready," Maria calls, and in a few minutes we sit around the kitchen table, everyone passing plates, eating, talking, laughing. I watch and feel like I'm in the audience, not part of the show, an outsider. It's not that I don't feel welcome, but it's just temporary and then I won't be part of their family anymore. I'll miss this. I'll miss them all, but I will be home, with Jenny, where I belong.

"Why do you look so sad, Meg?" Mateo asks.

"I'm not sad," I say. "I was just thinking." All of a sudden it's silent and all eyes are on me, waiting. "I'm thinking how lucky I am to be here. I've never had a family like this before."

Maria looks around the table, then turns to me. "We are a put-together family. And we are very lucky to have each other."

She looks around the table again. "We are a family not because of blood, but because of what we mean to each other."

I blink a few times as her words sink in. I should know that better than anyone. That's exactly what Jenny, Gene and I were for a while, a put-together family. And now Jenny and I. That's what Jenny has been trying to tell me all this time. I finally get it.

Susan and I walk into Jenny's Saturday morning to the smells of coffee and cinnamon. Jenny walks out of the bathroom smiling, says hello to Susan, wraps me in a hug and asks how I'm doing. Her hair is brushed back and she's wearing a little mascara and blush, white slacks and a sleeveless pink blouse.

"You seem happy," I say. "And you look nice."

"Thanks." She gives me a genuine smile that lights up her eyes, something I haven't seen in a while.

I almost ask if she has a date, half joking but half serious. I'll wait until she tells me. I set the white paper bag I brought with three brownies on the kitchen table, take off my jacket while she pours two mugs of coffee. There's a bread cooling on the counter next to the stove.

"You baked?"

"Cinnamon bread. It's for later."

"What's later?"

Jenny looks away, towards the counter. "Nothing. It's still hot."

Why is she acting all weird over cinnamon bread? I lift a brownie out of the bag and put it on a napkin, pick up a mug of coffee and bring them to Susan, settling in the living room with her book.

When I walk back out to the kitchen, Jenny is sitting at the table, a cup of milky coffee in front of her, half her brownie gone. My brownie sits on a napkin at my place across from her with a glass of milk. I sit and take a sip of milk. "I have a couple of things to tell you."

"I have something to tell you too," she says. "You first."

I take another sip of milk. "First, thanks for sending the letter. It was from Jack."

"I figured. I didn't open it."

"I know."

"What did he say?"

"Mostly that he was sorry for everything."

"He should be."

It wasn't until weeks after Jenny's trial that I told her about staying with Jack's mother and how she thought I was his sister Alicia. Jenny thought it was pretty twisted, which it was, I guess, but I like to think of it as an act of kindness. I also told her it was Jack that gave that anonymous tip, not Eric. She said the only thing that surprised her about that was she didn't think of him first.

"He was basically writing to say goodbye, and to tell me his mother passed away."

"I'm sorry about that. Really. But hopefully she's at peace now."

"That's what Jack said too. He wasn't a bad guy, you know. He really cared about me."

"I never trusted him. A grown man befriending my 16-year-old daughter. He basically put you back in the foster system. He got me arrested and wanted me in jail."

I take a sip of milk, a bite of brownie. I don't want to argue about Jack. We've done enough of that. Jenny will never know the Jack I knew. "It's over. I just wanted you to know he's sorry about how everything turned out, and he's glad he met me, glad for our friendship."

Jenny stares at me a few seconds. "That's it?"

"Just that I probably won't hear from him again. I can bring it over next time if you want to read it."

"That's okay. You said there were a couple of things?"

"I want you to know I get it now. I'm sorry I didn't get it before."

"Get what?"

"That we were a real family, that we *are* a real family. Maria calls her family a put-together family. She says what makes a family isn't blood, it's what they mean to each other."

"That's what I tried to tell you a thousand times. How come you only get things when other people tell you?" She smiles when she says this, and I am so glad to see the angry Jenny seems to be long gone.

"I don't know. But I get it now. All that time growing up, you, me and Gene. We were a family, right?"

Jenny's face changes, darkens. She takes a deep breath, sighs it out.

"What?"

"He came by the other day."

"Gene? He came here? How was he?"

"Filthy dirty and desperate and drunk, looking for booze and money, probably for drugs. I know you always thought he was some great guy, and sometimes he was, but not anymore. He's really bad news and we can't have anything to do with him, especially with me on probation. You understand that, right? We can't be anywhere near him."

It takes me a minute to process this. Gene. I haven't seen him since he left us at that motel when I was what? Eight? For a long time I wanted so badly for him to come back. "How did he find us?"

"The internet he said. I guess everyone's information is just out there." Jenny gets up and refills her coffee. "He actually scared me a little. I don't think I have ever seen him so strung out and desperate, looking for something to drink, looking in the medicine cabinet for any drugs. Anything. I made him a couple of sandwiches and told him not to come back."

"Is he homeless?"

"I have no idea, but I wouldn't be surprised. And don't start feeling sorry for him. Gene has always been about himself. He's a junkie and an alcoholic and he'll do anything he can to get a fix. Including using me and you. I told him to go away and not come back, but that doesn't mean anything. If he comes anywhere near you, call the police."

I can't believe we're talking about Gene. "You make him sound dangerous."

"He is."

"Then shouldn't we call the police? Get a restraining order or something?"

"I have a friend taking care of it."

I finish my milk, trying to process all this. "What friend?" I can't imagine who it could possibly be, but maybe this *friend* is why she's so happy. Is that who the cinnamon bread is for?

Jenny brings her mug over to the sink, rinses it and puts it in the strainer. "You actually met him before. Agent Peters."

It takes me a minute, but I do remember a guy in a suit, acting like he was in charge of the world, making me feel like a criminal. "The FBI guy? Wasn't he kind of a jerk?"

Jenny laughs. He was just doing his job. He's really a nice guy, and he's going to talk to Gene for me. Can you believe I called the FBI for help?" She sits back down, sips her coffee and looks past me, out the window.

"So he's nice, huh?" I stare at her until she looks at me, her face red. I don't know when I've seen her this happy. Here she is with half a life and she's this happy.

"Nice visit?" Susan is standing in the doorway, smiling. "Thanks for the brownie and coffee." She puts her mug in the sink, throws away her napkin while Jenny walks me to the door.

"Promise me if you see Gene you won't let him anywhere near you, okay? Until Charlie gets this straightened out, Gene will be looking to worm his way into our lives. He'll only hurt you. More than he already has."

I look into her worried eyes. "I promise."

She gives me a tight hug. "See you next week."

When she lets go and we back away, I smile. "Charlie, huh?"

Her cheeks redden again. "See you next week."

Chapter 29

"I'm surprised Gene hasn't tried to see you. I figured he'd be hanging around the neighborhood, hoping to *accidentally* run into you." Jenny and I are sitting at our usual places at the kitchen table, me facing the window and Jenny facing the door. Jenny spoons sugar into her coffee and waits for me to answer. It's her way of asking without asking.

"I promise I'll tell you if I see him." I feel Jenny's eyes on me as I go to the refrigerator for orange juice and pour myself a glass. When I sit back down, she's still staring at me. I look towards the open window over the sink with the sheer white curtains blowing in, and listen to the sound of a siren in the distance. Finally I ask, "What?"

"I'm sorry," she says, "that Gene turned out to be such a bum."

"It's not your fault how he turned out. I'm glad he hasn't tried to see me. I don't want to see him if he's like you said. Maybe he's not even around anymore."

"Oh, he's around. Charlie found him. He said Gene's renting a room not far from here. Some cheap place, probably full of junkies like him."

"Did Charlie talk to him?"

"He warned him. He told Gene he was being watched, that he was a person of interest in an ongoing drug investigation. I feel better knowing Charlie is looking out for us."

I'm about to ask how she and Charlie are doing when my cell phone rings.

Jenny sets her coffee down and glances at me, watches me talk, mostly "Yes" and "Thank you" on my end. As soon as I end the call, I tell her, "I got a job."

"You didn't tell me you were looking for a job. What about school?"

"I wasn't really looking. I mean, I was thinking about it, then the other day I went into Rosie's to get a muffin and there was a sign that said they were looking for part time help. So I filled out an application. I didn't want to say anything unless I got it. It's only two hours a day after school, and four hours on Saturday. Rosie wants me to come in tomorrow morning to train, and she said she'll put me right to work. She said her granddaughter quit, said she found a real job. 'Doesn't get any realer than this,' Rosie said."

"You'll be waiting tables?"

"Mostly, or working behind the counter, and whatever else they need." Jenny and I used to go to Rosie's sometimes for the chocolate chip pancakes. It's a small diner, two blocks over, and is always busy. I can't believe I have a job. My first job.

"Okay," Jenny says. "I like Rosie's. Breakfast and lunch. No booze. No drunks hitting on you."

Rosie is in her 70's at least, and reminds me of a bird. She's tiny, not even five feet, with a pointy nose, and weighs maybe 90 pounds, if that. She's always moving, and has more energy than anyone I know. Her skin is wrinkled like someone way older, but I think it's from all her smoking. She said she cut down to five cigarettes a day last year when the doctor told her to quit. "He's been telling me that for 20 years now, and I'm still kicking."

After a few shifts, I'm surprised how natural it feels being here. Rosie's brother Jay is the cook. He's a quiet man who seems perfectly content at the grill, cracking eggs with one hand, flipping pancakes, frying bacon until it's crispy but not burnt. People mostly order bacon and eggs over easy or scrambled. What I mostly do is fill mugs of coffee. People drink a lot of coffee. A couple of regulars sit at the counter and read the newspaper, take their time with their muffin or slice of pie. Every Tuesday a group of retired teachers come for lunch and take the booth in the corner. They stay at least an hour, laugh a lot, and always leave a generous tip.

On my third Saturday, about a half hour before we close, a guy in a black hoodie walks in. When he pushes his hood back and stands in the doorway for a few seconds, I recognize him and my heart starts pounding. Gene. I'm standing behind the counter at the cash register, handing change to a girl not much older than me, bouncing a baby on her hip.

Does he know I work here? Is he looking for me? Gene looks around for a few seconds, his eyes darting everywhere, skirting right past me. He looks just like Jenny said—dirty and strung out. His face is a lot thinner and he needs a shave, but it's him. I take a deep breath, calm myself, thankful he doesn't know me.

He takes a seat at one of the booths along the wall, the one closest to the door. I watch as he pulls a menu from behind the napkin dispenser, sets it down in front of him to study. My heart is pounding hard. There are still a few customers there, finishing up, and I'm relieved when Pete walks in. He's one of my favorite regulars who told me once I remind him of his granddaughter.

I don't know what I'm so afraid of anyway. It's not like Gene will hurt me or anything. And obviously he doesn't even know I work here or he would have come up to the counter and asked for me. Am I afraid because of what Jenny told me? Or am I afraid because I don't know who he is anymore? Is he anything to me? What surprises me most is that I'm not glad to see him. For such a long time, I would have given anything to see him again. When did I stop wishing for that?

I take a deep breath and walk over with the coffee pot and the smile I put on for customers I don't know. Maybe he won't even recognize me. "Coffee?"

He glances up for a second. "Yeah, thanks. Cream and sugar."

I turn over his mug and almost fill it, pull out a handful of little creamers from my apron pocket, set them down. "Sugar's on the table" I point to the dish next to the napkins.

He looks up at me more closely then. Does he recognize my voice? "Wait." He grips my arm and stares at me. "I—Margaret?" He takes in my whole face now, my hair, my eyes. "It is you. Hey." He smiles and has deep crinkles around his eyes that weren't there before. "You don't recognize your old man?"

I pull my arm away and take a step back, pretend I don't know him for a few seconds as I stare back, then I just say. "Gene."

"You don't seem all that glad to see me. How ya been? Look at you. All grown up. I've been meaning to get in touch. Hey, I saw Jenny. She tell you? Can you sit for a minute?"

"I'm working. Do you want to order something?"

"Aren't you glad to see me? I missed you. I missed my girls. Didn't you miss me? Even a little?"

There are so many things I had planned to say if I ever saw Gene again. They changed over the years, from telling him how much I missed him and wanted him to come back, to telling him how disappointed and hurt I was when he left us, to telling him to go to hell. But I still remember him being sweet to me when I was little, carrying me around and bringing me little presents. Right now, though, all I feel is sorry for him and a little scared and I don't want to be around him.

"Are you going to order something?"

Gene looks down at the menu and his voice changes from nice to a little rough. "Bacon. Scrambled eggs and toast. And pancakes."

I scribble it on my pad, walk away, and have a sick feeling in the pit of my stomach. I put the order slip in the window and stay behind the counter. I take Pete's order, his usual chocolate milk and a blueberry muffin, and he asks if I'm okay.

"I'm good," I tell him with a smile I don't feel, while my eyes keep darting back to Gene. I don't want him to catch me staring at him, but I can't help but look and remember the last time I saw him, how he talked to me like I was an adult, how he said he couldn't do it anymore, as if everything was Jenny's fault. Nothing was ever his fault. I didn't understand why Jenny was always so mad at him, and I wanted to be on his side. Before he left I remember he told me to take care of Jenny. As if he needed to tell me.

Pete turns to look at Gene, asks, "Is he giving you trouble?"

"No," I tell him. "I'm fine." I will be, as soon as he's gone.

When Gene's order comes out, I carry it over to him like he's just another customer. I shouldn't be surprised he's back now, now that we don't need him anymore.

Gene puts his hand on my wrist as I set down his plates. His nails are dirty and need cutting. I pull my arm away. Why do guys think it's okay to do that?

"I know you're mad at me. Jenny is too, but, come on, aren't you even a little glad to see me? Aren't you even gonna ask how I'm doing?" He has that same smile that Jenny and I fell for so many times.

"You just took off and left us. It's been almost nine years. You never came back, never checked to see how *we* were doing."

"Has it been that long? I didn't mean to be gone so long. I mean I didn't plan it. I've been looking for my girls for a long time."

I'm sure. "Enjoy your breakfast." I walk away, feeling strong. He and his lies can't touch me, can't hurt me.

When I refill his coffee, I feel his eyes on me but I don't look at him until I ask if he wants anything else. He must have been hungry; he ate every bite.

"Where's the bathroom?"

I point down to the end of the counter. "On the right."

He nods and stands and I take out my order slip, total it, leave it on his table while I go back behind the counter, near the register. I don't clear his plates yet. I made that mistake once on my second day and the woman got angry, said she wasn't finished, even though all that was left was a piece of crust. Rosie said her breakfast was on the house. She wasn't upset at me, just said, "Don't clear the plates til they're out the door, honey."

Pete is finished and takes his time laying money out on top of the check. The only other people are two women finishing their tea at the small table by the window. Pete and I both look over when Gene comes out, watch him walk right past his table towards the door.

"Excuse me," I say loudly. "You haven't paid."

Just as Gene is almost to the door, Pete gets up and blocks his way. "The lady says you didn't pay."

Gene tries to look all innocent, like he made an honest mistake. Skipping out on the check is something we did a lot when I was a kid. He made it seem like a game. "Oh, sorry," he says, as he steps back to his table, picks up the check, searches his jeans pockets and pulls out two crumpled dollar bills. He stands there for a few seconds, then turns and looks at me. "I'm a little short here. Do you think you could help out your old man?"

Pete turns to me, raises his eyebrows. "This is your father?"

"No. He's not." I could never explain who Gene is, how I believed he was my father for a long time. I don't know what he is to me now, and I don't know where this strength is coming from, but I'm glad I'm not that shy little kid he was probably expecting.

"Do you want me to call the cops?" Pete asks.

I stare at Gene, so embarrassed, for him and for myself. "No, that's okay." I walk over and snatch the check out of his hand. "I'll take care of it."

"I appreciate this," Gene says. "I'll pay you back soon as I can. I promise."

"I don't want your money. Or your promises. Just don't do this to me again." My voice is strong, but I'm shaking inside. All this time, having a dream in my head of the person I thought he was. Not that I thought he was perfect, but I thought he was better than this.

Chapter 30

Meg hangs her purse and jacket on the back of a kitchen chair, comes to stand by me at the counter and puts her arm around my waist, her head on my shoulder. I glance over at Susan, who opens her eyes wide, gives me a tight smile and a silent wave and slips into the living room. This can't be good.

I set the coffee pot down. "What's up?"

"Gene."

I knew it. I hold her close for a long minute, her body shaking with silent sobs she must have been holding in a long time. I was hoping Gene would just slink away and leave her alone, maybe even be too ashamed to show his face to this innocent girl he abandoned. "Come sit."

Meg wipes her eyes with her hands, grabs a tissue and blows her nose. "I don't know what I'm crying about."

"Where did you see him?"

"He came into Rosie's on Saturday. He looked just like you said, kind of dirty, needed a shave, but he wasn't wasted. Hungover, maybe, but he didn't seem drunk or anything. Tired. He didn't recognize me at first, then when he did he was all friendly, expecting me to be glad to see him. I always thought I would be, but I wasn't." Her eyes fill again and I reach over and squeeze her hand.

It's all my fault she's so hurt. No matter what Gene did when Meg was a kid, no matter how many times he took off and left us with nothing, I always took him back like he was some prize. That's what she grew up with. I thought so little of myself I accepted whatever Gene did, as if I didn't deserve any better. I never thought enough about how it affected Meg. "You're grieving a person who doesn't exist. I'm not sure he ever did. He was never that person we both wished for and pretended he was."

Meg looks down at the table. "He actually scared me a little." When she looks up at me, her eyes are dry. "I mean, it was Gene, but he was like a stranger. It was weird."

"Did he give you the line about looking for us? Missing us?"

"He said he's been searching for us for a long time. As if I'd believe that. Anyway, I waited on him just like I would anyone else, then when he was done, he tried to take off without paying. Pete was there and stopped him."

"That bastard. I can't believe he would do that to you. Me, yes, but not you."

"It was so strange seeing him. He acted like everything was normal, like nothing's changed, as if all these years haven't gone by since he just deserted us. He actually thought I'd be glad to see him."

I shake my head. "That's because we always were. But to go in there, where you work and do that to you. I could kill him."

"I think he's already killing himself."

"Well he doesn't have to do it in front of you. I'll be talking to Charlie later today and I'll tell him. Maybe we do need a restraining order."

"It wasn't like he knew I worked there. He didn't even recognize me at first."

"But then when he did, he decided it would be a good idea to try and stiff you."

"I think he would have done it no matter who it was. I mean, he obviously came in with no money, no way to pay. How could he do that? And just expect to get away with it?"

If she only knew about all the times Gene and I did that in the early days, before Meg, then even with Meg when she was too little to realize. Did we think we should get a free pass? Did we think we were entitled? More likely, we didn't think at all. It was all fun and games back then, and we never thought about consequences. "He's been doing things like that all his life. Thinks he can get by on his charm. And he has, for a long time."

"He wasn't all that charming."

"You should have called me right away. Charlie would have been there and arrested him."

"It happened so fast. It didn't seem real. And to tell the truth, I felt more sorry for him than angry. He seemed so desperate."

"If he comes in again, call me, okay?"

"I don't think he will. I wish he wasn't like that. I wish I could have talked to him. I feel like I don't even know him, and he was a big part of my life for such a long time. He called himself my *old man*. Pete asked me if Gene was my father and I said no. I didn't even have to think about it. But Gene made it seem like he was. When he saw he wasn't going to be able to just walk out on the check, he said, 'Think you can help out your old man?' He was like a father to me, right? I mean, that's how it felt when I was little. I thought he was my father."

"Of course you did. It was what I hoped for, that somehow we would just become a family. I was so naïve. You asked me once when you were little why you called him Gene instead of dad or daddy, and I told you that was how he wanted it. Gene and I never talked about having a family. I just wanted it so much I made myself believe he wanted it too. I don't think being an actual father was ever something he wanted. Way too much responsibility."

Meg nods like she understands, but how could she?

"Do you want me to get Charlie involved? Keeping Gene away?"

"No. I don't want to get Gene into trouble. I doubt he'll ever come back to Rosie's after what happened. It was just breakfast, and he looked like he probably hadn't eaten in a while."

Even with what he did, Meg wants to stick up for him, protect him. I get it. I did it for years, made excuses, forgave him. Every single time. "You're a good person. But please don't fall for his victim act. He chose to go in there and order food he knew he didn't have money to pay for. He didn't care who—What?"

Meg is staring at me, eyes wide. "I just realized, isn't that what you did? That night in the bar when I had to call Jack? You ordered drinks and you knew you didn't have the money to pay for them."

I can't believe she's bringing this up. It feels like a punch in the stomach and it feels like a lifetime ago. It also feels like it happened to someone else. But she's right. She's absolutely right. "As much as I hate you comparing me to Gene, you have a point. I was so upset that night, and I did do that. There's no excuse for it. But the difference is, I'm not that person anymore. I hope you know that. Gene is, and I think he always will be."

"I really feel bad for him."

"I know you do, and I get it. I really do. This is what he does, makes people feel sorry for him. Nothing is ever his fault. He's not worth getting upset about, not worth one more tear."

Meg goes to the sink, lets the water run and fills a glass. She stands there looking out the window at the gray sky before she turns to me. "Do you feel anything for him at all?"

"I feel a lot of things. I feel sorry for him, too, that he ended up like this. And I feel angry for the way he treated us, all those times he took off, leaving us for weeks at a time with nothing to eat. And how do you think I feel about him walking out on us, leaving us with practically nothing after he convinced me to sell our baby, promising we would have a better life?"

Meg nods. She looks so sad. I know she wishes Gene were a better person, but all the wishing in the world won't change the past and won't change who he is.

"When you said he didn't want to be a father, was it basically about me? I mean, was it too much, having two kids? If you didn't have me, do you think he would have wanted to keep the baby?"

"It definitely wasn't about you. And as far as giving up the baby, not having the responsibility was part of it, but it was mostly about the money."

"I wish we could have kept the baby. I'm sorry if you don't want to talk about it, but since I've been living with Maria and Miguel and the boys, I can't help but think about him, what he might be like, how our life would be so different."

"It's probably good for me to talk about it. It hurts me every day, but I have to believe I did the right thing and that he has a good life. I know it has to be better than we could have given him. I couldn't bring him to that trailer, to that life. It was bad enough I put you in that situation. I couldn't watch another child go hungry. And it didn't have to be that way. If I hadn't put all my faith in Gene and none in myself, everything could have been different. I could drive myself crazy with all the *could haves* and *should haves* and *would haves*. It doesn't matter now. I'm just thankful I have you."

"Me too."

"I didn't tell you that when Gene came over that day, he told me some story about Sam having a picture on his desk of a woman and a baby, tried to tell me he thinks it's my son. He said if I could loan him a few bucks he'd try to find out from Sam. Like I said, he's always looking for a quick buck."

"But Sam must know. He must know who adopted him and where he is. He arranged everything, right?"

"And what if he does? It doesn't matter. I mean I gave him up, signed him over, we took money for him. It's a done deal."

"But wouldn't you want to know how he's doing? I wonder if he knows he's adopted. I wonder if he would want to meet us."

It's funny how the conversation went from Gene to the baby. And I'm actually okay with it. Maybe it's about time. I get up and pour two cups of coffee, hold one out to Meg. "Do you want to give this to Susan?"

As she reaches for it, there's a sharp knock on the door that startles us both. That same sharp knock. I look through the peephole and there's Gene. I set my coffee down while Meg brings Susan's to her and I open the door, not afraid anymore, just angry. “I can’t believe you have the nerve to come here after what you did.”

Gene doesn’t even try to step in. He’s wearing a backpack and holding something in each of his hands. He looks down at the floor, then up at me. He actually looks sorry, but I know better than to buy his act. “I came to apologize to Margaret, and to you, before I go. Is she here?”

Meg steps over to the door but stands a little behind me. “I’m right here.”

Gene holds out a $20 bill. “I’m sorry about breakfast the other day. I put you in a bad spot.”

Meg hesitates a couple of seconds before she takes it. “It’s okay. Thanks.”

“And this is for you.” He holds out a photo.

“What’s this?”

“It’s our son.”

I take it, hold it with both hands and stare at this picture of a little boy dressed in blue shorts and a yellow tee-shirt. His hair is a little lighter than mine, big dark brown eyes and a shy smile. “Where did you get this?”

“I swiped it from Sam’s office. I thought you’d like to have it.” He holds up his empty hands. “No strings, I promise.”

“How do I know it’s him?” I stare at this smiling little boy, his innocent eyes staring right into the camera. He could be my son. Or he could be anyone. “And why would Sam have a picture of him after all this time?”

Gene looks down at the floor again, then back at me. “Sam’s sister has him.”

“I don’t believe you.”

“Why would I lie?”

I laugh, not because it’s funny, but because he would even ask. “Why? Because that’s what you do.”

Gene shrugs. “Okay. Believe me or not. It’s up to you. I just thought you’d want to know.”

I stare into his eyes and he stares right back. "Sam told you this? He told you this is our son?"

"Not in so many words, but remember I told you about the pictures in his office? I asked him about them, who the kid was, and he said he was his sister's. I remembered him saying something when you were pregnant, something about how it's too bad people who want kids can't have them and how his sister was trying to adopt. Anyway, it all fits."

I don't know what to say. I look at the picture again as a thousand thoughts go through my head.

"Anyway," Gene says, "I'm heading down to Mexico. I have a buddy down there who's doing pretty good, working in some resort renting paddleboards and jet skis to rich kids. There's nothing for me here but trouble." He looks at me, reaches out and touches my face, looks at Meg. "Have a good life. You both deserve it."

In a minute Gene is gone and Meg and I stand there, staring at the picture of this sweet little boy who might be my son.

Chapter 31

Jenny takes long strides into the kitchen. She's wearing a dress I've never seen before, bright blue, fitted at the top and flared at the bottom. She looks so pretty. I can't remember the last time I saw her in anything but boot-cut jeans or wide-leg pants for the past year. She's in her bare feet, and when she sits, she crosses her legs then lifts her right foot in the air.

At first I think she wants me to notice she's painted her toenails bright red, then I realize: no ankle monitor. "When did you get it off?" I ask.

"This morning. Thanks to Justin. Feels good to have my leg back."

"You look beautiful. You look happy."

"How could I not be? My daughter is coming home in a couple of days. I've finished my home confinement. I'm actually looking forward to starting my community service at the women's shelter. When the judge said community service, I pictured myself in one of those ugly vests, picking up trash along the side of the road."

"You're lucky. And the women at the shelter are lucky to have you."

"Thanks for saying that. If it wasn't for you, I probably would have ended up there myself."

In the four months since we saw Gene, Jenny hasn't mentioned her son or Sam or finding out if Gene was telling the truth about her son. She framed the picture Gene gave her, though, and has it on her dresser, so part of her must believe the little boy is hers. Ours. The couple of times I asked if she wanted to go see Sam, try to find out if what Gene said is true, she said, *not today*. I don't push it.

I think she's afraid that Gene was lying and she'll find out the boy isn't her son, that Sam has no idea who adopted him or where he is and he's lost to her forever. And at the same time, I think she's afraid it is him and that he has no interest in knowing her, or, even worse, that he won't want anything to do with her. This way there's enough distance and uncertainty that she can believe her son is happy and she did the right thing, while holding on to the real possibility of meeting him one day.

I have thought a dozen times about going to see Sam myself, see if Gene was telling the truth, but I won't do anything behind Jenny's back, not ever again, even though I would love to know for sure. I wonder if he would consider me his sister. Would I be able to make him understand that even though we're not related by blood, we have a bond that feels just as strong? Would he be able to understand how blood really has little to do with being family? Maybe not right away. It took me a long time.

"What do you want to do for your birthday?" Jenny asks.

"All I want is to come home."

This makes her smile, but it only lasts for a few seconds. "No, really. I want to do something special. This is a really important one. It doesn't even seem possible you could be turning18."

"What I would like is for us to go talk to Sam, see if he'll tell us anything about the baby." Ever since Gene came by with that picture of the little boy it's been haunting me.

Jenny doesn't look surprised, or angry, or afraid. She stares at me, then her smile is back. "You're something, you know that? Is this for you, or for me?"

"Both of us. I thought maybe we could just see whether or not Gene was telling the truth. It won't hurt to ask, right?" As I say this, I realize it could hurt. If Gene made it all up it would definitely hurt. It could take away the only true hope Jenny has to hold onto about her son.

"I'm as ready as I'll ever be. Let's do this."

I call Sam's office to see if he's there, hang up when he answers. We call an Uber and are there in about 40 minutes. Sam stands when we walk in, glances around as if he's looking for an escape. He has probably done so many shady things in his life he's always nervous things will catch up to him.

Sam looks from Jenny to me, back to Jenny. "Well, this is a surprise. Meg. And Jenny. I have to say, Jenny, you haven't changed a bit. To what do I owe this visit? Are you ladies in need of legal services?"

"I think you know why we're here," Jenny says. "Or you should."

Sam cocks his head, frowns. "I'm afraid I'm at a loss here."

"I want you to tell me about my son." Jenny says, her voice strong. I didn't expect her to be so confrontational from the start, but it makes me proud of her.

"I'm not sure what you think I can tell you."

Jenny sits and I do too, even though Sam didn't invite us to. "I want to know if you sold my son to your sister."

Sam's face gets red, but he recovers quickly. "First of all, if you're talking about the child you gave birth to, you signed away all parental rights. I'm under no obligation to divulge who adopted your son."

"Adopted? Don't you mean bought?"

"Jenny. We had a perfectly legal arrangement that you willingly signed. I'm not sure what you're after here."

"We just want to know if he's okay. If he's happy," I say, trying to take the tension from the room, the conversation.

Jenny reaches into her purse, takes out the picture Gene had given her. "Is this my son?"

"Where did you get that?"

"Gene. He said he got it from you. Actually, the word he used was *swiped*."

Sam shakes his head, looks away, then sits and looks across the table at us. "Your son is doing well. As I said, I am under no obligation to divulge any information, but since you already seem to know, I see no harm in telling you that much. Unless of course you plan on trying to contact him and disrupt his life?"

"Does he know he's adopted?" Jenny asks.

"Not that I know of."

Jenny looks at me, then back at Sam. "I wouldn't do anything to disrupt his life. I promise. I gave him up so he would have a better life than I could give him. You know that. But can you tell me about him? And about your sister?" Her voice is softer now. "Would you? Please?"

Sam sighs, looks at the picture and takes a deep breath. "My sister lost her husband about a year before she adopted David. That's what she named him, after her late husband. It was sudden. A heart attack. He was only 41, and she was devastated. They had been trying to have a child. When David died, something inside her died. She went into a deep depression that lasted months. Then she came to me asking if I could help her adopt a child."

"Why would she ask you? You're not an adoption agency."

"I don't know if you're aware, but the adoption process is long and drawn out and very difficult, especially for a single woman. Not impossible, but it would have taken years at the very least. The wait to adopt a newborn is especially long. My sister thought I could help cut through the red tape, help her jump through some of the hoops. I promised to do what I could, then shortly after that, Gene came to me, told me you were pregnant and he didn't know how the two of you could afford another mouth to feed. It was like providence. I saw a solution to both problems."

"So you decided to sell my son to your sister?"

Sam shifts in his seat, looks away for a few seconds. "My sister had received a substantial life insurance settlement and was more than willing to pay whatever it took. And I will tell you, Jenny, when I put that child in my sister's arms, she got life back in her eyes. I think I can honestly say that child saved her life. And I truly believe she saved his."

"So, he's happy and doing well? He has a good life?"

"She dotes on that boy. She couldn't love him more if he were her own flesh and blood."

"Thank you," I say. "That's all we wanted to know." I put my hand on Jenny's arm.

Jenny keeps her eyes on Sam. "Do you think she'll ever tell him about me?"

"I don't know, Jenny. He's only 12. I think it's a little early to say."

"I understand." Jenny stands, holds her hand out to Sam. "Thank you for telling me. And thank your sister for me, for taking good care of him. And if she does tell him some day that he's adopted, and if he ever wants to know me, when he gets older of course, I'm here. I would love to meet him."

Sam walks us to the door, wishes us luck.

On the way home, Jenny is so quiet. I had hoped she'd feel better knowing the truth, but maybe now she's afraid her son will never know her, that his adopted mother will never tell him about her, or that he won't want to meet her knowing she gave him away.

"Are you okay?" I ask.

"I was thinking of everything you went through to find your birth mother, how badly you wanted to find out who she was and why she gave you up and if you were wanted. It made me so afraid of losing you. I don't want my son to have those questions and doubts, and I don't want him to ever think he wasn't wanted. I also don't want his adopted mother to feel threatened like I was. I wish I could talk to her. And to him."

"When I was a kid, I used to write to him. I thought if I ever got to meet him I wanted him to know he had a big sister who loved him. I don't know whatever happened to those letters, but I remember how they made me feel connected to him somehow. We could write to him."

That night, Jenny and I sit across from each other at the kitchen table with paper and pen and the hope that David will someday want to know us. When we finish we swap and read each other's letters, neither of us embarrassed about the tears.

Dear David,

If you're reading this, you know you were adopted. My name is Jenny, and I am your birth mother.

The first thing I need you to know is how much I loved you and wanted you, and that giving you up was the most difficult, most painful thing I have ever done. I wanted you to have a good life, something I wasn't able to give you. I couldn't bring you into a life of poverty and chaos. My life was pretty much a disaster back then, but I wanted to keep you more than I have ever wanted anything in my life.

I also want you to know you have a sister. I named her Margaret, after my grandmother, but we call her Meg now. She wanted to be your big sister more than anything. She was too young to understand then why I made the decision to give you up, but I think she understands now. She is doing well, graduating high school in a couple of months, then going to college. She got a full scholarship to UMass Amherst and is planning to study to become a teacher.

The last thing I want you to know, and probably the most important, is that even though I carried you for nine months and gave birth to you, the person who raised you is your mother. Yes, I am your birth mother, and we are and always will be joined by blood. My love for you is deep and forever, but your adopted mother is your mother too, maybe even more than I am. Please don't let knowing about me, and someday maybe knowing me, take anything away from her. She deserves every bit of love and respect and loyalty a mother can have.

If you ever want to meet me and Meg someday, just tell your Uncle Sam. He knows how to contact me.

With love,

Jenny

The only background sound is the ticking of the clock on the kitchen wall. It's like the world has stopped as we both reach out to this child we have never met, this little boy we love so much.

Dear David,

We haven't met yet, but I am your sister, Meg. I hope when your adopted mother tells you about me that you will want to meet me. I can't wait for that day.

My mother, Jenny, is writing you a letter too, and I'm sure she's telling you how much she loves you and how hard it was to give you up. I was almost six when you were born, but I remember being so excited to have a little brother. I loved you from the minute Jenny told me she was going to have you, and was very, very sad when Jenny didn't bring you home. I was too young then to understand why she had to give you up, but I totally understand now. She wanted a better life for you than we had. Please don't ever think it was because she didn't want you or love you, because loving you was the reason she gave you up.

One more thing I want you to know is that I'm adopted too. Even though Jenny isn't my biological mother, she has always been my true mother. It took me a while to understand that, but it is the truest thing I know.

I hope I get to meet you some day and that we can get to know each other. Your Uncle Sam said you have a really good, happy life, and I'm glad for that. It's what we always wanted for you.

Love,

Your sister, Meg

Jenny and I read our letters over one more time before we fold them and slip them together into an envelope. I watch as Jenny writes *David* on the front, then puts it in an envelope and addresses it to Sam, along with a short note to him, saying that if and when the time comes that his sister tells David about being adopted, he might want to know why and how it came about, and maybe, hopefully, want to meet us. Mostly, we want him to know that he was always loved.

It's a short walk to the mailbox, and once we drop the letters in, Jenny takes a deep breath and turns to me. "Okay, what do you want to do now?"

I look into the eyes of this woman who raised me, and all I see is a deep and true mother's love. "I want to go home."

About the Author

Norma Murphy was born and raised in Lowell, Massachusetts, where she lives with her husband. A former public school educator, she is the author of two previous novels: *The Price of Secrets,* winner of a Pencraft Award for Literary Excellence, and *A Better Life,* which chronicles Jenny and Meg's beginnings. She is working on her fourth novel. You can connect with her on Facebook, or on her web site, norma-murphy.com.